The Adventures of Lew and Charlie Vol. II

By Maurice Decker

Mesa Gold

First published January 1928

Wolves of the Birch Woods

First published November 1928

Tamarack Trail

First published December 1929

ISBN 978-0-936622-34-7

Table of Contents:

INTRODUCTION:

Lew and Charlie are two stand-up guys who rely on their out-door skills to survive in the wilderness hunting, trapping and fishing. They also solve mysteries, catch crooks, and rescue damsels in distress. Perhaps best described as an old-fashioned adventure serial, the stories ran for 35 years in *FUR-FISH-GAME Magazine*. Over the years, Maurice Decker wrote 36 novella-length Lew and Charlie adventures, all broken into monthly chapters with cliff-hanger endings. They last appeared in the December 1961 issue.

In 1985, to mark the magazine's 60th anniversary year, the editor revised and republished one of those stories in its entirety, all 11 monthly chapters. When the story was coming to a close, readers who had become hooked on Lew and Charlie flooded the magazine office with letters asking for another story. Due to that outpouring of requests and enthusiasm, the adventure serial was revived and continues to be a favorite with the readers of *FUR-FISH-GAME*.

Those who don't like waiting a month between chapters have long asked for a Lew and Charlie book. But the stories never were published as anything other than monthly magazine install-ments—until now.

Volume 2, the second book in the series, takes up right where Volume 1 leaves off, following Lew and Charlie west as they battle a gang of crooked cattle rustlers and almost lose their lives discovering the truth behind a fabled Navajo river of desert gold. Then the boys head north for a winter of wilderness trapping that leads to a showdown with murderous fur thieves, and finally a battle with a thieving timber trust that is trying to steal the Native Cree homeland.

I'm happy to say that The Adventures of Lew and Charlie just keep getting bigger and better. Enjoy!

– Jeff Kirn, Publisher

Mesa Gold

Chapter 1 – Bottomless Sand

Towering mesas crowned with cedar and pinyon, brick-red cliffs cut straight as though sliced by a giant sword, burning sand, cracked dry lake bottoms and a dark wind rushing through the desert night—this is the Arizona Northland. It is a land of beauty and drabness, of pleasure and hardships, as are all lands of romance and legend. It also is the home of the Navajo.

A few traders have posts on the edges of the reservation, and the desert rats—prospectors for gold—plod behind freight-loaded burros. The pick and shovel are symbols of their faith in a "strike" which will rival the pot of gold at the rainbow's end.

It was early April, and the morning desert air was biting cold. But a few hours more would put the sun overhead and stifling heat would radiate from the sand. Ten feet from a rough trail which wound like a thin ribbon through the buttes stood a small touring tent. An ash-choked fire smoldered before the open door, and behind sat a dusty car.

A tousled head was thrust out into the morning air. Its owner sniffed cautiously and then emerged with a quick step, and a loud whoop. "For the luvva Mike! Get up, you sleepy birds! Can't you see I'm rarin' to eat and it's after five o'clock?"

He turned and surveyed the tent door impatiently. The canvas shook as someone struggled to throw off the stupor of sleep. A muffled voice replied, "You needn't get all worked up, Lew. You sound like one of those Spanish roosters crowing in the Hopi village. This is the first time in a week you beat Jim and me out of bed. I'll be out in a second."

Yawning, Charlie also emerged into the morning sun. "You're right about being hungry, though. I wasn't so starved even when we ran out of grub down on Big Thunder."

Lew grinned and asked, "Where's the kid?"

"Let him sleep," advised Charlie. "He needs it. After I get breakfast, you can call him."

He poked carefully in the ashes and laid a pile of thin cedar on top. Then he blew long and steadily until a small flame shot up.

"And so this is the West," grinned Lew.

"Don't you like it?" asked Charlie, beating up a gallon can of pancake batter. Crouching before the fire, he skillfully tossed up golden brown discs of cornmeal and wheat flour, piling them on a warm plate nested in the hot ashes.

"Oh, it's pretty good so far," conceded his partner. "I'm a bit like Jim, though. Sort of disappointed. Poor kid, his trip will be spoiled unless he sees a town shot up and the inhabitants carried feet first up the hill."

A youthful voice spoke from the tent. "You know I don't want to see anyone killed. But I would like to see some real gunplay. Those cowboys in Flagstaff didn't even carry guns, and they wore nothing but plain old blue overalls."

Charlie choked back a laugh at that, "You mustn't mistake movie cowboys for the real thing, Jim, and if you had looked close, you'd have seen a bulge on each man's hip under those overalls. I'll bet a ten spot those boys were heeled properly."

"Don't worry, kid," Lew chimed in. "We haven't seen the real West, yet. I'm expecting better stuff, too." Then he gazed longingly at the big brown cake Charlie had just tossed out of the pan.

Hungry campers have no business with conversation at meal time, and for a few minutes silence pervaded the camp. Then Lew strolled over to the car, took out and unfolded a large sheet of paper. "I wonder where the deuce this road goes, anyway," he speculated. "I can't find it on this map."

"And you won't," retorted Charlie, eyeing the crusted red mud on the car wheels. "I tried to drive a little sense into your skull back at the last fork, but you were determined to follow the roughest trail."

"What did we come out here for, anyway?" Lew grumbled. We wanted a good vacation after our winter's work trapping Big Thunder Valley, didn't we? We could have just stayed in St. Louis and blown our fur money."

Then a happy thought brought the grin back to his face. "I can still see you tucking away that stack of twenty-dollar bills. You chewed the fat half a day with that fur buyer."

Charlie grinned in turn at the compliment. "Remember you wanted to ship them and save the railroad trip to the fur market? Not me, my boy. When I go through a winter like that one, I'm going to get my money's worth. I figure we made another four bills by coming along with the pelts."

"Well, we can't stand around all day patting ourselves on the back," retorted Lew. "You hustle the stuff back in the car while Jim and I take down the tent and give the car its daily dozen with the grease gun. She's a hard looker, but, boy, didn't she pull through the sand on the edge of the last dry lake bed?"

Charlie slid the last cake over on Jim's plate and started to scour the fry pan with clean sand. Lew flattened the tent and rolled it into a compact bundle and then started to grease the car. It took them just ten minutes of steady teamwork to break camp.

Lew started the motor, warmed it with staccato gusts of acceleration, and then they were off. "The Trail of Romance," shouted Lew as he swung the wheel to miss a jagged rock in the road. But he didn't swing quite soon enough, and the tire collided with the stone and exploded.

Lew craned his neck out around the front fender to gaze ruefully at his work. Charlie grinned and commanded, "Get out your tools. Seems like we are having more flat tires than romance."

"That old casing was done for before we started," retorted Lew. "I wanted to throw it away but you said to save the new tires for the real bad roads."

"Here comes a man on a horse!" Jim declared. "Wonder if he's a real cowboy?"

The others grinned at this youthful enthusiasm. "Jim still thinks he's the Skagway Kid from Hell Roarin' Creek," whispered Lew, and Charlie nodded. They had stopped teasing him about running away from home in search of the Wild West adventure depicted in movies and books.

This was no cowboy advancing slowly down the trail. This was a Navajo, judging from the color of his blanket. The leathery face was bronzed and glazed by three score years of desert wind and sand. An older man, yet hale and hardy, he sat erect in the saddle and looked every inch the desert warrior. He stared at the travelers. Then he spoke in a deep voice.

The words were in the Navajo tongue and unintelligible to them. Seeing this, the man began to sign out his meaning. Charlie watched with growing admiration. The lean graceful hands were acting out a story.

"He says there's a stiff grade ahead, a sharp descent where the road goes down a mountainside," said Lew. Then he nodded and waved his hand in airy acknowledgement of the other's courtesy.

Seeing he had made himself understood, the Navajo pressed his pony with his knee and started on. Charlie looked after him thoughtfully. "I'm not so sure you hit it, Lew. We'll keep a close watch ahead. I don't like this trail, anyway. A lot of them on the map are plenty hard to follow, but this scratch in the ground isn't even listed."

"Don't croak," admonished Lew. "Ten to one the only adventurous thing on this trail today will be that other front tire blowing."

After changing the tire, Lew slipped the car in gear and they started off again. He didn't realize that Fate was about to hand him adventure in bunches—a wallop he would never forget.

Jim watched the Navajo as long as he could. Every Indian held his whole-hearted attention. "Yep," said Lew, glancing over his shoulder at the boy. "Think the old cannon you packed would down him? He looks like a pretty tough piece of shoe leather to me."

"Don't tease him," cautioned Charlie. "You know we had the same ideas when we were his age. Jim has turned out pretty well. Last winter on the trapline came as near to making a man out of a boy as anything I ever saw."

For several hours they bumped over the trail, scanning both sides for any sign of water. Last night's camp had been a dry one, and although there were still a few quarts of water in the two big flax desert bags tied to the car, they began to watch a little more anxiously as each mile passed without sign of a spring.

"Isn't that water yonder?" Lew asked, pointing to a clump of trees a little larger and greener than those on the plain. Then he saw a faint glint of sunshine glancing off of water and jammed on the brake. They all jumped out, grabbed the water bags and started on a trot.

It was a tiny spring but dammed up with a wall of red clay into a fair-size pool, sufficient to water a dozen head of stock. Charlie noted a line of dirty-white salt encrusting the edge. The bitter water was not very satisfying. They drank sparingly and filled just one of the bags.

"There is surely one sweet spring within the next fifty miles, if this blasted road lasts that far," said Charlie. "We've got the advantage on the men who established this trail by horse. Fifty miles is a fair day's reach for them, and they want to find water everyday. Fifty miles is only two or three hours for us."

At several places the trail was covered with drifted sand. "I see this road changes every time the wind blows," remarked Charlie. "Remember the railroad track we saw down South, the one that had oil sprayed on the right-of-way to stop the blowing sand drifting over and burying the rails?"

"We'll soon leave the sand behind," answered Lew. "I see higher ground ahead."

Lew dropped the car into second gear, and they climbed steadily to the top of a large plateau. The cedars began to dwindle, and finally loose gravel supported only dwarfed sage and greasewood. They topped the summit into a blast of cold air that whistled with vigor until it was blowing a regular gale of hard, sharp snow crystals. "Where the dickens is my coat?" Lew grumbled as he stopped the car. "Did you ever see anything like this?"

"The snow won't last long," Charlie said. "See, it melts as soon as it hits the ground. In half an hour we'll be going down the other side of this plateau, and then it will be as hot as ever."

The road over the plateau was smooth and hard, and they sped along at a good rate. Ahead loomed a mountain range shrouded in shadows of purple and gold. "See those peaks, Jim?" asked Lew. "They only look about five miles off, but you can't trust your eyes out here. Don't ever start out walking for some place that looks an hour away. You may not get there the same day."

They reached the edge of the plateau and started down a sharply winding descent. "Here's what old Rooster Feather was telling us about," declared Lew. "Gosh, it doesn't look dangerous. I suppose he thought we never went down a mountain grade before. But it was kind of the old gent to warn us."

Below lay a long, wide valley, and clumps of live oak and brush indicated a watercourse through the bottom land. "What are those?" called Jim. His sharp eyes had caught sight of tiny dots moving across the valley floor.

Charlie took out his binoculars and scanned the valley. "Cattle, sure as I'm alive," he said. "Must be an honest-to-gosh ranch, Jim. Couldn't be anything else this far from decent roads."

Jim bounced up and down on his seat. "Let her go!" he urged.

"Calm yourself," admonished Lew and then added, "This grade is steeper than I thought." He was compelled to apply the brakes every time they rounded a hairpin turn. Down and down they went until the road flattened out and they shot across the valley floor. Desert heat enveloped them again, and they shed the coats.

A fringe of live oak crossed the road. "There's water," said Charlie. "Stop her, Lew, and we'll fill the radiator and the bags."

The slow stream was maybe twenty feet wide but scarcely a

foot deep. Lew had been dreading a deep ford and grinned in relief. In bridgeless country, streams are always a source of worry.

The trail crossed at an oblique angle, but Lew wheeled straight across and the car gave a lurch then stopped abruptly with the front end settling into the riverbed.

"What the?" began Lew as the motor died and the car sank up to the hubs. "We may have to jack the blamed thing up and push it out," he finished.

"You didn't have enough speed to carry you across," Charlie observed." And why couldn't you follow the trail?"

"I wanted to cross at the narrowest place," explained Lew. "Anyway, I had plenty of gas on. The sand must be awfully soft. I don't understand ..."

A sharp cry from Jim made them turn around. The boy was standing up on the rear seat pointing at the water.

"We're going down!" he cried the alarm.

The rear fender was already nearly out of sight, and they could feel the car slowly but steadily sinking.

"It's quicksand!" yelled Charlie. "Jump for the bank! Quick!"

Jim cleared the sand with one wide leap, and Lew sprawled on the ground after him.

But Charlie took a moment to rummage hastily through the baggage and threw out two small packs. Then he jumped, but as he jumped, the front end of the car lurched and he fell short, full upon his stomach in the quivering sand. He felt the deadly suction drawing him down and floundered towards the bank, worming his way over the horrible stuff. Then a strong hand gripped his wrist, and a second later he was on firm ground with Jim and Lew bending over him.

"Look!" cried Jim, pointing to wide, oily bubbles that were breaking up around the top edges of the car. Then, with a horrid sucking sound, it vanished.

Chapter 2 – The Golden Quill

Charlie, Lew and Jim watched the quicksand swallow their car and entire outfit, quiver like a bowl of jelly, and then quiet into an even surface as innocent-looking as any sandy river bottom.

No trace of the car remained.

"I've heard of bottomless pits," Lew shuddered, "but this is the first I ever saw, and the last, I hope."

"If you had hit it any harder the car would have jumped out so far we never would have reached solid ground," said Jim.

"This is what the old Navajo was trying to tell us," Charlie said. "He knew we were strangers and tried his best to help us miss it."

"What will we do now?" asked Jim anxiously. "Everything is gone. Will we die out here?"

"Hardly," said Lew. "I figure we're only about a hundred and fifty miles from the last settlement. The only thing to do is to start back on foot and hope someone gives us a lift. Otherwise, we'll just plod along until we get somewhere."

"Why not keep on ahead?" asked Charlie.

"Ahead?" cried Lew. "In this desolation?"

"You forgot the herds of cattle we saw from the plateau top," Jim reminded him.

"The kid's right," affirmed Charlie. "Cattle means a ranch, and a ranch sounds like grub and saddle horses to me. My guess is we find them within ten miles."

"I hate to take that chance," answered Lew. "But if things go wrong this time, can't lay it on to me."

Charlie grinned. "Hand me those two sacks I tossed out of the car," he directed. Lew's face relaxed into easier lines after Charlie untied the canvas bags and started to unpack their contents.

"Those are our backpacking outfits," declared Lew. "I'll hand you the medal for quick thinking and bravery, old-timer."

"I took a risk," Charlie agreed, "but they're worth it. We've almost got Robinson Crusoe beat. Here is a featherweight tent of waterproof silk. We can pitch it like a lean-to and it'll be big enough to shelter three.

"Here's a wool blanket apiece. We'll show Jim how to roll up in one so it makes bed and cover both, and so his feet don't stick out.

Next comes my lightweight cook kit, everything I need to toss up grub on the trail."

"That is if we had any grub," grumbled Lew.

"You didn't let me finish," protested Charlie. "In that water-proof bag is a bunch of grub, selected to give the most food for bulk and weight. Tea, rice, cornmeal and bacon. I reckon that bag is going to be mighty popular before sundown tonight."

"How much grub in that bag?" asked Jim.

"Enough to last us three days if we don't knock over a few rabbits or sage hens, and a week if we do."

"Where's the gun to shoot game?" asked Jim.

Charlie grinned again. "You won't catch me unheeled in the West, my boy. I've read too many Hell Roarin' Creek stories for that." Jim grimaced at the dig but then couldn't help but grin.

"Here," went on Charlie, patting his shirt, "is my .45 auto slung under my left arm—out of sight but not out of reach. And here is what we pot meat with." Digging down into the largest bag he pulled out a short-barreled .410 shotgun.

Lew looked at the little gun with frank scorn. "You might as well heave a rock," he snorted.

Charlie repacked the stuff, slung one bag over his shoulder and handed the heavier to Lew. Then they waded carefully into the water, following the oblique course of the established trail and keeping as far from the quicksand as possible. Charlie probed into the streambed with a cactus stalk before each step.

"I'm glad that's over," said Lew when they had reached the other side. "I wonder if the cattle ever fall in it?"

"They do," answered Charlie. "When those big bubbles were breaking up around the car, didn't you smell the rank odor of decaying flesh?"

"Seems like any rancher who knew his stuff would fence it off to keep the stock out," said Jim.

"That's my idea, too," said Charlie. "I've been wondering what sort of a ranch this may be."

He filled a small canteen from the river. "Better take a good drink before we leave," he advised. "This is a small can for three men to share."

It was warm and slightly bitter, but desert travelers cannot be too choosy. They drank deeply.

The trail followed the river for a half-mile then turned straight towards the peaks on the horizon. As they rounded a turn, Charlie stopped. "I hear a rustle in those live oaks," he whispered and then stalked noiselessly down to the riverbank, the short shotgun held ready for action. He disappeared from view; then came a whir of wings and a quick shot. Three sage hens soared away.

"I hope he got one," exclaimed Jim. Before Lew could answer, Charlie appeared with a plump bird in hand. "This will help stretch rations," he said with satisfaction.

Lew looked at the watch strapped to his wrist. "It's eleven o'clock. We had an early breakfast. Why not stop and eat before we leave this water?"

His proposal was instantly approved, and as he cleaned the bird, Charlie built a small cook fire and prepared a pot of tea, "Tea," he said, "saved our lives the time those half-breeds drove us through the northern barrens for days."

Lew nodded. "It's funny how even in the tropics men find hot tea more invigorating than ice water."

For several hours they tramped steadily through the deserted valley. The trail faded until it was a mere saddle path. Jim began to puff, and Charlie stopped. "Sorry, kid. Sit down on this pack and catch your breath."

The report of a gun sounded far ahead in the valley. It was faint but unmistakable. "Maybe somebody's shooting coyotes," said Lew. "The valley has folks in it after all ..."

He stopped as four more shots followed with a rattle. "Must be burning him on the run," he resumed.

"Maybe it's rustlers," cried Jim hopefully.

Lew frowned at that. "I never did see anybody so bent on finding trouble. All I'm looking for now is a friendly ranch where we can buy horses and grub. What will we do then, Charlie? Ride straight up into Utah?"

"That's my plan," his partner answered. "A ride across northern Arizona into Utah clear to Salt Lake would be some stunt. But we've got all summer, and this air is just the stuff for you after having pneumonia last winter."

Lew had suffered a bad attack of the trapper's scourge last winter in Big Thunder Valley.

They started on again. The trail led them through a flat upon which were scattered huge boulders of a red chalk-line stone. "Hello," Lew declared. "There's a horse!"

A pinto pony stood off the trail. It threw up its head and snorted, backing away and then standing with quivering withers. A blanket was strapped to the animal's back, and it pawed nervously.

"What the deuce is it doing?" asked Lew. "Must have thrown the rider and run away."

"No," said Charlie pointing. "The rider is there on the ground."

They ran forward, and Jim shuddered when he got close and saw the crimson stain spreading slowly through the sand.

"He's shot through the side, I think," said Charlie in a low voice filled with concern.

The man opened his eyes. He was a brave of maybe thirty years, a Navajo. His face was calm. There was no pain or protest, merely a questioning look.

Jim bent over and held the small canteen to cracked lips. When the man had drunk, he looked at the boy, and seeing the tear-filled eyes, smiled faintly.

"Give me the first aid kit, Lew," commanded Charlie.

He knelt and cut away the bloody shirt. The heavy caliber ball, probably from a revolver, had plowed cleanly through the man's side, missing the vitals but leaving two holes that each bled profusely. Charlie stopped the bleeding with balls of gauze. Then he bound a heavy bandage about the man's waist to hold the pads in place. The Navajo made no sign of approval or protest.

"What can we do for you?" asked Charlie.

"Maybe he can't understand English," broke in Lew.

"I understand," the Navajo finally spoke. "You whites can be very thorough in your education of the red man, even to the extent of sending him to college—before you shoot him down like a coyote."

They stepped back in surprise at that.

"Who shot you?" asked Charlie.

"And why?" added Lew. But he stopped at the look of black anger that swept over the face of the Navajo.

"Boss Hetter shot me because I would not tell him where we Navajos wash the gold from the mountain streams. I am Wai-ton of the Sun Rock tribe."

Raising himself on one elbow, he poured out more words with blazing emphasis. "Someday we Navajos will sweep down from the mountains and kill him and his rustlers like sheep. Then the real ranchers will know the truth of Blazing Butte Valley. That it is bad white men and not the red who drive their cattle north."

He lay back, exhausted. "But you are good men. I see it in the face of the boy."

Blood welled from his lips as the effort of speaking proved too much. Finally, he whispered, "If my tribe comes for me, I live. If not, I pass with the sun. Light a fire and send the smoke sign: three puffs, three times repeated."

In a few minutes they had a pile of greasewood burning, and then they piled on resinous brush until thick smoke rose as straight as a pillar into the cloudless sky.

"Get the blanket from his pony," said Charlie. Lew approached the pony but the animal snorted and reared. The Navajo put two fingers to his lips and whistled. The pony stopped, and shivering visibly at the strange touch, allowed Lew to unwrap and lift the blanket from its back.

He held it over the swelling smoke, cutting off the rising column. Then, jerking it away quickly, he released smoke in a balloon-like puff that rolled and twisted into the sky. The blanket was put back and another cloud released until there were nine billows rising in groups of three. The smoke balls held their form as far as they could be followed with the eye.

It was hot and tiresome, but Lew began again after a five-minute interval and stuck to the job for an hour. Then the Navajo called to him. "That is enough. They will come."

An hour passed, and then Jim pointed. Through the heat they could see a cloud hovering close to the ground, rolling toward them.

Wai-ton opened his eyes.

"My brothers come," he said simply, although from where he lay on the sand he could not possibly see them.

"His ears are keen enough to catch the beat of hooves on this soft ground," whispered Charlie.

As the riders approached with incredible speed, Charlie saw the rifles they carried across their ponies' manes, ready for instant use. At a hundred yards they circled once and then came riding swiftly in.

They reined in their mounts and each man slid to the sand, rifle in hand. At the sight of the prostrate Navajo their faces set into stern lines, and Charlie instinctively reached for his gun. These were not men to trifle with.

"Steady, my brothers." Wai-ton spoke. "These men have helped me. Their hearts are right, especially the younger."

The Navajos grouped about, talking swiftly in low tones. Then they strapped a pad of blankets on Wai-ton's pony, and lifted him carefully up. Not a sound escaped his lips, although the move must have hurt him sorely.

He called them over as he lay across the pony's back. Searching through his thick, black hair, he found something and handed it to Charlie. "Take it," he said. "A medicine man is worthy of his fee."

Then he turned to Jim. "You have shown compassion for a wounded Navajo. Take this." He pulled a thong of deerskin from around his neck. Dangling from the end was a small disc. His companions straightened instantly at the sight of the charm. Each brought the flat of his right hand to his forehead in a salute.

"The sign of the Sun," Wai-ton continued. "Every mountain and desert man will respect the wearer. Show it when you need help from a red man."

Then the band started off at a slow walk, back toward the mountain peaks. The last glimpse they caught of Wai-ton his face was still calm, hanging from the side of the pony.

Charlie fingered the gift from the Navajo. It was an eagle feather quill, stopped with clay at the open end and filled with tiny grains that glittered in the sun and poured over each other like oil.

"Gold dust," he exclaimed. "Just lift it, Lew."

"Pretty good pay for a little first aid," Lew remarked. "I'd guess it at forty dollars."

"You are being way too conservative," answered Charlie. "Let's see what you got, Jim."

Jim handed him a round disc of black, glass-like stone the size of a silver dollar but thinner. The surface was glazed as though the flint had been subjected to terrific heat, and the surface had softened and run. One side was smooth; on the other was the figure of the sun with wide rays carved in relief.

Charlie drew his hunting knife across the stone. To his surprise, the keen steel slid over the glazed face without making a scratch. "What the deuce can this be?" he asked. "It looks like obsidian yet it doesn't seem brittle. And it looks hundreds of years old."

"I'd rather have another quill feather filled with gold dust," Lew replied.

"Those rustlers ought to be hung," Jim said vehemently. "Shooting a man for a little pile of gold dust."

"Well," said Lew, " I'm not expecting any hearty welcome at the rustler's ranch. Your wild stuff will start soon enough, Jim."

"They won't bother us," answered Charlie. "They'll be glad to sell us horses and get us out of the way. What do you think of the Indian now, Jim?"

Jim hesitated before speaking. "He was different from those I read about in stories."

"He was a college man," said Charlie dryly. "I always thought the Navajos were peaceful, but I'd hate to have that gang on my tail. They might be part Apache. The Apaches were the hellcats of this state."

They tramped until nightfall, and Charlie directed Lew to set the tent 50 yards off the trail, behind a big rock that broke the desert night wind. After a quick meal, which for all its quickness made an alarming hole in the grub sack, they rolled up in blankets and slept.

In the night the wind increased, and a gust whipping about the tent loosened a stake, waking Charlie. He rolled out and hammered the stake back in the sand and piled stones on top to help hold it.

He looked at his watch. It was half-past three and the moon already was fading out of the sky. A gray dusk settled over the valley, the dark before the dawn that is the darkest part of a desert night. He lay back and tried to sleep but a new sound caught his ear, a creaking and thudding that grew more audible between gusts of wind.

He crawled out of the tent and looked down the trail at a black line of horsemen filing slowly past the tent. He could see the drooping shoulders of riders who slouched and dozed in their saddles as the horses walked slowly on.

They were coming from the peaks that crowned the northern horizon. Charlie crouched in the sand and counted ten lean, wiry men. Just as the last rider swung abreast, he reined in his horse and turned in the saddle. Even in the gloom, Charlie thought he could see hard features under a growth of beard and caked alkali.

Chapter 3 – A Rude Welcome

Charlie crouched closer behind the rock as the mysterious horse-man stared his way through the desert night. An uneasy feeling played up and down his spine. If these were cattle rustlers, and he suspected they were, they might resent his spying upon them.

Rustlers were usually good with a gun, even a pistol shot from a moving horse.

Charlie's imagination carried that on with singular clearness until he thought he saw the gloved hand settle over the hard butt of the big gun swinging from his hip. Then the arm straightened, and the rider spurred his horse forward to catch up with the rest. Charlie breathed with relief. As soon as the muffled hoof beats faded out in the dusk, he stood and brushed the sand from his clothes.

Standing beside the tent, he watched the first sign of sunrise, a faint rosy glow over the mountain rim. He remembered how hot it would be after day broke and decided it was time to awaken his companions and get an early start.

They rolled out, grumbling, and Lew was particularly indig-nant, but Charlie persisted until he was fully awake. "Our water is gone," he explained. "We can't carry half enough in one canteen, and we must find more before the sun starts broiling us."

While Lew packed the light tent, he told of the line of horse-men passing in the night. Lew shook his head gloomily. "I knew we should have gone back. I suppose those birds will cut our throats and pitch us into some canyon."

"If you insist," replied Charlie, "I'll take the blame for this one. But we still have to get going."

They walked over to the trail. "Now which way?" asked Lew.

"We follow the horsemen," Charlie replied. "Their ranch can't be far away, for if it was, they would have camped and not pushed on until morning."

The day broke with all the splendid color of a desert sunrise, and the hoof marks turned sharply from the trail and struck out across the plain. They followed, tramping up to the summit of a low ridge. There on the plain was a huge herd of cattle, slowly spreading out in all directions. The steers had begun to feed, picking at the scant bunches of forage as they walked.

"Must be thousands of them," Lew whistled. "The owner must be a millionaire."

"Or a rustler," cautioned Charlie dryly.

As they walked down through the cattle, Charlie studied them closely. "What brand are they carrying?" asked Lew.

"Several," answered Charlie. "I've seen three different marks, and one that clearly had been altered. My guess is these cattle have been stolen from across the southern plains, maybe clear down to the Texas Panhandle. Boys, we seem to have stumbled on rustling done in a big way."

"You still think we ought to just burst in on them uninvited?" Lew asked.

"We can't do anything else," Charlie replied. "We must have horses to get out of here. Look, there's the ranch."

Through the milling cattle they caught sight of a cluster of buildings and the tall pinyon posts of a corral. As they walked closer, they noted weathered bunkhouses and sheds grouped about one large structure, evidently the headquarters of the boss. The buildings were built of cedar logs and roofed with sheet metal. There was an air of newness about everything.

"Won't be long, now," said Lew. "Get the old cannon ready, Charlie. We'll die with our boots on, at least."

"Dry up," said Charlie.

Smoke was pouring out of a stovepipe that leaned precariously from the side of a long cabin. This they took to be the cookhouse and mess hall. They walked past it up to the big building and halted before the wide veranda. Just as Charlie set his foot on the step, a shout from the corral drew his gaze.

The gate swung open and out galloped a rider, bearing straight upon them. His sombrero flapped in the wind and shaded his eyes until he was but a few yards off. "Whoop-e-e-e-e!" he yelled in surprise, and pulling back on the reins, brought his pony up with a cruel jerk. The animal slid forward, throwing dirt in the faces of Charlie and his companions. Jim involuntarily darted around behind the other two.

"What the ..." the man began as he looked them over. Then he burst out in a harsh laugh.

He was tall and rawboned, his cheeks burnt a dark brown by desert sun and wind. A sandy mustache drooped from either side of his mouth, and his eyes were frosty blue. Hard lines about his jaw told his character as plainly as words on a printed page.

As Lew later put it, "He was one tough hombre."

"Pilgrims!" he cried derisively. "Boys, come look what the wind blew in for us!"

Jim stood behind Charlie, eyeing the rough rider with obvious trepidation. The Wild West was unfolding before him a little too quickly now.

The rustler looked past Charlie to the fear in the boy's eyes, and a look of cruel humor came into his own. He wheeled his horse around to where the boy stood. Reaching down, he grasped Jim by the collar and started to drag him up to the saddle. Charlie struck the fellow's wrist with a clenched fist. Jim dropped back to the ground on his hands and knees.

A flush of blood-black red flooded the rustler's face, and he swung cat-like from the saddle. Charlie faced him in silence.

"What yuh mean by that?" the rustler inquired through clenched teeth. The man was bad clear through, and Charlie clearly saw that trouble would be the outcome regardless. He decided to bring things to a head at once.

"I won't watch a man pick on a boy," he answered shortly.

The rustler eyed him with the look of a natural bully. "What's about yoreself? Yuh seem almost full-grown," he sneered.

Then he stepped forward and his high-heeled boot turned in the sand, throwing him slightly off balance. Charlie seized the chance and struck him full in the mouth.

The rustler fell back on the ground but bounced up like a rubber ball, cursing fluently although quietly. Charlie stepped back. The man was twenty pounds heavier than he, but he had the advantage of youthful grace and the other was handicapped with tall punching boots. Charlie's half-moccasins fit his feet as snug as gloves.

The rustler waded in, his long arms cutting the air as he endeavored to clinch with Charlie.

Charlie was a cool boxer, but as the rustler advanced upon him, he suddenly realized just how little he knew about rough-and-tumble man fighting. He concentrated to keep his head clear and his feet moving. He saw an opening, and jumping in, struck two quick blows — right and left — that rocked the rustler's head from side to side. A loud shout burst from the crowd of punchers who had streamed out of the mess house and formed a rough circle about the fighters.

"Catch 'im, Sandy! Don't let a kid roll yuh like that!"

The jibes of his companions made Sandy madder than ever, and he thrashed about like a demon. The crowd pushed in closer until Charlie was hampered for room and began to fear his footwork would soon be of no avail.

Jumping back to avoid a savage rush, he collided with one of the spectators. The rustler seized the chance and sent a heavy blow straight from the shoulder. Unable to sidestep, Charlie shifted just his head and let the blow strike his face at a glancing angle. His head still snapped back and his eyes blurred. Then he stepped forward and sent two uppercuts, one of which luckily found the mark and stopped the deadly clinch that had started to descend upon him.

The circle was crowding smaller every second, and Charlie knew he must do something at once.

The rustler stopped to regain his breath and then started a quiet, easy stalk that chilled Charlie's blood in his veins. He decided to risk everything on one coup. Stepping quickly back, Charlie met the man's rush with a powerhouse pivot blow. Swinging upon his heel, he put every ounce of strength and the full weight of his body into a clenched fist that landed fairly upon the point of the other's jaw. This time the rustler sprawled across the ground and did not bounce back up. Charlie sprang to his side, ready to renew the fight in case the blow had not ended it.

A drop of blood oozed from the fallen man's ear, so terrific had been the blow. He stirred feebly and then settled back on the sand, motionless. Charlie gently rubbed his swelling knuckles. The hand was badly sprained.

A cool silence had settled over the other punchers. Their faces contained none of the satisfaction that comes from seeing a fair fight ended well. Charlie whispered to Lew and Jim, "Set your backs against the house."

The rustlers muttered among themselves and then in a body pushed forward. Charlie reached under his arm for the gun slung there, and was just starting to draw when a slim figure pushed through the rest. Even in his first brief glance, Charlie noted the absolute lack of expression in this face, the almost colorless eyes. The man was clad in spotless riding breeches and shining puttees, and he shouldered his way through the rustlers with careless indifference, elbowing them out of his path with astonishing ease. Big, burly punchers fell back as though moved by a giant hand.

Instantly, Charlie knew this had to be Boss Hetter, the leader of the rustler gang.

His colorless eyes flitted over them, and he demanded, "What are you doing here at my ranch? Where did you come from?"

Charlie stepped forward and briefly told of the loss of their car, how they had walked to the ranch looking for horses.

As he spoke, Hetter's eyes played over him. Charlie gathered that they could see through any bluff or lie. Here was a man no one could fool. When Charlie finished speaking, Boss Hetter walked back to Sandy, who now sat upon the ground rubbing his jaw.

"Get up, MacTare," he commanded. "Since when did I appoint you our welcoming committee? If you can't ride today, go back to your bunk."

Then he turned back to Charlie.

"Had breakfast? No? Come in and eat with me." Then he led the way up on the cool veranda where a table was set with silver and linen, an immaculate breakfast service in perfect keeping with the mien and appearance of their host.

Hetter snapped his fingers and called, "Mingo!"

An aged Chinese shuffled out, his strawboard slippers pattering across the floor. His sure manner bespoke vigor in spite of the age wrinkles on his face.

"Three more!" commanded Boss Hetter. Then he motioned for them to be seated and started to pepper Charlie with questions that at first seemed merely of casual interest, but which upon second thought revealed inquisitive search. Where was their home? How long had they been on the road? Had they had any trouble on the trail before reaching the ranch?

Charlie took the position of spokesman, and choosing his words carefully, returned answers that were truthful yet told as little as possible. He carefully avoided any mention of the Navajo or the line of horsemen who had passed in the early morning.

Mingo soft-footed in while they talked, bearing platters of fried steak, hot biscuits and coffee. The three travelers fell upon this feast with hearty vigor.

"Will you sell us three horses?" Charlie finally asked, and Boss Hetter nodded.

"I suppose you want horses that are well broke? If you get them, will you leave today?"

Charlie nodded. "We've a limited amount of money and must make it go as far as we can, so we can't stay long in any one place."

"What route north will you take?" Hetter's eyes flickered quickly as he put this question, and Charlie fancied it was of considerable more import than the casual tone implied.

"I don't know anything about the country north of here. Which is the best and shortest trail into Utah?"

"I'll show you," was the answer. Breakfast over, they walked out to the corral. Hetter ordered one of the wranglers to sort out three well-broken mounts.

As they waited for the horses, a mangy dog loped out from behind the mess hall, and squatting on its haunches, broke out with a dismal howl. Hetter turned with lightning speed, snapped a six-shooter from his belt, and fired in the same motion. Without apparent aim, the 40-foot shot bowled the canine over. It yelped once and then straightened out dead.

"Dogs get on my nerves," Hetter said simply, sliding the pistol back in its holster. "I told Sam to keep that one out of my sight."

Charlie, Lew and Jim were speechless. The man's hand had moved so swiftly their eyes could not follow. "Man," Lew whispered, "did you ever see such gunplay?"

"Never," answered Charlie. "Now I see why all those rough hombres got out of his way when he shoved through them."

Hetter was watching his man sort out the ponies for them when a stout figure emerged from the cookhouse and walked over beside the dead dog. A flour sack apron tied about his middle marked him as the ranch cook. He prodded the animal with a toe. Then he looked up at them, his face pathetic in its weakness, full and round with watery blue eyes, which with the swollen veins in nose and cheek indicated plainly the cause of his pitiful condition.

He asked, "Did Boss Hetter shoot 'im?"

Charlie nodded, and the man's lips trembled. "Poor Gip," was all he said. "He was the last friend I had." Then he shuffled back into the kitchen.

"I suppose you want saddles and bridles, too?" Hetter asked.

"What will all of this cost?" asked Charlie.

Hetter calculated quickly in his head. "Three ponies with saddles … an even hundred and fifty."

"Fair enough," answered Charlie. The man came up leading the mounts. They were small but wiry, just the kind for desert travel.

One, a piebald with a broad streak running down her nose caught his eye. "She is mine," he declared, gaining confidence as the transaction continued to go smoothly. With any luck at all, they would be on the trail north within the hour.

The wrangler grinned. "She's the orneriest of the lot. Look at that there glass eye."

Charlie pulled out his pocketbook, counted out the required sum and handed it to Hetter. But as he did, the eagle quill of gold dust fell at his feet.

Charlie stooped, picked up the quill and thrust it back in his pocket. But as he straightened, he chanced a swift glance at Hetter's face. The blank features were flooded with a vivid greed that chilled his blood.

A second later, Hetter was counting the money with seeming indifference, but Charlie knew the game had just changed.

Chapter 4 – The Rear Attack

Charlie silently cursed his carelessness in dropping the quill of gold dust at Boss Hetter's feet. But the thing was done, and he knew trouble was surely coming.

"Ride back to the trail and go straight north," Hetter spoke with seeming indifference. "Fourteen miles on you will find a huge mesa the Indians call Rain Rock. They go there to make medicine every year when the corn and beans burn in the summer drought. The trail divides at the Rock. Take the right hand. It is the best and quickest route to the Utah line."

"Thanks," replied Charlie. "We appreciate your help. Just one thing more. Can we buy about a week's supply of food?"

"See the cook," directed Hetter. "Good luck."

He ended the conversation at that by vaulting into his saddle, spurring his horse, and galloping off towards the herds of cattle that spread across the plain.

The three stared at each other in silence for a moment. "You pulled a boner there, old man," said Lew. "Did you see Hetter when that quill of gold dust rolled out on the sand?"

"I'll say I did," answered Charlie.

"Why shouldn't you have shown it to him?" asked Jim.

"He's the bird that shot the Navajo," explained Lew. "Don't you remember? And he shot him because he wouldn't tell where he found the gold."

"And now we're tangled up in it," Charlie finished for him.

"The thing for us to do is get away from here as fast as we can," Lew said. "Then, when we're out of Hetter's reach, maybe we'll go prospecting for a little gold ourselves."

"It's big country to go prospecting around blindly," answered Charlie. "Plenty have tried and failed."

He told Lew to hold the horses and took Jim with him into the cook's kitchen. Sam was bending over a heap of dirty plates and cups, muttering to himself. He jumped nervously as they entered.

"Howdy," Charlie greeted him. "The boss said you would sell us some grub. I would like a sack of flour, baking powder, beans, bacon, and some dried fruit."

"Sure," said Sam, "I'll fix you up. You orter have some canned tomatoes to drink when you get thirsty. Too much water founders a man in this heat."

"Give us some, then," agreed Charlie, and Sam shuffled about gathering the supplies. Then he piled the stuff in a heap on the table.

"How much?" asked Charlie.

"'Bout eight dollars, I guess."

"Here," Charlie said, handing him a bill. "Never mind the change. Buy yourself a little solace when you get to town."

Sam regarded him in silence. Then he inquired mildly, "What the blazes you doin' out here?"

"Just traveling," said Charlie. "We're going north into Utah."

"Wish I was going," Sam said. "If I ever git out of this hellhole, I'll stay out. Hetter tell you which trail to take?"

"Yes, up to Rain Rock and then turn right."

Sam's dull eyes cleared a bit at that, and his flabby lips settled into firmer lines. Then he spoke, after glancing about the room cautiously. "Bad things happen to strangers out there. Watch the ponies at night, and don't camp at Rain Rock. Thar's sweet water five or six miles beyond."

"What do you mean?" asked Charlie quickly.

Sam shook his head. "I've said too much already." Then his voice trailed off into an indistinct mutter, but Charlie thought he could distinguish the words, "When a feller shoots yore dog, the only friend you have left ..."

They carried the food out to Lew, divided it into three parcels and roped one to each saddle. As they worked, Charlie told Lew of Sam's warning.

"I'm going back and get a couple of water bags," announced Lew. "That one canteen is only an aggravation. Also, I'm going to see if I can buy a gun off that cook. One firearm in the family isn't enough. And maybe I can pump him a little more."

He ran into the cook shack, and a few minutes later emerged with a six-shooter strapped to his waist.

"This gun has seen a lot of use, but it's still sound. And Sam says it'll drive tacks at ten yards. He only had one box of shells to sell. Here's two three-gallon water bags." Then Lew added, "Old Sam was as mum as an oyster about Rain Rock and danger."

When Jim tried to mount his horse, he got one foot in a stirrup before the animal began to side away. He hopped along on the other foot, yelling, "Whoa! Whoa!"

"Get off and then mount from his other side," Lew advised. "Western broncos are mighty particular how you handle them. They have been trained a certain way in everything."

They loped down the trail and then turned north, riding close together. The ranch and cattle herds were soon behind, and before them lay majestic mountain peaks. When Charlie's horse shied abruptly from the trail, he brought it up with a jerk. Looking down in the trail, he saw a big rattlesnake coiled in thick loops, rattles singing a vibrant call while the flattened head swayed back and forth.

The thing was as thick as a man's arm and fully five feet long. Lew drew his gun. "Here's a chance to try this out," he said, and throwing down the muzzle, shot straight into the coils.

"Nice shot," commented Charlie. "You clipped his neck."

Their horses sped tirelessly ahead mile after mile. "Isn't this great?" said Jim.

"Wait until tomorrow morning," cautioned Charlie. "It's been a long time since I've been in a saddle, and I know I'm going to be pretty stiff. We'll have to take it easy the first few days. After we get hardened we can step on the gas."

"We've got to get clear of Hetter and his gang today if we can," replied Lew. "I'm in favor of going on half the night."

"Look at that dust over there," broke in Jim. "What's making it, cattle or horses?"

"Not cattle," said Lew. "The cloud is moving too fast. It must be men riding at a fast clip."

Charlie frowned. "I wonder if Hetter has sent somebody to cut in ahead of us. Remember what Sam said about Rain Rock? Maybe they'll ambush us there."

"It don't look good," agreed Lew. "What do you say to turning back and trying to shake 'em by going the other way?"

"Hardly," said Charlie. "These fellows know the country and the water holes, no matter which way we go. We'll fight it out if we have to. It's the Utah line or bust!"

"That's the stuff!" cried Lew. "What do you say, Jim?"

"I'm not so keen to see gunplay as I was yesterday," confessed Jim. "But I'm going to stick with you through it all."

"Bravo," applauded Charlie. "Nobody could say it better. Get out your glasses, Lew," he added. "See if you can look into that cloud of dust."

Lew trained his binoculars on the cloud, which swept up abreast of them about a mile distant. "Nothing but dust," he said. "It's thick and—whoa there. I can see ..." he lowered the glasses. "There's just one man, and he's riding to beat hell!"

"Maybe he's a messenger being sent ahead to stir things up," answered Charlie.

It was nearing midday, and the desert sun beat down upon them. Their ponies had slackened their gait to a shuffling trot, and they wisely let them pick their own speed. After more hours of travel, a dim mass loomed far ahead. Charlie pointed. "Must be Rain Rock."

The mass slowly sharpened in line and detail until they could distinguish a mesa colored dull red by the afternoon sun. "I hope there is good water," said Lew. "I've been ready to eat for three hours."

Their ponies shuffled on. Jim's sharp eyes first picked out the straggling clumps of live oak which mark the course of water. They rode straight for it until Charlie made the next discovery. A lean-to tent stood beside the pool of water. They circled about to the opposite side, horses pulling at the bits as eager noses turned toward the smell of water. There was no one home, but a pile of ashes and a heap of blankets indicated the tent had been used.

They rode right into the water, letting the horses drink until they began to swell the saddle girths. "Listen to those saddles creak," said Lew. "Suppose they'll founder themselves?"

"Not these ponies," answered Charlie. "They're used to going a day without water and then filling up like a camel. What do you think of that layout there?" he added, pointing to the tent.

"It's sure dirty," answered Lew. Big bones, scraps of hide and other filth littered the ground. They rode out of the pool and Charlie dismounted to refill a water bag. "We'll use this for cooking only, and boil it well. This place is a ways from being sanitary."

They rode along the mesa base, seeking the fork in the trail and the path to Utah. Rounding a sharp curve, they came upon three men squatted beside a dead steer, stripping off its hide with short, curved knives. They were swarthy, squat Mexicans, clad in greasy, tattered overalls. After staring back at them for a moment, one advanced a step and put on a wide smile.

"I am Pedro, boss skinner," he said by way of an introduction. "We follow the herd and shoot the cripples before the coyotes spoil the skins."

"Where does this trail divide?" asked Charlie.

"Hundred yards ahead," the man answered. "But you should

camp here at the water. There is no more for forty miles."

"Can't," put in Lew. "We are in a hurry."

"A dry camp is bad," the fellow answered. "Ahead nothing but heat and sand. Stay, and soon we cook some meat."

"How do you carry the hides?" asked Lew.

"Chuck wagon comes from the ranch. She bring us grub and take back the hides."

"Thanks for the offer," Charlie cut in, "but we cannot stop this early in the day."

The man shrugged and said, "You make a big mistake."

"Adios," said Charlie, and kicking his horse, pulled around the men. Then he half-turned in the saddle and watched them until another bend in the road hid them from view. "I don't know their game," he said, "but let's put at least a dozen miles between us and them."

"That's some job," Jim said. "Following the herd, killing and skinning the cripples."

"Those men are the lowest caste of the plains," Charlie explained. "And I've heard they are none too particular about shooting a healthy steer when they can't find a cripple."

"Let's get moving," urged Lew. "Sam said about five miles to the next water, and I sure feel like eating."

They reached the water late in the afternoon, a sweet spring that flowed out from the base of a gravely hill to form a little oasis. The tired horses picked ravenously at the sparse growth while their riders limped about, getting the cramps out of their legs.

"I'll bet my legs are an inch longer," moaned Jim.

"Just wait," said Lew. "The worst is coming tomorrow."

The sun finally set behind the range of hills leaving their camp in cool shade. They lay about the campfire, appreciating the warmth as the desert night chill settled about them. A jackrabbit, all ears and legs and standing as high as a small calf, trotted out and stood to watch them.

"Here's where I get some more target practice," Lew said, drawing his gun.

"Better save those cartridges," warned Charlie.

"Just try one shot," answered Lew, and then he fired.

The jack was hit but took off. Lew mounted his horse and followed. "I'm going to finish the job," he declared over his shoulder.

"Don't be gone long," cautioned Charlie. "There are too many tough hombres loose in this desert."

"I won't be gone ten minutes," Lew promised, galloping off.

But when half an hour had passed, Charlie walked out into the desert a few hundred yards and looked anxiously in all directions. The wind was rapidly filling the hoof prints of Lew's horse with blowing sand. Even if he could trail Lew, Charlie was loath to leave Jim alone in camp.

He returned to the tent and built up the fire to guide Lew home in case he lost his bearings in the gathering dusk. Then he sat in troubled silence. Jim fell asleep, but Charlie sat brooding over this most recent turn of events. Had Hetter's gang bushwhacked Lew? Had he fallen foul of the three Mexican skinners back at Rain Rock? When he found himself chastising Lew for his foolhardy ways, he finally muttered, "This won't do. I'll go crazy if I sit here worrying all night."

With a strong mental effort, he banished the dark thoughts and after walking back out of the circle of firelight, pulled a blanket about his shoulders and sat down to watch and listen. A coyote barked out on the desert, and innumerable faint noises filled his ears. Even in the desert where life is thinly distributed, the night wind carries a multitude of murmurs and whisperings. Once, Charlie thought he heard a faint shout and answered, but no response returned. He sat in contemplative silence as the moon rose over the range and flooded the desert with a soft, velvety glow.

* * *

Lew galloped after the wounded jackrabbit, brandishing his gun in the air. What he expected to be a short chase turned into a long one. "Look at him go!" he shouted in surprise, as the animal fairly flew over the sand in spite of the dangling limb.

He spurred his horse on, but the jack drew away until he lost sight of it in the dusk. He stopped and looked around at a forest of stubby cactus trees. "I've got to get out of here before I'm lost," he thought.

He turned back, peering anxiously ahead for a glimpse of familiar hills. But he had ridden much farther away than he realized. Still, Lew was sure of his direction, so he rode steadily ahead.

He was right in his sense of direction, but the horse he rode naturally veered to the right, and instead of heading for camp, Lew gradually drifted in a widening arc that brought him two miles south.

Finally, after he had ridden more than far enough, Lew realized he was lost. At first, he thought of riding in ever-widening circles to pick up his own trail or some familiar landmark, but he gave this up and halted.

"The sensible thing to do," he thought, "is to stop where I am until the sun comes up. Then I can either see camp or calculate how to reach it. That's what Charlie would do," he grinned to himself, "and is hoping I'll do."

His horse suddenly threw up its head, and as Lew bent forward to grasp the reins more firmly, a strange whirling noise smote his ears. Then a lariat settled over his shoulders and jerked him from the saddle. A second later he was being dragged over the sand behind a galloping horse.

Chapter 5 – Death in the Desert

It came so suddenly Lew scarcely knew what happened. Then the rope about his chest and arms, and the sharp pains that shot through his knees and thighs as rocks and cacti dug through his clothes, brought speedy realization of his plight—he had been roped off his horse and was being dragged across the desert!

He tried to reach his gun, but the taut rope pinned his arms to his sides. All he could do was throw back his head to try to save his face as he was dragged rapidly along.

Through the stinging sand he could just distinguish the dim outline of a horseman. Did the man intend to drag him to death?

When his despair was greatest, the speed slackened. A moment later he knew the man was checking his horse. Hope revived, and he then decided upon instant revenge for this foul attack. As soon as he could free his right arm, he would draw the gun from his belt. With the earth to steady his arm, he couldn't miss such an easy shot.

The horse was walking slowly now, a most welcome change from the ripping pace. In a minute more it would stop, and then …

But a quick hand plucked the gun from his belt, and a whistled command brought the horse to a stop. The man had slid from his saddle, leaving the horse walking on to keep the rope tight about Lew's arms while he secured his revolver. Lew rolled over and stared straight into the face of the ranch bully Charlie had soundly thrashed that morning—Sandy MacTare!

MacTare grunted his disappointment. "Dern yuh," he snarled. "I thought yose was thet cocky partner. But you'll do to start on," and stooping, he skillfully bound Lew's hands behind his back and lashed his feet together with heavy thongs.

MacTare chuckled evilly as he tested each knot. "Where did yuh git thet gold dust yore partner showed Hetter?"

"An Indian gave it to him," answered Lew.

"I suppose yuh expect me to believe thet Indians is in the habit of givin' their gold away? No, I got ter have somethin' better thun thet. Yuh might as well come across, son. We got ways ter make folk talk out here in the desert."

"That's all you'll get," retorted Lew, "for it's all I know."

''I reckon you'll change yore tune," said Sandy. "I'm goin' to roll yuh over in this sand wallow and let yuh lie thar until about mid-afternoon tomorrow."

He dragged Lew into a shallow pit in the sand and crammed a gag in his mouth. "Maybe by thet time yore memory will have freshened, what with the heat and thirst and scorpions and snakes."

He turned and mounted his horse, pausing for a parting word, "It'll be about a hundred and twenty in the sun by noon tomorrow."

Lew heard the soft footfalls of the pony thudding away in the dusk. He twisted his head and saw he was lying in a hollow scooped out of the sand by the wind. That wind now sucked down into the bowl and raised a thin flickering of sand. The stuff whirled about, and then settling, covered the toes of his boots. It was possible that by the next day he could be buried alive in drifting sand. And if the rustler did not return, the world might never know his fate.

He looked at the sides of the bowl. Were they too steep to roll up and out? Although he ached in every muscle and joint, he exerted all of his strength and rolled vigorously towards the top. But halfway up, the loose sand crumbled and he tumbled back in a choking cloud.

Lew was still hopeful. His injuries were not serious although painful, and with hours of cool night ahead, he had time to find some means of escape. Systematically, he tested every knot that bound his hands and feet. MacTare evidently had experience tying up captives, and Lew soon knew he had absolutely no chance to slip these bonds.

An hour passed slowly as the moon climbed a cloudless sky. He wondered what Charlie and Jim might be doing. Why, he might be within a half-mile or less of camp. The gag choked back the shouts that rose to his lips. He could only grunt in his throat and nose, sounds too faint to carry a hundred feet.

A faint rustle jerked him alert. Then a strangely repulsive odor filled his nostrils, and Lew's heart chilled. He turned his head and stared into the cold, unlidded eyes of a rattlesnake. He held off the natural impulse to roll back and away from that venomous death. The muscular serpent was coiled within three feet of his face, easy striking range. Lew knew his only chance of life was to feign death. Snakes do not strike dead men. But any motion, even the flickering of eyelashes, might bring the fatal spring.

The yellow-brown folds seemed to slowly swell, and he knew the snake was coiling. The rattles sang an angry warning, but by iron force of will, Lew lay still. He closed his eyes. Perhaps the light in his stare had aroused the snake's ire. Every moment he expected to feel the sting of venom-loaded fangs. His heart pounded so loudly he felt the rattler surely must hear it.

Finally, he could stand the suspense no longer and peeped out from under his eyelashes. The snake had turned and was retreating back over its own slippery coils. With difficulty, he refrained from moaning. With the snake out of view, Lew decided he should try to sleep an hour or two. Rest would refresh his body and clear his mind. He closed his eyes and dozed off.

A sharp gust of wind awoke him as a miniature whirlwind spun over the sand bowl, lifting and leveling the red grit. He looked down and saw his legs covered with two inches of sand. He decided against any more sleep.

Something glinted by his foot, a small object that reflected the moonlight. The sand shifted again, and sitting up, he saw it was a half-covered tin can. The top had been cut open with an ax, and the points pried outward. Some prospector had halted his burro here out of the wind and eaten a meal of canned pork and beans.

Naturally, the thought of food made Lew hungry. Then hope flooded his heart. Upon such small tricks of fate are nations lost and lives saved. Lew wriggled to get his bound hands overtop of the can. His weight pressed it firmly into the sand, and arching his back to make working room, he began to saw the thongs that held his wrists across the sharp-edged tin.

The tin was soft, and too much pressure only bent the points, so he had to depend upon constant sawing back and forth. His hands slipped often, and the jagged tin bit into his flesh, but he kept doggedly on. Every ten minutes he had to stop and gain new strength in his wrists and hands.

It seemed as though he had worked for hours before the thongs slipped a fraction of an inch, but they were still secure when he tried to pry his hands apart. Streaks of crimson were diffusing in the sky overhead when the soft "pad-pad" of a horse caught his ear.

Was MacTare returning already? He wormed about and saw a horse looking down at him. He noted in surprise that the saddle was empty and then recognized his own pony. It had wandered about since he was dragged from its back by MacTare's lariat.

Hope again filled Lew. Here was a quick way to reach camp the moment his bonds were cut. He began his work with fresh vigor. He could feel the warm blood from gashed wrists run down his fingers. His head began to swim. The gag in his parched mouth was becoming unbearable as the sun rose and heated the dry desert air.

He felt more than heard the horse's feet beating upon the ground, and then a voice—MacTare! The rustler had returned in time to thwart Lew's escape. He gave a mighty jerk at the thongs but they held. The rustler stood over him looking down with an evil grin.

"Wasn't expectin' me so soon, eh?" He removed the gag from Lew's mouth and unstrapped a canteen from his saddle. Lew lifted his face eagerly, and MacTare poured water in the sand beside his face. Lew sank back, ashamed of the eagerness he had displayed. He set his teeth and silently awaited the other's next move.

"Not ready to talk?" asked the rustler. "Well, I reckon I'd better go on and not come back until sundown. Got a little business over thar by them hills, anyway, soon as the rest of the boys catch up. Maybe yore partner or the kid'll be more talkative. I might even forget to come back this way if we git what we're after."

At the thought of the rustler torturing Charlie and Jim, desperate anger flared up inside Lew. He gave a terrific pull at his bound hands, felt the thongs give and then part. His arms shot out from under him and wrapped around the rustler's feet. The surprised Mac-Tare hit the sand hard but then kicked and rolled cat-like out of reach. Lew's hobbled feet prevented swift pursuit, and MacTare scrambled to his feet, drawing a knife.

"I'll fix yore face so your own mama won't know you," he promised. Lew struggled to his knees, eyes fixed on the evil glitter of the knife. Then an angry whir behind MacTare caught his keen ears, and Lew saw bulging coils whip about the rustler's leg. The man screamed once, and an ugly flat head darted against his thigh. MacTare had stepped on the giant rattler, and the reptile was taking swift vengeance.

The rustler kicked wildly, lost his balance and toppled over. The snake uncoiled from his leg and glided up over the edge of the crater under a clump of sage.

Lew waited, but MacTare lay still on the sand. Surely even a rattlesnake bite would not paralyze a man so quickly. But MacTare did not move even when Lew hobbled over and swiftly jerked his gun from its holster. Twirling the cylinders to count the loaded chambers, he prodded the prostrate form with his toe. Then he rolled the man on his back and saw that MacTare had fallen on the point of his own knife, his weight driving it through his heart.

Lew pulled out the knife and used it to slash the ropes from his ankles. With a short run, he gained the top of the sand bowl. The big snake rattled a warning as he passed the sage bush. Lew hesitated with gun in hand. Then he smiled with a wry grimace.

"I guess I've killed my last rattlesnake. Think of it. An empty bean can and a rattler! I never would have believed I would owe my life to such a combination."

Lew examined the rustler's mount. "I guess my own horse is better," he said. "You look like you've had some pretty hard riding." Then he pulled a short rifle from the saddle scabbard, searched through the saddlebag and found a box of shells. Satisfied with these finds, Lew walked to his own horse and mounted.

The range of hills where they had camped the night before were plainly visible now, and he galloped towards them, remembering the words of the dead MacTare: "As soon as the rest of the boys catch up with me …"

He must hurry to warn Charlie and begin the run for their lives. As he rode, he looked back over his shoulder in the direction of the ranch. There it was—a low cloud of dust hovering where earth and sky met, a cloud raised by hard-riding horsemen.

When he saw Lew galloping into camp, Jim shouted with joy. But Charlie's face remained rather stern as he asked, "Where the heck have you been?"

"I'll tell you as we ride," Lew broke in. "You'll have plenty of time to bawl me out later, but Hetter's rustlers are only about five miles back, burning leather to catch us. Come on, let's go!"

As they rode he told them of his ordeal, and when the tale was finished, Charlie reached out his hand and said, "I won't bawl you out this time, old-timer. You deserve a hand for coming through as you did, and if MacTare hadn't roped you alone, he probably would have sneaked up on our camp and got us all."

"It sounds just like a story," cried Jim, his eyes bright with admiration. But then his face darkened, and he asked more soberly, "What now? Will they keep after us?"

"I think they will," replied Lew. "We'll either have to lose them in the mountains or reach someplace where we can stand them off. We won't last long out here in the open."

They rode in silence for an hour. Charlie looked back over his shoulder often, and the ominous sign of pursuit dogged their trail. Their pursuers were still miles away, but the gap had narrowed, and Charlie wondered at that. Their horses were fairly fresh from a night's rest while those ridden by Hetter's gang must be jaded from a long night journey.

"How far off are they?"

"About five miles," calculated Charlie. "Maybe less."

At his words, Jim dug his heels into his pony's flank and shot ahead at a furious gallop.

"Whoa there!" commanded Lew. "That's exactly what you must not do. We can't outrun those fellows. All we can hope for is to keep our lead until nightfall or we run into something to help us out. If we crowd the horses, they'll be played out by noon."

The sun was blazing down with all its force, and their horses' gait gradually slackened. Had Hetter deliberately given them horses with limited endurance? As a matter of business, he might have shocked off his poorest riding stock, but Charlie was inclined to give him credit for more sinister motives.

It seemed as though they lost speed every hundred yards, and the hovering dust cloud was drawing in on them. An hour later, Charlie decided their lead had been reduced by more than a mile. At that rate, they would be overtaken long before sunset.

He searched the plain ahead, looking desperately for a place where they could hide or, with their backs against a wall of rock, stand off the rustlers. Nothing but the dreary sameness of desert met his eyes, that and the haze-shrouded mountains in the distance.

"We won't make the mountains," Lew finally said. "And these horses won't hold out until night. How's it going to end, Charlie?"

"Don't give up hope. But those horses behind must be made out of iron. Watch them …"

"Say," Lew interrupted. "What's that ahead? A canyon?"

A rift was slowly opening in the ground before them. At first, they could see only a narrow line, but at half a mile, they could clearly see it was wide and deep and extended as far as they could see to either side.

"Maybe it's the Grand Canyon," said Jim.

We're hundreds of miles from that," answered Charlie. "I just hope there's a path down and water at the bottom when we get there."

They rode up to the rim and stopped. Lew pointed to the opposite wall of the canyon, to hundreds of small openings in the sheer rock face. There were hundreds of them arranged in tiers, one above the other, the top row being hundreds of feet above the bottom.

"Cliff dwellings!" exclaimed Charlie. "And, boy, do those

caves in the rock look good to me. Hurry! Let's get down and over to them. If we can hide before Hetter and his gang arrive, it'll take them a week to find us."

The trail swerved over the brim of the canyon and zigzagged down to the valley below. Urging the horses forward, they crowded down the hazardous path. "If we could only hide the broncos," said Lew, "Hetter would never know what became of us. See any water?"

"Not yet," Charlie replied. "But I think the horses smell it. See how they've picked up since we started down? I'm afraid we'll have to turn them loose. Hetter will guess we've taken to the caves, but it'll still be a job to smoke us out."

They made the bottom and spurred the jaded animals across to the opposite side. "Look at the ladder," cried Jim, pointing to a pair of cedar poles with lashed crossbars. "Somebody must live here."

"The cave dwellers are long gone," Charlie replied. "That ladder might be hundreds of years old. Cedar doesn't rot in this climate. Or maybe some archeologist made it while exploring the caves. Anyway, it's going to come in handy for us."

Then he looked back anxiously, fearing he would see their pursuers riding up to the canyon brink, but the skyline was clear.

"Here's water," called Lew. It was a small pool in the shade of the wall, and the horses strained eagerly towards it.

"Jump off and fill the canteens," commanded Charlie. "Let the brutes drink while we strip off the food bags and the saddles."

They jerked off the riding leather and equipment, working in feverish haste. "Turn the horses loose," snapped Charlie. "Hit them a whack on the back and start them down the valley. We must get this stuff up in a cave before Hetter shows up. Sharp now!"

He sprang up the ladder, testing the rungs. They were stiff and sound. They hauled their stuff up twenty feet to the first cave mouth.

Lew looked up, calculating the climb. "We've got time to make another story," he decided. And drawing up the ladder hand over hand, he planted the bottom on a ledge of rock and started up to another tier twenty feet higher.

"Just like a fireman scaling a skyscraper," he grinned down to encourage Jim.

It took six trips to carry all of their stuff up. "Do we have time to make another story?" Lew asked. "The higher we get, the safer."

"Pull that ladder in, now!" Charlie ordered in a low voice. "I hear them coming!"

And just as Lew dragged the last foot of cedar into the cave, horsemen crowded the opposite canyon rim. They drew back in the deep shadows of the cave. "Lie quiet," commanded Charlie. "Rustlers might have night glasses that reach back in these shadows. But if we don't move, maybe they won't spot us. The horses got a fair start. Maybe Hetter won't pay any attention to them."

Then the sharp report of a high-power rifle rang across the valley, and Charlie's horse, the piebald with the glass eye, stumbled and fell kicking in the sand. "The devils," whispered Lew. "They are shooting the horses!"

Two more shots and all three were down. "Whoever it is can shoot some," was all Charlie said, though Lew could feel his partner's seething anger. "They're taking no chances. I will say Hetter is a thorough chap."

"What'll he do next?" asked Jim fearfully.

"We'll soon see," answered Charlie in grim tones. "But things don't look quite so good now that our horses are gone. All they have to do is camp at the water pool, and thirst will drive us down to them. Even if we do shake these fellows, we're half a thousand miles from anywhere. If there's as much desert ahead as we've come over thus far, we will never get out on foot. What do you say, Lew?"

Chapter 6 – Holed Up in the Cliffs

L ew looked over to the opposite wall of the canyon at the armed horsemen lining the rim and then he gazed back into the shadows of the cave dwelling that sheltered them.

"Well," he replied to Charlie's question, "I think we could be a darned sight worse off. This rock wall over my head and at my back makes me feel pretty good, and we made it just in time. The horses are gone, but they wouldn't have lasted another half hour. No, I feel a heap better than I did an hour ago when we were burning leather just to keep ahead of Hetter's gang. Water is the only weak part in our present setup."

"Exactly," said Charlie grimly. "Water is going to decide this business. It usually does in the desert. Hetter will block our way to water, for sure, and I don't see how we're going to stop him."

"We can get the ladder out tonight and keep climbing," suggested Jim. "Maybe we can get to the top and sneak away in the dark."

Charlie shook his head at that. "We can't start out over the desert on foot. They would run us down as easy as a coyote taking a wandering lamb."

"Seeing as we may stay awhile," Lew said, "I've always wanted to explore an ancient cliff dwelling. Jim, suppose you lie here with my rifle and watch Hetter and his gang. Charlie and I will take a look back in the cave."

The mouth of the cave extended maybe ten feet and then opened into a larger room.

Lew carefully darted his pocket light over the room. The walls were smooth, carved out of the cliff by ancient masons. "This must have been the living room," said Lew. "Look! There's a stone fireplace," and he played the beam across a heap of oblong stones, still crusted with soot.

"There's ash still in it," he exclaimed. And, sure enough, charred bits of wood also were scattered about. Behind stood an earthen jar skillfully fashioned from clay with a twisted loop over the top to serve as a handle.

"Looks like this cave has been used recently," said Charlie.

"Not necessarily," answered Lew. "I have read about archeologists finding seeds in the clay granaries of cliff dwellers, stuff that had been stored a thousand years, and the grain actually grew when they planted it. In this dry climate, everything stays about as it was in the beginning."

"I know all that," Charlie replied, "but still, there's something fresh about this fireplace. Let's go farther in."

The cave narrowed again, forming another short passageway, and then they found themselves in a second room, larger and wider than the first. Again, Lew played his light over the walls and ceiling, but when he lowered it to the floor both exclaimed in surprise. A file of footprints could be plainly seen in the dust, running, straight into the black shadows beyond.

"Gosh," said Lew. "I never thought footprints could be preserved this long."

"They can't," declared Charlie. "Those tracks are fresh. The desert wind still blows in here and would cover them in less than a week. Look how sharp the edges are cut. I'll bet a good hound dog could find enough warmth in them to follow with his eyes shut. No, this cave has been used within the past few days—or hours."

They started to go forward when a low cry from Jim brought them running back to the mouth of the cave. "They've reached the pool underneath," he said. "I should have guarded the pool," he added. "I could have covered it with the rifle."

"No use," answered Charlie. "When the sun went down, they would have walked right in. Don't worry, Jim. You didn't fall down on the job a bit."

"What will we do for water?" asked the boy.

"Our bags will last another day if we are careful," Lew said, "and I have an idea to get more. Water doesn't worry me as much as those footprints back in the cave."

As he told of their discovery Jim listened in wonder.

He stopped suddenly as a voice called up from the valley below. It was Hetter, and the absolute lack of expression in the tones only made the words more sinister.

"I'm going to give you boys one chance to come clean. No Indian ever just gave a white man gold. I've spent three years trying to find that gold, killed a dozen men who crossed my path."

He paused to let those last words sink in. Then he continued. "You may think you're safe, but I explored these ruins thoroughly when I first came to the ranch. If you think I'm bluffing, I used night glasses to see you in the cave where you are hiding, and if you check, you will find four passageways leading out of the rear room. How will three of you watch all four tonight?

"Tell me straight how and where you got that feather quill of gold dust, and I'll put you on three of my best horses and send you back south unharmed. If you don't, we'll drag you out, tonight or tomorrow, and make you talk. It won't be pleasant. Take half an hour to think it over."

Charlie, Lew and Jim sat silently staring at each other, each feeling a tiny prickling of fear play up his spine.

"There's one thing about that guy," whispered Lew in an effort to regain his natural, easy manner. "He's reliable. I think we can bank on the part about getting dragged out and made to talk."

"Doesn't matter," said Charlie, "we can never make him believe this accursed gold was merely handed to us as a present. We'll have to see this business through, same as if we did know where the Navajo found his gold dust. I wish we did know. It's tough to have to fight like this for nothing."

"We aren't fighting for nothing," cut in Lew. "Man, can't you see we're fighting for our lives? That fellow meant every word, except the part about sending us back unharmed if we tell what he wants to know."

"I'm going back to check on those passages," Charlie said, and then he ran inside with the light. In a minute he was back.

"Hetter's right," he said grimly. "Four narrow passages, and the footprints lead straight through the center one. We must move out of here as soon as night is dark enough to cover us. The quicker we find a cave with but one opening, the better I'll feel."

The odor of burning wood came up from the valley, and presently Lew sniffed the air like a coon dog on a trail. "Smell that steak frying?" he asked hungrily. "We haven't eaten all day. Let's feast on the fatted calf, Charlie. I prefer to face trouble on a full stomach."

"Your fatted calf is going to be plain bacon," Charlie said, "But look around. I'm guessing there's a pile of wood back of the fireplace. I'm going to run back down those passageways and see if one leads to a smaller, less accessible cave."

The crackle of burning cedar followed Lew's search, and Charlie decided to go ahead and make a quick exploration of the main passageway leading out of the back. Carrying the flashlight in one hand, his gun in the other, he followed the footprints.

The passage pitched abruptly down at a steep angle. Though

the walls grew rough, the floor was smooth as pavement. Flashing his light down, he saw a trough worn down the center. This was likely the main path down to the bottom of the canyon, probably leading to the water pool below. Generations of cliff dwellers had worn it in the rock as they walked down in the course of daily life.

Charlie thought he must be near the level of the canyon floor now, and he was right, for the path turned to horizontal, and ahead a brighter spot glowed. The cave opened but a few yards above the pool, a slit in the cliff so narrow Charlie wondered if maybe he and Lew could pile it full of rocks and seal the way.

Then he remembered the three other passages and their need to hurry. It would be impossible to block them all in time. He turned and noiselessly ran back up into the cave. As he ran, he wondered who had left the trail of footprints. Had one of Hetter's men been in the back room watching them? The idea sent another shiver up his spine.

A coupe of minutes later, he stood looking down on smoking plates of bacon and hot tomatoes Lew was setting on the cave floor. Long shadows were shooting across the canyon with astonishing speed, and the air was chilling rapidly. Lew threw on more wood, and the fire blazed up cheerily.

"Notice how this smoke sucks up?" he asked. "This cave is more like a sieve. What did you find?"

"I found enough to make me want to get out of here as quickly as we can," Charlie replied. "Let's eat fast, and as soon as the night will cover us, we're going to use the ladder to climb up. I don't know what we'll find, but trying one of the passageways will likely lead us square into an ambush."

"This meal made quite a hole in the water supply," said Lew. "I've got a scheme to get more before we climb up. In a few minutes, it will be dark enough to try."

"Work fast," cautioned Charlie.

While they waited for night they packed their outfit into the two pack sacks and pulled the ladder to the mouth of the cave, ready to climb. Then they sat listening and watching the large room with four black mouths of danger through which a horde of armed rustlers might rush at any second.

Finally, Lew stood up, walked to the room and brought out the big clay jug. He tied a rope to the twisted handle and then stepped to the mouth of the cave, balanced himself over the pool of water, and lowered the jug.

Presently, Charlie heard a faint splash. Then he heard a bump and another as Lew pulled the water-filled jug up the side of the cliff. But a rifle cracked in the valley below, and Lew scrambled hurriedly back inside.

"They were watching all the time," he said ruefully. "When I got it within three feet, they practically shot it out of my hand. Come on. Let's get out of here while we still can."

"We can't try the ladder for a few minutes more," Charlie cautioned. "If they could still see well enough to hit a jug they could easily pot us off of the face of the cliff. We'll just have to sit here and wait a while longer.

Jim walked back to the fire and piled on more wood. Then he ran back at full speed. "I hear somebody coming through the passageway!" he whispered fearfully.

"Quick, Lew! Stand up the ladder," commanded Charlie, leaping to his feet. Then he stepped into the opening that led to the inner room. "Send Jim up first, and then follow with the pack sacks. I'll cover you!"

Lew dragged the ladder outside and stood it against the cliff, planting the bottom as firmly as he could on the narrow shelf of rock. He motioned for Jim to climb, but before the boy reached the ladder a shout from Charlie whirled them about.

A group of dark figures were rushing from the inner room, and they heard a sharp command in Hetter's voice, "Remember, don't kill them all!"

The rustlers' tall shadows flashed across the walls as they cut in before the blazing fire. Charlie rolled one with a quick shot through the thigh. The man behind him also stumbled over the fallen one, but the third cleared both with a mighty jump that carried him clear past Charlie out into the mouth of the cave. Then he sprang at Lew, but as he did, Jim stuck out his foot and tripped him. He fell headlong into the ladder, knocking it over and down into the canyon, where it landed with a clatter.

The rustler clutched frantically at the ledge as he sprawled forward, and for a moment Lew thought he would check himself. But he followed the ladder with a different kind of thud when he landed on the rocks below.

Charlie was swinging his rifle now, clubbing at the men who jammed into the narrow hallway. With the ladder gone, Lew knew they were fighting for their lives. He drew his revolver and fired point-blank into the face of the nearest rustler.

"Stop clubbing," he told Charlie. "The ladder fell. We're trapped, and we'll have to shoot our way out."

Then Jim screamed from the mouth of the cave. "There's a rope coming down the cliff from above!"

"What the ..." began Charlie, and then he shouted. "Climb it kid! We'll follow! Run, Lew, and grab our stuff! I can hold them a few seconds more. If you don't," he added as Lew hesitated, "none of us will get out of here."

Seeing the sense of his words, Lew fired twice and then ran as the crowd charged Charlie. He reached the mouth of the cave, and, sure enough, a twisted hide rope swayed back and forth. He jumped up, and catching hold above his head, pulled himself up behind Jim.

Charlie pumped the lever of the rifle until a click told him the magazine was empty. Then he struck the first face before him. A hand grabbed the stock and jerked him forward, but he dropped the weapon and leaped with every ounce of his strength to the cave mouth. Just as he grasped the rope, a man dove at his feet, and hugging him about the knees, pulled him back.

Charlie knew in a second more he would be a captive. He pulled out his hunting knife and slashed the arm that held him, and the grip relaxed. A sharp kick, and he was free. Then his arms worked like pistons as he pulled himself up the rope, holding legs high above the clutching hands below.

Charlie swiftly drew himself up to the end of the rope, where Lew grasped his collar and pulled him over on his face. "Are you hurt?" Lew demanded. "I was just starting down to help when you got clear."

"I could hardly hold him back," a familiar voice spoke, and looking about, Charlie stared into the eyes of Wai-ton the Navajo, dimly lit by a small fire back inside the cave.

"Not sure why you're here," was all he could think to say, "but mighty glad to see you."

"Red Eagle, my foster brother, brought me here to recover from Hetter's bullet," Wai-ton explained. Then he motioned to a Navajo youth sitting by the fire, maybe four years older than Jim but already a man in his tribe.

A scraping sound jerked his attention back to the face of the cliff. The rope was quivering. "They're climbing up after us," whispered Lew, as he reached for his six-shooter. But Wai-ton waved him back and squatted beside the end of the rope, knife in hand.

Heavy breathing sounded from below, then a hand reached up, and Wai-ton calmly slashed the strands of twisted hide. They snapped like a bowstring, and a wild cry pierced the air, followed a moment later by another heavy thud.

"Two, perhaps more on it," Wai-ton said calmly. "Come inside. They will not bother us anymore."

Charlie glanced about the cave, noting that there was no inner room, just a single passage leading back into the cliff. The Navajo, following his eye, said, "You were not so lucky picking your cave. We were in an even safer cave, up near the top of the cliff. As soon as night fell we climbed down with our lariats. I was ready to swing over the edge when they rushed you. Then I saw your ladder fall and swung my rope down, hoping you would see it and use it."

"You saved our lives," Lew said.

Wai-ton dismissed that with a wave of his hand. "Tell me—why is Hetter after you?"

Charlie quickly told the tale, repeating Hetter's claim of years spent looking for the Navajo gold mine.

Wai-ton grunted in disdain. "The pig can search the desert for a lifetime and not find a grain of gold unless I show him where to look. I alone of the Navajo nation know the secret. And I wish I had been deaf when it was whispered to me by my dying father.

"In my father's time, gold was used only in religious ceremonies. The white man's whisky and lust for gold have ruined my tribe. Now, Navajos cut each other's throats for a handful and what it will buy at the trader's post.

"I have made my last trip to the Valley of Heat for gold. I swore this before Hetter shot me. The gold has only brought my people trouble and death."

The fire flickered up, revealing a face set in lines as stern and hard as the rock upon which Wai-ton sat. Then the Navajo looked searchingly into Charlie's eyes. "Would you like to know the secret of the gravel beds, where a man can wash out not ounces but pounds of gold?"

Chapter 7 – The Valley of Fire

Charlie, Lew and Jim all jumped to their feet and cried as one, "Yes! Tell us where you find the gold!"

The Navajo, eyes flickering as if he inwardly mocked their eagerness, replied, "It is not only a matter of knowing where to go. You must have the stamina of the antelope. You must be as immune to heat as the lizard. It is a long, hard path through the Valley of Heat, where the winds blow straight from the gates of hell!"

"We'll take our chances," Lew replied. "You said you don't want any more of this gold, and you do not want your tribe to have it. Then give us the chance, that's all we ask."

"The gold is but forty miles from here," answered Wai-ton, "mixed with sand and gravel in the bed of a dry river, so thickly you can see it glint in the sunlight, nearly a third pure gold. But those forty are miles over soft, sucking sand that is too loose to hold a horse; the only way is walking in the broad moccasins we Navajos have worn for generations.

"Tomorrow, I will take you to the trail—if after you hear the rest of my tale you are still willing to try. The cave above us has a tunnel leading out on top of the cliff. We will start early, before sunrise, and be miles away in the desert before Hetter knows we are gone."

"What will you do, then?" asked Charlie. "It looks like we brought a heap of trouble at our heels and dumped it on your door."

"After I have shown you the trail," replied Wai-ton, "I and Red Eagle will wait in the caves. I evened up the score in part last night, but the balance against him is still big. Hetter will not find me until I am ready to exact that revenge. Now, listen carefully. I will not have time to repeat this in the morning.

"I will walk with you over the loose sand until the trail becomes plain enough for the eyes of white men to see. Before I leave you, I will show you a line that you can run by compass, straight to a water hole twenty miles away. This is the only water, and it cannot be depended upon. Many years ago, the hole in the rock stayed full the year around. Now it goes dry for weeks at a time. No one knows why.

"When you reach this water hole tomorrow at midnight, if it is dry, you must turn back immediately while what water you have carried lasts. If you keep on, you are as good as dead, for there is no more water ahead.

"If you find water, take all you can carry and save every drop the rest of your way, for you must carry enough to last you through the valley and then back again. There is no water where you will find the gold. That ancient river has been dry for ages."

"How will we find the trail from the water pool?" asked Lew.

"I have piled rocks in signal cairns," answered Wai-ton, "two to the mile. They look like other piles of stone, unless you know how to read them."

He gathered a handful of stones from the cave floor, forming them into a curiously shaped mound. "Study this. If you know what to look for, you will not miss it. When you reach the river of gold, do not lose your heads and stay too long. You may sleep several hours, but stay no longer. Do not overload yourselves. Take only what you carry easily. Then pray you find the pool full on your way back. If it has gone dry, there is no hope, and the accursed gold has claimed three more lives.

"You will find dead men along the trail, sun-dried mummies. One, a man of my own tribe and my friend, spied on me in his lust for the things gold will buy. He started across the Valley of Fire alone. I found his body on my next trip. He had used part of his precious water to wash gold from the sand in order to carry more."

Wai-ton rose to his feet. "We sleep now," he said simply, crossed to the back of the cave and lay down beside Red Eagle. He pulled his blanket over his shoulders without another word.

"What do you think?" Lew asked Charlie. "Will the gold we can carry be worth the risk, if it's mixed with sand?"

"I'm too tired to make a decision now," he replied. "We'll sleep on that question."

It seemed to Charlie that he had scarcely fallen asleep before Wai-ton shook him and whispered in his ear. "It is time to start. Be quiet. Sound travels in the night air."

He looked at his watch. It was three o'clock. He aroused Lew and Jim, repeating the warning, and they made brief preparations to start. The Navajo looked over their packs and advised them to leave behind every article that would not be absolutely necessary. He frowned at Lew's determination to carry a gun, saying, "You cannot fight thirst with bullets." But Lew flatly refused to go without his six-shooter. The rest of their outfit fit in one light pack. This and the water bags comprised their load.

Wai-ton walked to the mouth of the cave, grasped the end of a leather lariat that hung down from the cave above, and pulled himself up hand over hand. They followed and presently stood inside the upper cave. Here Wai-ton said, "The boy should stay with Red Eagle until you return."

"That's a good idea," answered Charlie.

Jim begged hard to accompany them, and Charlie finally said, "It's plain foolishness, Jim. You'll hold us back." But the boy protested until Charlie finally gave in rather than waste more time arguing.

Wai-ton beckoned them to follow and took them back in the narrow cave to a large clay jar so tall and broad it resembled a cistern. "We keep this full when we stay in the caves," he explained.

Then he brought forth three more water bags. This made a load of two each, a stiff load, but as he pointed out, a load that would be lightened all too quickly. "Use the empty bags to carry back sand and gold from the river bed," he said.

After he filled the bags from the jar, he rubbed each in the thick dust covering the cave floor. "What's that for?" asked Lew.

"Water bags sweat so evaporation cools the water, but you cannot risk losing even an ounce," Wai-ton said.

The cave narrowed until they were walking with heads and shoulders stooped. The air was close, and soon they followed their guide on hands and knees. He finally stopped, thrusting up one arm, and then disappeared through a small patch of light. They followed, squeezing through a hole no larger than a badger's den. They found themselves on the plain a hundred yards back from the canyon.

Wai-ton spread a low sagebrush on top of the hole, covering it completely. The Navajo walked on, and they dropped in behind. Now that they had started, all doubts of the wisdom of their dangerous expedition had vanished.

The ground grew softer underfoot, and presently they were ankle-deep in sand. Wai-ton pulled out four pairs of curiously made moccasins, donned one and handed a pair each. They put on the strange foot gear, which was made of stiff cowhide with soft sheepskin uppers. They were twice as broad as a man's foot, but padded cleverly so they fit with fair comfort.

"They make me think of snowshoes," grinned Lew.

They hung their other shoes around their necks. Lew suggested they leave them, but Wai-ton shook his head. "You will need them to cross through the Valley of Heat," he explained.

For a while they walked easily along. But the sand became looser than ever, and once more they were sinking to their ankles. Every step was an effort.

A single shaft of light from the rising sun shot over the rim of the distant mountains, and lighting the air about them, disclosed a remarkable sight. They were traveling through endless low mounds of sand, heaps that stretched out as far as they could see. It was pure sand—not a cactus, greasewood or shrub of sage to break the monotony. The sand shone ghastly white, a death's head hue in startling contrast to the soft shadows that still enveloped the mountain peaks.

Wai-ton strode ahead, picking his way first this way and then that, never hesitating. His manner was so sure, they felt absolute confidence even though they could discern no trail. Mile after mile dragged by, and the rising sun brought stifling waves of heat radiating up from the sand. Great drops of perspiration beaded their faces, but the cheeks of the Indian were as dry as the sand itself when he stopped and turned to them.

"Time to drink," he said, and raising his water bag, gulped down but two mouthfuls. They imitated him and drank sparingly, remembering they would need every drop for the return trip if they found the water pool dry.

"Say," Lew called ahead to Wai-ton. "How are we going to find our way back across the sand? I haven't a blessed idea of the way we came to get here."

"If things go right, you will be back at sunset on the fourth day, and I will be waiting for you at the same place I leave you. Come straight back from the pool by compass, and you will find me."

He walked two hundred yards farther and stopped. "Give me the compass," he said. Sighting carefully over the small dial, he glanced at the sun and then back.

"Here," he said, handing the instrument to Charlie, "run a course straight ahead two points north of west, and you will go directly to the pool. Sight in two hills ahead to keep the line straight. You must not miss it. The pool lies on the edge of the valley, and when you first see black, burned stones, watch for it."

He looked into their faces. "May the Sun God spare you today. I hope the gold you bring will repay your effort." Then he left them.

"Well, we're on our own now," said Charlie. "Let's have another small drink and then push on. How you standing it, Jim?"

"Fine," replied the boy. His lighter body weight had been a big

46

help in crossing the loose sand.

"Did you ever see such navigating?" Lew marveled. "Over wastes of sand without faltering or hesitating once? And he was so sure of every step I haven't the slightest doubt we will come straight to the water pool if we follow his directions."

"That was instinct," said Charlie, "developed over generations of desert life. The Northern Indian can pick his path through a wilderness of spruce or birch the same way. If it had been anybody else, I never would have risked our lives by trusting that we will reach water after crossing this sea of sand."

"Just thinking about it makes me thirsty," Lew replied. "I could drink a gallon of water right now."

"Don't think about water," cautioned Charlie. "Think of all that gold, instead. Maybe we can make another trip after this one."

"I don't think so," said Lew. "Something tells me this is going to be our last jaunt, so let's make it count."

They started on, Charlie carrying compass in hand, sighting a course between sand hills with careful accuracy. Instead of skirting the largest, he led them straight overtop, afraid to lose the course by circling. This made walking harder, as the drifting stuff was loosest, sliding and rolling under their feet.

The hills were getting lower, and in another hour they were walking on a desert bed that was nearly level. The sand was as soft as ever, but for some reason it had not drifted. Noon came with the sun straight overhead, and the choking heat brought gasps of fatigue as they walked slowly on. Finally, Charlie stopped.

"I'm not hungry," he said, "but I think we should eat a little to keep up our strength."

Lew dropped the pack he was carrying and sat down in the sand, but he had scarcely landed when he jumped up with a cry. "The stuff is red hot!"

Charlie opened the pack and took out a large square of dried meat Wai-ton had given them for desert travel. He cut off a slice for each and opened a can of tomatoes.

"Tastes like dried venison," Lew commented, washing it down with the warm tomato juice.

"With no added salt," answered Charlie. "Wai-ton knows his business when it comes to the desert."

Lew swallowed his last bite and then said, "I wonder sometimes if I'm really out here or if I'll wake up and find myself chugging along in the old car. Boy, hasn't a lot happened in just four days?"

"Why didn't we wait until night to cross the sand?" asked Jim. "It would be cooler, then."

"True," conceded Charlie, "but the dickens would come when we tried to sleep during the desert day. I would rather do my walking now, with the prospect of a cool night's sleep ahead. Wai-ton gave us until midnight to reach the pool. Then a night of sleep with plenty of water will leave us fit for the last half of the journey. There won't be loose sand, I take it, but the heat will be even worse."

"How could it be any hotter than this?" groaned Lew.

The miles passed slowly. They stopped more often to drink small swallows of their precious water. It was nearly half gone, and Charlie warned his companions to preserve the last half in case they would need it to make a return trip from a dry pool.

Charlie carried the boy's water bags and shoes, and he was thinking that when they started from the pool in the morning, he would leave Jim behind. This would give the boy nearly two days of rest with water before the return, and he felt sure Jim would need it.

After a seeming eternity, the sun sank slowly behind the mountains, bringing relief from the heat and glare. Charlie doggedly held to a course of two points north of west, eyes aching with the strain. He pressed forward with increased speed, for he knew they must reach the pool before night was too far along. It would be hard to follow a compass line in the dusk, but it would be impossible an hour later. They ate a brief lunch and started again. The sun was now below the horizon, and the sand was cooling fast.

When Charlie realized that an hour more would bring full night and he might be unable to read the compass, he quickened the pace again. They simply must reach water. They still had three full bags of water, but they must know as soon as possible whether they would be forced to turn back from a dry pool.

Dusk descended with a swoop that startled him, and he stopped short, no longer sure of his direction. Had exhaustion made him veer to one side or the other, until the compass line was no longer leading them to water? The fear of what this might mean smote him with appalling force.

"I'm not sure anymore," confessed Charlie. "I'm afraid we may miss the water. Wai-ton said we must hold exactly to our direction to find it."

"He should have thought that darkness would be a problem,"

grumbled Lew.

"He is so used to going without a compass, I suppose he never thought of that," answered Charlie. "Well, let's keep on. No good standing around now."

As they walked, Charlie suddenly swerved about an object lying in the sand. He gave it a single glance and called loudly. "Speed up, boys; we'll be to water in an hour."

Lew and Jim following in his steps shuddered as they glanced down at the dried skeleton of a man sprawled beside their path. They knew Charlie's encouraging words were intended to soften this shocking reminder of the peril they faced.

It appeared to be the skeleton of a white man, the bones covered with a thin, transparent layer of what once was flesh and skin. Charlie wondered why coyotes had not stripped the bones. No pack, gun or tools were visible, and he thought he could read the details of the tragedy. Water gone, the man had flung aside his equipment and rushed blindly across the sand until he fell exhausted.

But it looked like they were on the right path. This man had likely found the pool dry, and had not saved water for the return. An hour passed, and it was so dark Charlie could no longer lay out any course ahead. He stumbled over something, and looking down, saw a rock burnt black in color.

"We're there," he called. "This must be the edge of the Valley of Heat. Wai-ton said it would be covered with black stones. The water pool can't be far now."

"I'm going to strike a line at right angles to our course," Lew said. "I'll run down ten minutes by my watch, and if I don't find water, I'll backtrack over my own trail. You wait here so I don't get lost. Then I'll run a line the other way and back again. If I don't find water, we'll go on ahead a couple of hundred yards and I'll do the same thing again. That way, we can search a lot of ground without losing our original line."

"It's a good plan," approved Charlie, and Lew vanished into the dusk without another word.

"I hope he don't start off after another jackrabbit," said Jim.

Charlie grinned at that but then winced as a dry, chapped lip cracked open. Lew came back twenty minutes later. "No sign," he said shortly and then vanished again, this time on the other side of their path.

Thirty minutes passed this time, with Charlie pacing back and forth. If Lew was lost, how would he ever find him?

"I found it!" were the words that brought hope to his heart.

They ran towards the sound, Lew shouting at intervals to guide them, and presently came to a low pile of rock. Lew pointed down to a glint of water at his feet.

"Help yourselves," he invited, and they plunged forward and gulped down the warm liquid.

"Careful," Charlie warned Jim. "We mustn't drink too much." Then he started to splash handfuls in his face and over his arms. The water was warm but not bitter, without any of the white alkali about the edges.

"Why in the world is there a pool of water out here in the middle of all this sand?" asked Jim.

"I don't know," answered Charlie. "But I do know springs are often found in the last places in the world you might expect water."

The pool was six feet across and a foot deep, and they could see no sign of an outlet or inlet. The black rock piled around the edge looked like it had been placed by human hands.

"I can stand a meal, now," said Lew, as he straightened up and shook drops of water from his eyes. And then they attacked their scant supply of food before lying down beside the water. A cool breeze fanned their flushed faces, and they dropped calmly into sleep beneath stars twinkling in a cloudless desert sky.

The heat of the sun woke them in the morning, and sitting up with a jerk, Lew looked at his watch. It was eight o'clock. They had overslept three hours. As they swallowed a quick meal, Charlie proposed that Jim stay here at the pool and wait for them to return. He was expecting protest, but to his surprise Jim agreed at once. He realized that the boy must be worn out completely.

They refilled the water bags, and Charlie suggested that Jim build a low wall of rock to shield himself from the sun. Then they waved goodbye and left. "The kid has sure stood up fine," Lew said as they walked among the blackened stones. "I was afraid he wouldn't stay alone."

"We've got to get back on time," answered Charlie. "Or he'll worry himself sick and maybe even start looking for us. If he does, his chances will be mighty slim."

They were walking through a low valley where scattered black stone stretched as far as they could see. The rocks looked as though they had been subjected to terrific heat.

"This is Wai-ton's Valley of Heat, all right," said Lew. "Suppose the sun scorched the stones like this?"

"No," replied Charlie. "I believe all this stuff was thrown up by a giant of a volcano. We must watch carefully for the Indian's rock signs. There should be one a half-mile from the pool. If we don't find it in that distance, we start off to each side like you did last night."

"I almost passed by the pool," Lew admitted. "It was funny. I was walking along when I suddenly smelled water. I couldn't see it, so I circled around until I about fell in."

"Isn't that one of the trail markers?" asked Charlie, pointing to a pile of rock. Sure enough, it was a signal to mark the path, just different enough to catch the eye of one who knew exactly what he was looking for.

A slight wind had risen, and they recoiled involuntarily from the blast-furnace effect. "We can't stand much of that," gasped Lew. "Heaven help us if it blows a gale."

Charlie did not answer. But he, too, feared the result if the breeze gained force. It could be beyond human endurance.

The wind held steady, but it still was the longest day that either could remember. They had to walk much of the way with heads turned down, and each emptied a water bag so quickly Charlie became alarmed.

The path was now nothing but blackened rock over blazing sand. Their eyes blurred, their brains reeled, but they pressed on, watching for the next stone marker. Charlie was counting, remembering there were two to the mile, and when they had passed twenty, he called a halt. They had walked ten miles over the worst sort of trail, and it was mid-afternoon.

"We'll arrive after dark again," said Charlie. "Want to eat?"

"Hardly," said Lew. "What I want is barrels of water. My mind keeps wandering to ice-cold lemonade and ice cream and ..."

"Shut up!" commanded Charlie. "For Heaven's sake, try to keep your mind on other things. Right now, I'm thinking how I will spend my share of the gold. I expect to get there by midnight. Then we can sleep until morning, load up, and start back before sunrise."

The miles dragged slowly behind them until the sun set and the wind ceased as suddenly as it had begun. The sand cooled, and they walked at a faster pace, although both were badly tired out. Stubbles of beard fringed their bloodshot eyes and seamed cheeks.

"Gosh," said Lew. "I hope I don't look as bad as you."

"Don't worry," was the answer, "you do."

At dusk they started having trouble finding the trail markers, and several times they were forced to swing back and forth to search for them. And then, hours after the sun had set on the Valley of Heat, they climbed a gentle hill and before them in the moonlight lay the dry riverbed filled with sandy gravel and water-worn boulders.

They had reached the river of gold.

Chapter 8 – Gold in the Gravel

At the sight, Lew did exactly what Wai-ton had warned against. He lost his head, and whooping shrilly through cracked lips, fell on his knees and began clawing at sand and gravel. Charlie bent over, picked him up by sheer strength and set him on his feet.

"Pull yourself together, Lew," he commanded in a stern voice. "This stuff isn't going anywhere. We've got a short time to sleep before dawn breaks, and you are going to lie right down and take advantage of it.

"Look here," he continued, holding up his single filled water bag. "We each used two coming over and we had all we could drink before we started. We've got only one to get back on—and we're going to start out thirsty. I hope that'll bring you to your senses."

"I guess I did go blooey," Lew confessed. "But maybe this isn't the place? We might be a mile up or down from where Wai-ton digs his gold."

"We aren't far off," answered Charlie. "Look over there," and following his pointing finger, Lew saw a skeleton doubled up on the sand less than fifty yards away.

"Gold and death," he shuddered. Then he grinned ruefully. "Good thing I'm not superstitious. I'm so tired I bet I could lie down right beside that thing and sleep without one bad dream."

They swallowed a few drops of their precious water and resolutely corked the bags. Great as their thirst was, their weariness was even greater, and they fell instantly asleep on the sand.

Despite Lew's assertion, his rest was haunted with visions, the principal of which were cool waterfalls. Charlie awoke an hour before sunrise from his own dream, one that left him shivering.

"Wake up, Lew," he called, and Lew turned a haggard face towards him. Charlie winced at the bloodshot eyes and deep-lined features of his happy-go-lucky partner.

"Let's load up and go," was all Lew said.

They drank sparingly, ate a few mouthfuls of jerked meat, and climbed down into the dry riverbed. It had been a fair-size stream cutting a zigzag path across the desert. At one time, perhaps a thousand years ago, the burnt land had been a fertile plain with tumbling water pouring through this course, water that whirled among big boulders dropping the glittering specks of yellow metal it had carried from distant mountains.

Charlie stooped over, picked up a handful and let it run slowly through his fingers. He turned a blank face toward Lew. "No gold here," he spoke almost in a whisper. They dug deeper in the riverbed, testing at different spots, but not a sign of "color" could they see.

"Maybe it's here but we can't see it?" said Lew. "Gold would have to be pretty thick in sand for the eye to find it."

"No, it isn't here," answered Charlie. "Wai-ton said it would be much more obvious."

Lew groaned. "Did we come through all of that yesterday for nothing at all?"

Charlie sat down to think. They could not be far off the trail, for only a half-mile back was one of the Navajo's rock signal piles. Then he jumped to his feet. "I have it!" he cried. "What we want is a pocket below a sharp bend. That's where current would drop gold. Come on!" and he started up the dry bed.

Charlie stopped at a sharp curve and started to dig. He lifted a handful of sandy gravel and, as it ran over his fingers, they saw as plain as day vivid flecks of color mixed thickly with the dross. It was a rich pocket of virgin gold.

At first they were too excited to move. Then they dodged back and forth in the pocket, digging up sand at random and examining each handful. "There's tons of gold here!" cried Lew, and Charlie could not help but agree that the streambed was literally loaded with placer gold.

"Looks like it," he said. "But we can carry just so much, and we have to start soon. Fill up an empty water bag so I can see how heavy it is."

They scooped the rich pay dirt into a water bag. Charlie lifted it and realized that they could never carry more than one bag apiece across the Valley of Heat and the loose sand that lay between them and the Cliff Dwellers' caves. He looked over to tell Lew and saw him feverishly filling a second sack.

"That's it," he commanded. "One bag each is all we take. Remember what Wai-ton said. We can't drink this stuff, and twenty extra pounds might drag us down before we were halfway back through that inferno."

"Oh, what I wouldn't give for an airplane," sighed Lew, as he realized the wisdom in Charlie's words.

Charlie felt the same way but resolutely turned his back and started on the return trail. Would they return for more? Or would the river of gold lie here undisturbed for generations to come, guarded by wind-dried skeletons?

They tramped steadily through the burnt rock, through a daytime nightmare of blazing sun and torturing thirst. As Wai-ton had prophesied, their last drop of water was gone long before they reached the pool, and the only thing that kept them on their feet was the thought of drink at the end of the trail.

If the day before had been a long one, this one was immeasurable. Charlie lost count of the rock markers along the fiery trail, hoping that their strength would last until they reached the pool, or at least until night brought some relief.

If they had not been young and in splendid condition with muscles strengthened by outdoor living, they would never have endured that journey. And then night fell, the air cooled, and they began to talk. Their mouths were dry as dust, but after the long silence of the day, conversation, brief and short as it was, cheered them.

"Wonder if the Navajo could have stood this trip better than we did?" asked Lew.

"It wouldn't bother Wai-ton nearly as much," Charlie replied. "To the desert Indian, heat and thirst are just everyday matters. They never worry, and I know we have suffered a lot from worry."

"What do you think this gold is worth?" Lew asked.

"We are packing a lot of sand with it," Charlie began, "but offhand, I'd say five thousand dollars. It may run over, but not any less."

"I've got a handful of small nuggets in my bag that I'd say are worth a thousand themselves," Lew replied. "Not so bad ..."

He stopped talking when Charlie exclaimed, "What's that up ahead?"

Peering through the dusk of evening, Lew saw a figure moving slowly towards them. "It's Jim!" he cried. "Yo ho, Jim!"

There came an answering shout, and then the figure turned, ran back and disappeared. "What the dickens is he up to?" asked Lew.

They walked on with renewed strength, and Lew even attempted to whistle a little. But his lips were just too cracked and dry.

Then they saw Jim running towards them, and when he came closer they saw he carried something in both hands that he held carefully out toward them. "He's bringing us water!" exclaimed Charlie. "Did you ever see a kid as thoughtful?"

When he met them, they saw it was his hat filled with water.

"Did you get along all right?" asked Charlie.

Jim nodded and handed over the water. "Drink first, Lew," said Charlie, but Lew shook his head, and to cease useless discussion, Charlie lifted the hat and drank deeply. Never had water tasted so good. Then he passed the hat over to Lew, who buried his face in it.

When Lew stopped gulping, he emptied what water remained in the hat out upon the sand. Jim uttered a sharp cry, but it was too late. "What's the matter?" asked Lew.

Charlie studied the boy's face. "You shouldn't have done that," he told Lew. "That's all the water there is!"

"Pool went dry at noon today," Jim finally spoke in a trembling voice. "I had been sleeping all morning, or trying to, when I went over to get a drink and there was only a couple of inches left in the bottom. I was so scared I just stood there watching it sink away, until I happened to think there might be some way to save a little for you when you came. The only thing I had was my hat, so I filled it. I didn't even have time to drink much after I got the hat full. It drained away like that."

"Then you haven't had a drink since morning?" Charlie asked.

"I had a little after I filled the hat," the boy replied.

"My gosh," broke in Lew. "Kick me, somebody. I've been out in the desert only a few days, but I ought to know enough by now to never throw away a drop of water. Jim, I'd do anything in the world to get back that cupful for you."

"I'm not as thirsty as you are," Jim repled. "I've been lying in the shade all day resting. What I am worried about is how are we going to get back tomorrow."

"I want a look at the pool," was all Charlie said.

The bottom had grown as dry as the sun-bleached bones that guarded the fickle spring. Charlie sat with Lew and Jim on the rock wall. Each feared to voice the thoughts that were in his mind, although each knew the others were thinking the same. Twenty miles across soft desert sand and not a drop to drink. Each knew he would never make it.

Charlie started to pace back and forth. He was thinking, wracking his brain for some scrap of information he might have heard or read sometime back in his life, something about desert pools which might aid them now. Why would a pool suddenly run dry and then fill up again? Where did the water come from, and where did it go?

He jumped down into the pool and dug his heel into the sand. Where could the water go—but straight down? Maybe if they dug deep enough?

"If I had a shovel ..." he spoke the thought aloud.

"I know where there's one!" exclaimed Jim, and then he ran out into the desert. He came back shortly, carrying a short-handled spade.

"Where did you get that?" asked Charlie.

"I walked out in the desert this morning before the sun came up and found another dead man over there. A dead burro lay beside him, and this spade was tied to its back."

Charlie took the tool and started to dig a shallow pit three feet across, knowing the sand would only fill in anything steeper. He shoveled steadily a few minutes and then stopped, panting. He could only force his aching muscles to the task for so long.

"Your turn, Lew."

Lew took his place, and they changed off every few minutes, working frantically in spurts. As they weakened Jim also took turns and plied the shovel manfully. Charlie examined the sand every few shovelfuls, but it was dry as dust.

The digger stood in a pit up to his shoulders, and they were starting to grow discouraged when Charlie picked up a handful of fresh sand and detected a faint trace of moisture.

He jumped in to take Lew's place, throwing up sand like a badger. He dug a small well in the center of his pit, and water seeped slowly in from the sides.

Calling for a cup, he waited until he could dip it in the liquid that rose slowly in the hole. Then he passed it up to them overflowing. It was muddy, but water, nevertheless.

Jim drank first, and then they stood impatiently waiting for the well to fill until each had drunk his fill. "Get the water bags!" commanded Charlie. "This may not last."

They worked swiftly, filling the bags with water that oozed in with aggravating slowness. When the bags were full, Charlie called for their hats. "This will give us plenty to drink in the morning before we start back."

Then the well went dry.

"We were just in time," whispered Lew.

"Let's sleep," suggested Charlie. "I'm going to try to wake up before the sun, but I never was as tired before in my life. I'm afraid we'll all sleep until it roasts us awake. "

He was right. Nobody awoke until the sun was high in the sky and the heat unbearable. "Say," said Lew, as he rubbed his eyes open. "Do you know we turned in last night without eating a bite?"

"We haven't much left, but we might as well carry it in our stomachs as in our packs," Charlie replied. "Let's finish the jerked meat as we walk. I don't know how long Wai-ton will wait for us if we're late. If we miss him, we'll be in bad shape again."

And they started on the trail, Charlie laying out a reverse course by compass. They had traveled two hours when he noticed the sun disappearing behind a curious haze that was spreading through the sky. It was not a cloud but more like a veil of pink that screened the fiery heat. At first it made them profoundly grateful. But then the sky looked forboding, a dirty yellow streaked with black. "I'm afraid we're in for a storm of some kind," said Charlie.

"Well, it can rain all it pleases," answered Lew. "I won't mind one bit."

"It won't be rain," Charlie said. "There are no signs of dry washes out here, and you always find them in desert country that gets rain. Listen …"

A faraway hissing, grinding noise seemed to be building, faint yet of such a tone it filled them with awe. "What's that?" asked Lew, lowering his voice to a whisper.

But before either of his companions could reply, he pointed ahead and cried, "Look there!"

A dark cloud that reached from the desert floor to high in the sky was sweeping down upon them. It was still a mile away, but they could see twisting, curling waves whipping at its edge.

"A sandstorm!" exclaimed Charlie. "This is going to get rough."

The storm swept across the desert with relentless fury, and the grinding, hissing sound swelled into a mighty roar. Now they could see huge funnels of sand being sucked high into the air.

"Lie down and cover up," shouted Charlie. Then, as they started to obey, the huge cloud veered suddenly to the left.

"It's going to miss us," Lew cried. "We won't …"

A hoarse shout sounded out in the maelstrom before them, and turning startled eyes, they saw a figure lurching towards them. It was a man holding an arm to cover his face, stumbling out of the maelstrom of wind and sand, clothes shredded into fluttering flaps.

"Is it Wai-ton?" asked Jim

And then the figure tumbled clear of the storm, which swept by to one side. His arm dropped, and at twenty yards they stared into the haggard features of Hetter, the boss of the rustler ranch. And when he saw them, a bellow of rage burst from his lips, and whipping a gun from his belt, he leveled it at Charlie's chest!

Chapter 9 – Saved by the Sun God

It certainly was a queer tableau, this unexpected meeting in the desert. Although it seemed they stood silently for minutes, it really was but a short second more before Lew went for his own gun. But Hetter swung his ready pistol on him, with a snarl so dangerous Lew automatically dropped his hand.

"Careful, Lew," whispered Charlie out of the side of his mouth. "He looks like he has gone crazy mad."

There was a wild look in Hetter's erstwhile expressionless eyes. "Dern you!" the man was screaming. "You thought you fooled me when you sneaked away from the caves! But you didn't. I followed your trail, and I've been waiting for you to bring back the gold for me. I know you've got it. Be quick before I shoot you down!"

His voice leveled to a high-pitched scream, and his features twisted with passion. It was as though his true nature had broken through the icy mask that covered it before.

Charlie threw the bag of gold he carried, not to where Hetter stood but a few yards away, craftily placing it so the man would stoop before him when he went for the treasure. "There it is," he said calmly, and then bracing his muscles, waited for Hetter to make his move. But Hetter merely glanced at the gold and flashed his wild eyes back upon him.

"It can lay there until I'm ready," he said. "I've got other work to do. I'm going to put you in the ground with that Navajo who fooled me so long. Oh, I caught him!" he sneered as he noted the change in their faces. "And when he wouldn't tell me how to follow you, I shot him dead this time."

Hetter took a step forward and jerked back the hammer of the single-action pistol. He pressed the trigger, but no shot followed. Blank surprise came to Hetter's now expressive face, and then with a demonic cry, he threw the gun at Charlie's head. It missed by inches. Lew reached for his own weapon, but Charlie caught his arm.

"Don't shoot the man—he's crazy, lost his mind in the hell of that sandstorm!"

Hetter stared at them a second, and then, throwing his arms over his head, turned and rushed back into the maelstrom of sand. They stood amazed. Then Lew walked over and picked up the gun.

"Action clogged with sand," he said.

"He's a goner, now," Charlie said. "We couldn't save him even if we tried, and I must confess I don't feel much like risking my life for the like of his. Not after he shot Wai-ton."

"Say," Lew said slowly. "That means there won't be anybody waiting to guide us through the sand dunes."

And then as they stood thinking of this, the sandstorm veered and swept over them, howling like a thousand banshees. They dropped flat on the ground and wrapped their heads as best they could.

Flying sand rasped their legs and backs, searching out every thin or loose place in their clothing, grinding off skin to rawness. The wind heaped the drifting stuff over them, and they were forced to rise and shake off the accumulation to keep from being buried alive. If the main body of the storm had struck them, they might not have survived. As it was, in less than thirty minutes the storm had passed.

They slowly lifted their heads and found the air clear, although a strong wind still blew, and the sky remained overcast the same sickly yellow. They stood and commenced to shake sand from their clothes, dogging it from their eyes and ears and spitting out the grit in their mouths.

"Let's take a drink," said Jim thirstily, and he lifted a water bag to his mouth.

"Sure," agreed Charlie, "but remember this water may have to last us a long time. We must find the way ourselves, and while I can run our course by the compass a few miles, after that, we trust to chance. Wai-ton made too many turns for me to remember the trail."

Charlie took the compass from his pocket and leveled it in his hand. A sharp exclamation burst from his lips.

"What's the matter?" asked Lew.

"Clogged with sand," replied Charlie. Then he shook the delicate instrument, and removing the glass cover, tried to clean it in vain. The needle refused to obey the magnetic attraction.

"Well, I guess there isn't much more that can happen to us," said Lew gloomily.

"I know the general course," Charlie replied with a confidence he did not truly feel. "Come on! Every minute we lose standing here cuts down our chances of getting through."

He led them forward on as straight a line as he could. The odds were against them, but they struggled manfully, and presently, gathering hope from the encouraging combination of action and perceived progress, Lew found enough spirit to joke as they tramped.

They drank sparingly, but those few minutes in the sandstorm had sucked them dry, arousing a fierce craving for water. In spite of rigorous restraint, the water bags lightened with alarming speed.

Finally, dusk swept over the dunes, and Charlie called a halt. "Wai-ton left us somewhere near here," he said. "Can either of you remember which way we turned the last time he changed course?"

Lew scratched his head. "I believe we turned right," he ventured. "If we did, we should turn left a little ways ahead." Then he lifted his water bag. "I figure we have enough to last until the middle of tomorrow forenoon. That gives us twelve hours. We better rest, eat what grub is left, and keep going until morning."

Charlie only nodded his assent.

They rested an hour, ate and started out. The moon filled the desert with ghostly shadows, and their minds kept turning back to Wai-ton, the brave Navajo who had saved them and then put them on the trail to gold. It was difficult to accept that a snake like Hetter had taken such a life.

The sand was loose, and even though they wore the broad-soled moccasins that better supported their weight, the grind was wearing them down. Charlie could feel his strength ebbing.

"We must rest more," he finally said. Then he whispered to Lew, "We've missed the way. The caves would be within sight, if we were on the right trail."

"I know," Lew whispered back. "But I thought we could keep on until we came to some sort of water. I'm afraid Jim won't last much longer."

The boy looked up at that. "What are you whispering about?" he asked. "You might as well tell me if we are lost."

"There's still a chance," Charlie answered. "We may miss the caves, but I don't mind that so much. There may be a dozen rustlers still camped there waiting for us. No, we'll go straight from here and find water within ten or fifteen miles. That only means about five hours of tramping. Can you do it?"

"Sure," answered Jim.

"Hullo! What's this?" Charlie said as he bent over and looked closely at the sand. "Coyote tracks! The first sign of life out here. Let's follow. Maybe he's headed for water!"

As they trailed they realized the coyote had been trotting ahead with a purpose. Not a foot to the right or left did it swerve. They stopped frequently for short periods of rest. And then an hour past midnight, Charlie sighted a small gray object that whisked off and disappeared in the gloom.

"That's him!" he cried. "What do you suppose he is doing?"

When they reached the place they saw sign of a recent camp. The small heap of ashes was still warm, and scattered about were scraps of meat and bone. This was what had brought the coyote, and Charlie examined the ground carefully.

"Looks like a party of four or five men," he said. "I wonder who they are, and where they went?"

"Well," said Lew, "this gives us something to work on, at least. We can follow their trail. A coyote might wander fifty miles over the desert, but a bunch of men is going somewhere. Think we should drop this sand and gold?"

"Better hang on to it a while longer," advised Charlie. "We've carried it over the worst of it already. Come on."

As they traveled, they noticed the sand growing firmer. A rosy glow in the east indicated the approach of morning when they stopped and drained the last few drops of water from the bags. They had covered a wide stretch during the night, pausing only for short periods of rest. They decided to take a longer rest now, and Charlie urged Jim to sleep if he could. As he glanced about, Charlie rubbed his eyes twice before he believed what he saw. "That looks like mountains ahead!" he exclaimed.

"Mountains, sure enough," cried Lew. "And mountains almost always mean water!"

They jumped up, all thought of rest gone, and as they struggled ahead, Charlie knew they would not be able to stand much more. He was gambling everything on those low hills ahead.

The trail was cut plainly in the sand before them, the men who made it walking single file, each placing his feet neatly in the footprints of the man ahead. This made Charlie believe it to be a party of Navajos, and he devoutly hoped they were headed home.

When they approached nearer, they saw a narrow defile in the mountains and realized the trail led straight towards it. "There's a valley on the other side of those mountains," said Lew. "A valley filled with plenty of water. I can hear cattle now. Can't you?"

"No," said Charlie. "But I hope you're right."

They walked through the narrow pass and Jim let out a sharp cry of disappointment. Before them lay a sunken valley of burnt white soda, alkali and parched black rock. It was a miniature Death Valley, even worse than what they had been struggling through. The other end was lost in heat waves that swelled up from the desert floor.

After the first bitter pang of despair, a dull fatigue seized them. Lew dropped his load and staggered over to the shady side of the slope. The others followed. "There's no use wading into that inferno," he said dully. "What the devil are those men going down through there for, anyway?"

Charlie could think of no answer to that, nor any solution to their predicament. They were too exhausted to walk, and meaningful rest was impossible without water. Still, he endeavored.

"Let's sleep a couple of hours in the shade here," he advised. "Don't give up. This trail leads somewhere. After we rest, our brains will be clear and we'll find a way out."

They kicked off their shoes, opened their shirts to cool off, and then lay behind the rock that warded off the rays of the sun. Their fatigue was so great that in spite of the thirst that consumed them, they all three fell asleep. And they slept so soundly that a rifle shot in the valley below failed to arouse them.

But if it had, and they had sat up, they would have seen four figures toiling across the burnt soda plain straight towards the gap in the mountains where they slept, and the foremost carried something heavy across his shoulders that bent his back.

Moccasin feet are noiseless in the desert, and Lew did not awake until a jerk at his belt roused him. Sitting up, he stared into the faces of four desert Indians. With a cry of alarm he reached for the gun that was already gone.

At this cry, Charlie and Jim awoke, and as they moved, the four figures leveled short rifles, one grunting a sharp command which though in a strange tongue could mean but one thing.

For a second Charlie thought he was having another nightmare, but as he watched the lean, cruel faces, he knew this thing was real. They were short, wiry men, tanned nearly black by desert sun and wind. They were clad in tattered, dirty blankets. They had eyes as cold as those of a rattlesnake.

On the ground beside one man lay a small deer, its freshly cut throat still oozing blood, and hanging from the shoulders of each swung a large water bag of deer skin tanned with the hair on. At the sight, Charlie's mouth quivered, and he made a motion, pointing to his mouth and then to a bag. But the leader who still held Lew's gun only grunted, and stepping forward drew a short, keen knife.

Charlie's face paled as the Indian stepped directly in front of Jim. As he bent over the boy, Charlie gathered his muscles, resolving to at least die fighting.

Then a startled cry burst from the Indian. He reached swiftly and grabbed the curious stone disk on the thong around Jim's neck, the disk Wai-ton had given Jim back at their first meeting.

Now the man spoke swiftly to his companions, who crowded about, feeling the stone and scrutinizing it with keen gazes. Then they straightened, and in unison brought up arms in the same salute given by Wai-ton's fellows when they saw him pass the object to Jim.

The fierce eyes softened, and the desert dwellers relaxed as they offered water bags all around. After that, one of the Indians pointed to the dead deer and made a gesture that invited them to eat. Charlie and Lew both nodded vigorously, and while one of the desert men carved thin slices of venison from the haunch, another pulled a small bundle of cedar roots from his blanket and kindled a fire. In a minute the smell of broiling meat filled the air, and the three realized how empty their stomachs were.

They watched the Indian broil the meat with less wood than a white man might use just to start a fire. The Indians continued to talk in low tones, turning about every few minutes to look and point at Jim, who still wore the charm around his neck. Lew watched in open-mouthed wonder.

"Hang on to that thing like it means your life," he told Jim. "Because it probably does."

After they had eaten and drank once more from the skin bags, they felt new strength coursing through their veins. Then the Indian who had discovered the stone charm about Jim's neck stood and looked at them with questioning eyes. Pointing, he swept an arm out in a wide circle that covered a fourth of the horizon, and waited as though for an answer.

"He is asking us which way we want to go," volunteered Lew.

Charlie took charge of the situation, and with a few concise gestures imitated a man riding horseback. The Indian evidently understood, for he nodded, and picking up the deer carcass, stepped off with his followers in single file.

Charlie, Lew and then Jim fell in behind.

"I don't even care where they take us," said Lew.

"Me, too," agreed Jim.

The Indians led them back through the mountain gap with a slow, seemingly lazy gait that covered a lot of ground and taxed the three of them to keep up. After two hours, the leader offered his water skin to Charlie. He drank and then passed the water to his companions. After they had drunk, the Indian slung it back over his shoulder and resumed walking without bothering to take his own drink.

"Evidently, these fellows are regular camels," Lew observed.

That night they camped beside a spring at the base of a low mountain. "We must be a long ways from our old trail," said Charlie. "I don't remember seeing any mountains like these."

When they awoke the next morning, one of the Indians was skinning three prairie dogs. Charlie shuddered a little when the cooked quarters were dished up, but he ate a small piece, and the meat proved better than he expected. Then they filled the skin bags, which had grown rather flabby the day before, and started out before sunrise.

The desert grew less bleak. At noon, they topped a swelling plateau and saw a narrow valley marked with squares of green alfalfa, and in one end a neat array of white ranch buildings.

Lew whooped out loud.

The Indian pointed to the ranch and then started to turn back. With a burst of gratitude, Lew unfastened his bag of sand and gold and offered a generous handful. The Indian looked at it curiously, at first, and then refused with a gesture of disdain. Then they all saluted the symbol hanging around Jim's neck and turned silently back into the desert.

"Let's go down there and see if we can buy some horses, grub, and a map out of this country," Lew exclaimed.

"I'm with you," Charlie agreed. "Let's head home, and then I think a winter trapping up North in the snow and ice would be the proper thing. How about it?"

"You can bet your bottom dollar!" Jim chimed in with a grin.

The End

Wolves of the Birch Woods

Chapter 1 – The Old River Rat

Old Jean Labady lowered his rifle as the soft splash of canoe paddles reached his still-keen ears. He scowled, grumbling under his breath. Old Jean was fishing, and while he ate fish regularly, he had yet to cast his first hook and line. When fish were needed, the old river rat shot them with his rifle.

River bass swam lazily in the deep pools of the Big Beaver, which flowed a hundred yards from his cabin. The concussion of a high-power bullet striking the surface typically stunned one or two, which then floated belly up—that was fishing, for Old Jean.

He lived a hundred miles from the nearest game warden, and for half a century had done about as he pleased. But the approaching canoe made him hesitate. Old Jean feared no man, yet as his hair had grizzled and his face had seamed, he had turned to guile rather than bravado. While it was unlikely a game warden was coming, there would be plenty of time to fish later.

Hunting season was close at hand, too, though dates on a calendar didn't mean much to Old Jean, either. It was Indian summer in the great Northwoods, with squirrels and grouse butter-fat.

As the birch-bark craft rounded a slow curve in the river, his equally keen eyes recognized the paddler. "Pierre Baptiste," he grumbled. "And the fool be drunk again."

Pierre was drunk—exuberantly singing snatches of French-Canadian songs. Yet no matter how intoxicated he might be, he could still paddle like the very devil. Pierre had a stroke of his own, a peculiar twist of the spruce blade, never lifting it from the water but drawing it edge forward for the next stroke. In the bow sat Marie, his young Cree wife.

They were on their way home from the fur post at Elk Bend, where they had been outfitting for the coming season. Home was a wide expanse of well-watered birch flats a hundred miles down the Big Beaver, the trapping rights to which Pierre had inherited when his father passed away.

The other Frenchmen respected Pierre, and Marie held the respect of the Indians because of her grandfather Big Bull. Tales of the chief's deeds were still told in the caribou-skin tepees. Consequently, Pierre had little trouble defending his trapping ground, though he always brought heavy bundles of furs to the Post. And for the last three years, in addition to the furs, he had laid before the factor's inspection a bundle of caribou skins tanned to the last degree of suppleness by Marie.

At one time vast herds with tossing antlers had migrated down from the frozen barrens. But this had ceased 20 years ago, and since then, few hunters had been lucky enough to shoot even one a year. Some whispered that Pierre had discovered a hidden yard where caribou were still plentiful in the fall and winter. Others said he ran miles up into the barrens on snowshoes and shot caribou where they still migrated in mile-wide herds. But Pierre was wary, and none had learned where he shot caribou in such numbers.

Pierre caught sight of Old Jean, and hailing him, turned the nose of the canoe with a flip of his paddle. Marie spoke a quick protest and strove to return the craft to its former course, but Pierre outmanned her with his quick stroke and shoved the prow of the birch boat upon the bank.

"Ho, Jean!" he called. "Your fren' Pierre has come."

He climbed unsteadily to his feet, passed the sullen woman, and stepping ashore, pumping Jean's hand vigorously. He was tall and slender with blue eyes and fair hair, a sharp contrast to the thickset, swarthy Jean.

"You're drunk," Old Jean spoke shortly. Then turning to the Cree woman, he added, "Why don't you roll him in the river?"

Pierre laughed heartily at that. "Sure," he agreed. "Why not? But Pierre work hard all winter. Now we enjoy life."

"You would not have to work so hard if you took a trapping partner," Old Jean suggested smoothly. "You have ground too beeg for one man. I go along this fall, yes?"

Pierre sobered noticeably at that. "Not this year, my fren'. Maybe next."

Old Jean turned and started back to his cabin. "I suppose you stay here tonight?" he asked in a voice that offered no welcome.

"Sure," Pierre answered brightly. "What for I stop if not to stay with my fren' Jean?"

The men soon sat before the open door of Jean's cabin. Like the homes of most bachelor trappers, it was ill-smelling. Pierre produced a bottle of spirits, and then bid Marie in a mix of French and Cree to prepare the evening meal. At that, Old Jean jumped up with his rifle and ran down to the river. A gunshot rang out, and a few minutes later, he returned with another nice bass.

Disdaining the filthy utensils in the cabin, Marie brought her own kettle and pan from the canoe and started a fire in the rusty sheet-iron outdoors stove. Marie fried the fish in crisp brown chunks.

Old Jean watched Pierre with mounting resentment. "Drunken pig," he muttered, and then frankly studied the woman's face for any reaction to his words. But Marie's features did not change.

A shout from Pierre brought him to his feet, and looking down the Big Beaver, he cursed silently. Another canoe was rounding the curve, with a man at each end. Pierre was already waving them ashore, holding a whiskey bottle in welcome. "Fool," growled Jean.

After a few words between themselves, the men turned their canoe toward shore and beached it beside Pierre, who introduced himself. "I Pierre, the bes' trapper on the Beeg Beaver." And then he offered them the bottle.

They were young men, both tall and broad of shoulder, but one fully twenty pounds heavier than the other. They were dressed in plain flannel shirts and wool trousers that tapered and tied below the knee inside wet-proof moccasins of moose hide. Soft wool hats covered their heads.

The larger took the offered bottle and a small swallow of its contents. He passed it to his companion, whispering a warning, "Go easy, Lew. It's pretty awful."

"Do we even want to stop here, Charlie?" asked Lew.

"We can't very well get away now, not without being rude," said Charlie in the same low tone, and then they followed Pierre up to where Old Jean sat, still scowling. The Cree woman bent over the cooking fire, pan in hand.

Old Jean's eyes swept over the strangers. "Hunters from the States," he muttered to himself. "But canoe, she too beeg for hunters."

But he grinned a welcome, and when Pierre introduced and invited his new friends to dinner, Old Jean shouldered his rifle and marched back down to the river. They took Pierre's offered bottle again but this time only pretended to drink. Old Jean brought back another bass and tossed it to Marie. Then he sat down beside Charlie.

"You hunt moose and deer?" he asked.

Charlie grinned. "That's it," he said. "Yesterday a trapper told us we would find plenty of game about seventy miles down this river. How about it?"

"You go twice that far," Old Jean suggested. "There much moose and deer."

Marie served tea and biscuits with the fish. Pierre fumbled over his plate for a minute and then announced that he was tired and would rest a short time. Then he stumbled his way across the threshold of the cabin door, and Marie, jumping up, seized him by one arm and helped him inside.

"Our friend drinks powerful stuff," said Lew, keeping his face straight with an effort. Although Pierre had made a spectacle of himself, something about the man's good nature left him feeling amused by the light-hearted Frenchman.

Old Jean's face screwed up into its habitual scowl. "Pierre a fool for whiskey," he replied. "But he good man in woods. He bring more fur to Elk Bend than anyone."

They finished the fish and biscuits in silence, paying the ultimate compliment to the cook. "Gosh, it's great to eat something this good we didn't cook ourselves," Lew said. At his words, Marie's pretty features curved into a smile for the first time.

They stood up and looked towards the river. Old Jean spoke quickly. "You stay here tonight. Stay in cabin or out by fire—just as you like."

Charlie wanted to push on, but again, it was nearly nightfall, and he saw no way to refuse the invitation without giving offense. "I don't like camping in a crowd any better than you do," he said to Lew as they walked back down to their canoe. "But it would look bad if we didn't stay."

They pulled the craft up on the bank then brought blankets and a light silk tent back with them. They kindled a small fire some twenty yards from the cabin and made camp. Old Jean walked down and looked inside their canoe.

His keen eye took in the many bags and bundles protected by waterproof canvas, and when the two were busy, he kicked a couple of them. The clink of metal sounded under the cloth, and he muttered to himself. "Traps. These boys come north to steal the Frenchman's fur. That fool Pierre maybe stop them at the right place."

Inside the cabin, Pierre was snoring loudly. Marie had fetched her blanket from the canoe and was leaning back against a stump before the blaze with the wool about her shoulders. Old Jean studied her for several moments and then squatted down beside her. Not so much as a glance acknowledged his presence. Presently, Old Jean spoke. "You too good woman for Pierre."

Still, Marie was silent.

Jean resolved on a bold stroke. "You come live with me. Let Pierre guzzle his whiskey. When spring come, we go to Elk Bend and I buy you what you like. Pretty dress—anything."

Still, the woman did not stir. Old Jean waited expectantly, peering into her blank eyes. Growing bolder, he passed an arm about her shoulders. At that, her hand shot out and slapped him across the face with a smack like the noise made when a beaver whacks the water with his tail.

Anger swept over Old Jean, and he grabbed her roughly about the waist. But Marie slid from his grasp like a lithe panther and ran to the tent Lew and Charlie had pitched, Old Jean at her very heels.

Lew emerged from the low tent, and the woman ducked behind him for protection. "What's the matter?" asked Lew in surprise.

"She hit me!" sputtered the man. "Cat of a Cree, I'll ..."

"Easy, old-timer," soothed Lew, pushing him back with the palm of one big hand. "You and her man can fuss all you want, but you mustn't molest his wife."

Old Jean regarded him in dark silence. Then he wheeled about and went back to his hut. Charlie came up dragging a load of wood. "Don't mix up in anything that don't concern you, Lew," he warned, having heard and seen enough to get the picture.

"I couldn't let that old crow paw the girl," he replied. "Neither would you." Then he turned to Marie. "Why don't you slip inside the cabin where your man is and bolt the door while Old Jean is still out by the fire? It won't hurt him to sleep out one night."

Marie nodded, walked back and entered the hut. After she slammed the door, they heard the wooden bar settle into place. Jean looked up from where he sat with a baffled expression.

Lew and Charlie could barely restrain their laughter, but they knew it really was no laughing matter. "We should have kept right on down the river," Charlie observed.

"Things will be OK in the morning," replied Lew with his usual optimism. "Pierre will be sober enough to protect his woman, and Old Jean may forget all about this business. Anyway, I vote we break camp early and get away before they are even awake."

Charlie agreed heartily with that and then piled a mix of green and dry wood on the fire to keep it burning late into the night. Then they rolled up in their blankets under the open door of the tent.

Down by the cabin, Old Jean brooded. Pierre had once again refused to take him for a trapping partner, and his own traplines were growing thin in fur and game, much trapped and over-hunted. Pierre's land was rich in everything that makes the trapper's life easy—and then there was Marie.

He could not believe she had struck him when he offered to take her away from the drunken fool. Only ten short years ago, Old Jean was still catching the eye of every dark-eyed Cree girl along the Big Beaver. He saw himself as a wronged man.

Maybe the woman had only needed coaxing. Why did these strangers have to turn up now? And what business had they bringing traps into the country of the French and Cree? Thoughts of revenge began to creep into Old Jean's mind. He stole down to the river, paused beside the canoe of the two strangers and again poked a bundle with his toe. The big-bottomed freighting canoe clearly was loaded with a season's supply of trapping gear.

"Bah," he whispered to himself. "What liars!" Then he picked up a paddle and went to work, his silent actions cloaked by the mantle of night.

In spite of their intention to wake early the following morning, Charlie and Lew overslept. When the ringing of an ax brought them up with a start, the sun already was driving back the thick fog hanging over the river.

Charlie peered out of the tent first. Old Jean was yawning before the embers of his fire, and the cabin door was open. Pierre, or maybe Marie, must be swinging the axe. "Come on, Lew," he urged. "Let's get away from here."

They bundled their blankets and Charlie started down to the canoe with a load when a sharp cry brought him up. The ringing of the ax ceased, and Marie ran out of the cabin into the trees. Charlie dropped his load when he heard her cry out, and he ran after.

He found her bending over Pierre, who sat clutching a moccasined foot with both hands, blood streaming out between his fingers. His face was white, and Charlie immediately called for Lew. Between them, they carried Pierre to the cabin and laid him on the pole bunk. Old Jean watched with widening eyes as Charlie carefully cut away the moccasin and sock. The wound was deep, and he was considering the choices when Marie came in carrying a huge puffball. She shouldered Charlie aside and bound a piece against the wound.

"Hurt bad, old-timer?" Lew asked with sympathy in his voice.

"I no mind," he replied. "But how can Pierre trap? Fur is ready, and Pierre has a debt at the post."

"Oh, you'll be up on your feet before you know it," Lew tried to reassure him.

Pierre only shook his head and groaned.

Then Old Jean spoke from the doorway. "I cut a foot like that five years ago. Lay in camp two months before I could walk the trapline again."

Lew gave the man a dirty look and then walked back to their camp to finish taking down their tent. "Thank Heaven we can get away now," he told Charlie. "But the old rat was right. Pierre won't be doing much walking for a month or more."

"Whiskey has no place in a trapping camp," Charlie answered. "Look at the trouble Pierre has piled up for one day of foolishness."

Marie appeared silently at his elbow. "Pierre want talk with you," she said, and Charlie and Lew both realized these were the first words they had heard her speak.

"What do you suppose he wants?" asked Lew as they followed her to the hut. Old Jean had left to finish the wood chopping Pierre had started, and Marie began winding more strips of cloth about Pierre's gashed foot. The bleeding had ceased.

"That's a good stunt to remember," whispered Charlie, nodding at the puffball.

Pierre looked up and said, "Pierre in bad feex. If I no trap, others come in, and they take everything, ruin Pierre." He looked at their faces in turn. "Nobody I trust—but you."

At that, the boys started in surprise.

"Yes," nodded Pierre, quickly making up his mind. "Take my traps downriver and catch the fur. When I can come, we divide— Pierre take half, you take half. We both make good money, and Pierre pay his debt when the ice goes out in the spring."

Lew and Charlie huddled in a corner. "I don't like mixing in other people's business," Charlie began. "But we are looking for a place to trap."

"And here it sounds like a real good place is being offered to us," Lew chimed in enthusiastically.

"All right then," Charlie decided, and they turned back to the injured man who was watching them eagerly. "We'll take you on, Pierre. Tell us how to find your trapline, and we'll do our best."

"Good!" Pierre beamed. "Go down the river, counting the branches on your left. My line begins at the seventh branch and ends at the eighth. Goes back from river as far as the hills. I come as queek as I can."

"We won't need your traps," Charlie told him. "We got our own."

Lew brought their first aid kit to Marie, but she waved aside his bandages and iodine, preferring the native remedies of her people.

"Well," said Lew, as they loaded their canoe, "How's that for falling into something soft?"

"I don't want to be croaking, Lew, but I'm going to reserve judgment on that. Still, the proposition does look good."

They stopped in at the cabin to say good-bye to Pierre, noticed that Marie was missing and also the sullen silence of Old Jean.

"Gosh," Lew said as they walked back to the river. "I can't wait to get out of here. Hello … what's this?"

Marie was sitting in their canoe, paddle in hand.

"I go," she announced with a smile aimed squarely at Lew. "You good men. You need woman in camp. I cook and scrape fur—do much work for you."

Lew's face lengthened into lines of acute astonishment, mingled with something very much like embarrassment.

Chapter 2 – Shooting the Rapids

When a pretty young Cree offers to leave her husband and go with you on your winter trapline, what can a fellow do? Marie was good-looking, there was no doubt of that. She was straight and slender, her black eyes snapping with spirit. Charlie stood back, enjoying his partner's discomfort, wondering just what his next move might be. Lew was out on a limb, as the coon hunters like to say, and his customary self-assurance failed him completely.

"Say," stuttered Lew. "You've got a man to look after. What will he do if you clear out?"

Marie spoke softly. "Pierre? He always do fine. He and Jean drink whiskey all winter and fight all they please. We trap fur. Come," she finished with a smile, steadying the canoe for Lew to step inside.

"Can I go along, too?" asked Charlie, with a smile of his own.

Lew turned to him in desperation. "Tell her how it is," he begged. "Don't just stand there grinning like a tomcat."

Charlie thought fast. What would be the best way to get her out of the canoe without giving offense? Of course they had to turn down her proposition. If not, here was a fine chance to get into another scrape that could end badly.

Then Pierre called loudly from the cabin, "Marie!"

She jumped to her feet, hesitated, looking into their faces, waiting for some sign of acceptance. But they remained silent, and she sprang out on land. As she ran she called over her shoulder, "Wait, I be back soon!"

Lew jumped into the canoe with a haste that all but swamped it. "Wake up, Charlie! Grab that paddle and use it."

They shot out into the center of the river, where the current caught them and added speed to their steady paddle strokes. "Pretty busy half day," Lew finally grinned, his easy manner returning.

"Yesterday, we were drifting down the river, going nowhere in particular. Now we're headed straight for a dandy trapline — if Pierre told the truth."

"Marie would have come in handy," Charlie commented dryly, "chewing hides and scraping furs for you. And remember how good that fried fish tasted last night? Don't you think we should turn back and pick her up?"

"Shut up!" was all Lew could think to say, and Charlie quietly enjoyed the blush rising in his partner's cheeks.

"Now let's talk sense for a while," Lew continued. "Pierre said his land is about a hundred miles ahead. But we have to count the river branches, and it starts at the seventh on the left. How long will it take us?"

"Two days of easy downstream paddling," replied Charlie. "If we make fifty miles before camping tonight, I will be satisfied."

As they paddled, Charlie, sitting in the bow of the canoe, turned his head and held up a hand. A new sound had injected itself into the common sounds of the forest and the river. The dull rumble gradually swelled into a low-pitched roar.

"That must be our first portage," Charlie declared, and he turned the end of the canoe towards the bank. The river had spread out into a broad pool above the narrows, and they paddled close to the bank until, looking ahead, they caught sight of a twisting stretch of foam-flecked water.

"Time to land," warned Charlie, and they pulled the canoe up on the bank then unloaded their outfit for the portage. They lashed a paddle across the thwarts at each end to serve as yoke bars and then swung the craft lightly over their heads.

The portage trail was overgrown with weeds and low brush. To their left, the river tumbled over green-black boulders, swift as a mill race. "Doesn't look like this trail has seen much use," commented Lew. "I wonder if the voyageurs shoot this place?"

"I'd hate to try it," said Charlie. "There aren't many people living year-round out here, you know. It's early yet for the river trappers. They'll be coming along in a couple of weeks."

The portage was less than two hundred yards, but the load was heavy, and it took three trips before they were ready to launch again.

"One of these days, I am going to shoot that kind of white-water rapids," said Lew.

"Our load is too heavy," answered Charlie. "And our canoe is all wrong. It takes the right kind of light craft and two expert paddlers to make it through that kind of rock."

As they once again paddled downstream, Lew enthused, "Just smell this air. I wish we were trapping right now."

"We must hunt deer first, before trapping season opens," Charlie replied. "We need two or three on the pole for winter meat. We might even smoke a few fish. It's a job, but they make a nice change. We are a little light on grub, you know, on account of bringing all those traps. The Frenchies eat beaver, but I can't say it sounds good to me."

They paddled steadily until a high sun told them it was noon. Then they stopped for lunch, and Lew, casting out into the river, caught three slim river trout. Charlie brought out a kettle of oatmeal cooked that morning, and they ate heartily. It was their practice to bring from the morning camp a supply of cooked cereal or rice to eat at noon. After a short rest, they resumed their journey.

A flock of ducks arose from the river ahead and wheeled off over the timber. "You'll have to hurry, old-timers," Lew called after them, "if you expect to spend the winter in Florida."

Near the middle of the afternoon, the low roar of broken water again warned them of rapids, and they pushed the canoe over near shore. A huge boulder divided the channel ahead. Charlie pointed to it with his paddle. "The rapids probably start just behind that stone," he said. "We had better land now."

"Wait," urged Lew. "Let's take advantage of all the water we can. I'd a lot rather paddle and pack all this stuff a little less. Then he shoved ahead with a couple of vigorous strokes. The roar of the rapids grew louder, and when just a few feet from the stone, Lew finally said, "I guess this is all we better take." But as he turned the canoe, the sharp push of current on the side of the boat shot them ahead at alarming speed.

"Quick!" cried Charlie, and he sank his blade deep in the water, pulling with a mighty sweep of his powerful arms. Crack! A sharp snap sounded above the roar of the rough water, and glancing up, Lew saw Charlie staring at the broken paddle in his hands.

Their craft started to swing, but Lew caught it and straightened their course. "Turn off that rock," cried Charlie, leaning out over the side to push them off with his broken paddle handle.

Lew already was straining with every ounce of strength, but the bow swung directly at the rock, grated on the rough granite, and then they swept around and headed straight into the rapids.

They sped down the narrow torrent. Charlie called back to Lew, warning of partly submerged rocks. The water raised up on all sides of the tossing canoe in clean-cut masses of dark green. It seemed as if they would be swamped at any moment. But the buoyant canoe righted itself again and again, riding the waves like a cork.

Sitting in the bow, Charlie could see the worst was still ahead. Then they were flying between jagged points and ragged ledges, the water seething. With a set face and iron muscles, Lew was plying every trick he knew to steer them safely between the boulders.

Charlie, looking ahead, breathed a short sigh of relief. He could see the river widening out into a channel. If Lew could just keep it up a minute more, they would be through. That's when they crashed full into a hidden rock, and the canoe floor under his feet shredded.

Charlie leaped clear of the sinking canoe and was immediately swept downstream. Struggling to the surface, he gulped frantically to fill his lungs before again being pulled under the suffocating water. When the light began flashing in his closed eyes, he realized he was close to drowning.

If the canoe had struck farther upstream, they would have had no chance. But just as Charlie was losing faith, his feet touched something solid and his head emerged. Fortified by a gulp of air, he regained part of his strength. A second later, the current swept him against a breast-high reef of rock. Clutching it with both hands, he held his head and shoulders above the water.

Something heavy struck him in the back. Reaching instinctively about, he felt and then grabbed Lew's limp arm. Until that moment, he had been fighting so hard for his own life he had not thought of his partner. He held Lew by the wrist and used his free hand to work his way inch by inch along the rocky reef toward shore. It was desperate work, with the dead weight of his partner dragging him back and the current threatening to sweep them both into the churning depths. He strove as much as he could to keep Lew's head above water.

He struggled until he was wading only knee deep. Then he dragged Lew up on the bank and fell beside him. He wiped the blood and water from Lew's ashen face and feverishly pumped his chest, trying to drive water out and air into his water-logged lungs.

But Lew remained lifeless, and Charlie had about despaired when he saw an eyelid flicker. He redoubled his efforts, and Lew spit out what looked like a gallon of water then started gasping.

He struggled to a sitting position and asked, "What happened?" Then, remembering, shuddered violently and threw up more water.

"We're in a heck of a fix," he finally said feebly.

"Could be worse," Charlie replied. "I reached around just in time to grab you. Were you knocked out?"

"Must have been," said Lew. "All I remember is going down with the canoe."

"We almost made it," said Charlie. "You sure showed how to

handle a canoe in those rapids."

"I thought I was doing good," said Lew, "before we crashed. Did your paddle break? I saw you holding the handle."

"It broke at the low handhold," answered Charlie. "The wood had been cut a third of the way through."

"The devil!" exclaimed Lew. "Why didn't we notice before?"

"It was cut right under that leather drip cup," said Charlie. "And it must have been done last night."

"Old Jean!" Lew declared, realization flooding his features with a mix of disbelief and then something much uglier. "Let's go back there and wring Old Jean's neck!"

"The old cuss meant for us to drown," Charlie replied quietly. "He new the rapids lay ahead. But we've got more important problems to face before we can even think of revenge. For instance, where are we going to sleep tonight, and what will we eat for supper?"

Lew sat down on the bank. "Old Jean's time is coming," he said ruefully. "But you're right, Charlie. We have some tough sledding before us."

"First thing is to strip and wring out these clothes," Charlie continued in his business-as-usual manner. "If we don't, in a couple of hours the sun will be down and we'll be chilled through. Lord, I'm thankful we are wearing nothing but wool. How do you feel? Got any broken bones?"

Lew carefully worked his arms and legs. "Nothing but scrapes and bruises," he declared.

After they were back in damp but not dripping clothes, Charlie said. "Let's walk along the river and see if by any chance something from the canoe washed up on the bank. Come on."

Below the rapids the stream widened out into a stretch of quiet water, nearly as still as a long, narrow lake. They searched as they walked, looking out into the water as far as they could see bottom.

"I'm afraid it all went to the bottom," said Charlie. After they had walked another mile along the river, they agreed it was useless to search anymore. "Turn out your pockets, Lew. Let's take inventory of what we do have."

Lew placed what he found on the ground between them. It was a woefully small pile—a pencil and pocket diary, handkerchief, two revolver shells and a pocketknife.

"Where's your matchbox?" asked Charlie in surprise.

"Must have been in my coat," confessed Lew.

"Always keep it and the other necessary articles in your trousers," Charlie admonished. "It's easy to walk off and leave a coat, but no one starts off without his pants."

"Well," asked Lew. "What have you got?"

Charlie laid out his matchbox, handkerchief, a common nail and pocket comb. "I guess I shouldn't say anything," he remarked sheepishly. "I left some pretty important things in my own coat."

Lew picked up the matchbox. "We'll keep warm tonight, even if we don't eat," he said, opening it. Then he whistled sharply.

Charlie reached over, grabbed the thing from Lew's fingers and shook it. Nothing rattled inside. "I remember now. I emptied the box starting the fire last night. I was going to refill it from the big tin box in the duffle, but that nonsense with Old Jean and the woman drove it out of my head. I guess I've spilled the beans, Lew. I feel the chill coming on."

Towering spruces took on an aspect of menace. The river murmured in mockery, and a north wind smote their faces with the veritable breath of fear—promising the blizzards that would soon sweep over the land.

Chapter 3 – What the Woods Give

"Come on, Lew!" Charlie broke the deep silence that had enveloped them. "It is only a short time before night, and we absolutely must have a fire and a sheltered place to sleep."

"How about we rub two sticks together like the Indians do, until they blaze up in flame?" offered Lew. "I've read about it but never actually seen it done."

"And you never will," answered Charlie. "The Indians were too wise for such foolishness. They used a bow and drill. I know how it's done. But it takes the right sort of wood. And we don't have time to hunt it up. Besides, there is a quicker way—those two pistol cartridges of yours."

They had only gone a hundred yards farther when they found a big tree toppled over, the massive root wad still holding a thick mass of earth. There were piles of dry leaves along the trunk and limbs sticking up into the air where they had dried and seasoned above ground. Here was fuel and shelter both.

Charlie quickly broke off several dry, hard branches and peeled a square of bark from a yellow birch sapling.

"Use the knife, Lew," he directed, "to pry the bullet out of one of those shells. Go easy—that knife is worth many times its weight in gold to us."

Lew obeyed, and Charlie poured half the powder out and set it carefully aside on the dry piece of bark. "I kindled a campfire once this way with a handgun," he explained. "That nail and a stone will answer for hammer and firing pin, but we've got to find a substitute for a gun chamber. I'll notch the sides of two sticks so when they are pressed together, the hole will just catch the head of the shell."

He did so and then clamped the shell. "Stuff a ball of dry leaves in the end of the shell for a wad," he ordered. "If we shoot powder alone, it may blow out its own flame. But a wad of leaves may hold the spark until we can light this birch bark."

Lew struck the nail after carefully placing the point on the primer. The load went off with a sharp "poof!" and they both cried aloud in triumph. The leaf wad from the cartridge was smoking. Charlie laid the birch bark carefully over the smoke and began to blow gently. A second later, the bark burst into flame and he piled on

81

small sticks until a fire was blazing.

Charlie wiped out the fired shell, poured back the powder he had saved, and corked it with the bullet. "This will come in handy next time," he said. "Once we find a piece of flint we can make sparks with that and the knife blade. But the hardest thing about using flint and steel is to catch the faint spark in something that will catch fire. A few grains of powder will be wonderful. If we are careful, we may light a dozen fires with these two shells."

They worked quickly, dragging in a huge pile of fuel, enough to last through the night. When the woodpile was sufficiently high, they piled heaps of dry leaves up under the butt of the uprooted tree.

"Keep them back from the fire," warned Charlie, "and dig up some fresh dirt between our beds and the blaze."

"Say," Lew asked, "I don't suppose there's any chance of our eating tonight?"

"Why not?" asked Charlie. "It isn't such a miracle to find food in the woods. But if we want to eat tonight, we better get busy. "

"What do we do?" Lew asked. "Hunt with clubs?"

"We might club a fool grouse about sundown," agreed Charlie. "I've seen them sitting on tree limbs within club reach. Now let's both comb the timber for food. Don't stay out longer than an hour, though, and don't get lost."

"I know my woodcraft," retorted Lew. "At least I don't pack empty matchboxes."

"No, you don't pack any," grinned Charlie as he picked up a long, hard limb, and stepped noiselessly into the woods.

But the dry leaves rustled underfoot, and although he hunted diligently, the only living creature that crossed his path was a snake that slithered out of sight under a huge log.

"Hope we don't come to eating them," thought Charlie, with an involuntary shudder. It was too late for berries, and he did not find a single nut-bearing tree. The shadows deepened, and he decided it was time to return and pile more fuel on the fire.

Back at their camp, he heard Lew coming with all speed. "Bring a couple of blazing sticks," he grinned. "I found a wild beehive in a fissure in the rock, with big clusters of comb. We'll have to smoke them out, first, but then we can scrape off gallons of honey!"

Charlie picked up a couple of blazing brands and followed Lew, who soon stopped before a narrow crevice. "There," Lew pointed. "We can start the fire in the opening."

They gathered more wood, and when the fire was burning well, piled on damp, punky pine. Thick smoke arose, and they fanned it inside with slabs of bark. "Watch out," warned Charlie. "They may come out fighting mad."

"I don't think so," said Lew. "Not this time of year." A few bees did straggle out, but they seemed dopey from the smoke.

"Let's try now," said Charlie, brushing more dopey bees aside. Then he reached in and cut down large clusters of dark honeycomb, passing them out to Lew, who placed them on slabs of bark. Altogether, they estimated the weight of their find at 20 pounds.

After they returned to camp, Lew sat before the blaze with a bark plate of honey on both knees. "Things look a lot better," he said contentedly. "Say. How much of this stuff dare I eat?"

"All you can hold," answered Charlie. "Honey is naturally nourishing, and it will even help keep you warm. Tomorrow we'll make birch bark pails to hold what we don't eat tonight. That is if you leave any … and if a hungry bear doesn't come snooping into camp while we sleep."

Lew got up and threw another branch on the fire.

After they had eaten, they stored the rest on top of their windfall-home and covered it with more bark. Charlie bent up the edges of the bottom slabs to save as much of the liquid honey as might strain out of the comb.

The flames of their cheery fire pushed back the evening chill that rolled up from the river. "No wonder the ancients worshiped fire," reflected Lew. "We're in a rather bad fix, I know, but somehow as I lie here and watch the flames, I'm mighty easy in mind and don't dread what's coming one bit."

"We've made splendid headway," Charlie agreed. "If we progress as well tomorrow, by noon we'll have weapons for taking food and lines for fishing. What else shall we plan for tomorrow?"

"I say we don't turn back," Lew volunteered. "Let's get on down the river to Pierre's trapline. He must have a cabin there, and we may still be able to make a fur check."

"Exactly what I think," agreed Charlie. "We must have come halfway before the canoe wrecked. That leaves about fifty miles, maybe less. We can walk there in two days, and if we build a raft to float down, we could save time even if it took half a day to make it."

"It will take longer than that," said Lew. "Remember, we haven't a tool but my pocketknife."

Charlie, nodding at the fire, said, "We can do better than that. Fire is a most useful tool, as long as we control it. We will find some dry windfalls and then burn them up into the right lengths. There are always vines in the woods to tie them together. If we start early in the morning, we'll be launching at noon."

"When we find the cabin, then what?" asked Lew.

"We spend the winter," Charlie replied. "Pierre will be coming in six weeks or so, and if we can hold out until then, he'll have guns and axes and grub. There's a chance of his coming on the warpath, too, if he finds out that Marie wanted to ship out with you. But you didn't take her up, and I'm for sticking it out. Let's roll over now and sleep. We'll wake up quick enough when the fire burns down and the cold comes creeping in."

As Lew stood up, he backed into a sharp stub that ripped his sweater vest. "There it goes," he grumbled. "I'll have to tie these broken ends together or the whole thing will unravel."

Charlie sat up quickly. "That's it!" he cried. "We'll unravel the yarn in your sweater for fishing line. There must be a couple of hundred yards of it."

"Unravel my sweater?" Lew repeated. "I suppose I ought to be thankful my pants aren't knit from yarn."

"Don't complain," Charlie grinned. "It will help keep that stomach of yours full. We'll treat it with some of this beeswax. That will hold the fibers together and make it stronger and waterproof. You'll still have half a vest left. Where shall I begin—top or bottom?"

Lew and Charlie were so tired they rolled down in the leaves and were soon asleep. But the fire burned low long before midnight, and they both awoke shivering to pile on more wood. After the fire blazed again, they sat talking until the heat made them drowsy, and then they slept for a couple of more hours. Three times they did this, and then morning broke.

"I vote we get busy at once on a raft and reach Pierre's cabin as quickly as we can," Charlie said.

"I saw a couple of big trees blown over close to where we got the honey," said Lew. "Timber won't rot laid up on solid rock."

The found the trees and they were long, straight spruce about a foot in diameter. Charlie dug the knife blade into the wood. "Sound as a dollar," he declared, "and more than enough for six logs 12 feet long, which will float us and everything we've got. Get some fire, Lew. It takes time to burn timber through."

Lew ran back to camp and returned with as many blazing brands as his hands would hold. Charlie started a fire at each stepped-off mark, allowing a foot and a half waste at the burning joint. The timber caught slowly, but once it started, the blazes started to run along the sides of the logs. They kept plastering the trunks with wet mud, confining the blazes where they wanted them.

"Suppose we go back and eat some honey now," said Charlie. "These fires will be fine a few minutes without any attention. Then one of us must find some tough vines to tie it all together."

They started back, and when Lew looked up at the honey stash, he cried out with anger. A porcupine was plundering their sweet food. He dashed forward, and the animal wheeled clumsily, trying to carry a slab of honey-loaded bark away with him.

That was all the opening Lew needed, and he dealt the beast a killing blow with a stout club of wood.

"He sure has messed up our honey," Lew moaned.

"I don't know," Charlie replied. "I was dreading another meal of it. And he looks like a meaty young one, to me."

Lew dressed the animal with the pocketknife, wincing whenever he pricked a finger on a sharp quill. Then he quartered it, and they squatted before the fire cooking chunks on green sticks.

"This stuff is burnt outside but still raw in the middle," Charlie observed. "Maybe we can cut the rest in thin slices and broil it on a hot rock. But let's eat what we can now."

They hung the remaining meat high in a sapling and returned to the tree-cutting fires. Lew volunteered to go for vines and returned half an hour later trailing armfuls. Lew sorted them by size and length then braided thicker ropes from the strands.

As soon as the trees were burnt through enough to break sections free, they rolled them down to the riverbank and started tying them together in the form of a raft at the edge of the water.

They extinguished the fires reluctantly. But there was just no good way to carry burning coals on a wooden raft. Then they selected long, dry saplings to use as poles, leaped on and pushed off. As they edged one end out into the current, Charlie cautioned, "Go easy, Lew, those vines won't stand rough handling."

But contrary to expectations, the raft stayed surprisingly solid, and with the poles, they were able to keep it headed straight downstream. Charlie estimated they were making a good five or six miles an hour, much better time than walking and also much easier.

Late in the afternoon they heard it—the sound of white water.

"Head in to land," shouted Charlie, and they pushed and poled vigorously. But the current quickened, and the unwieldy craft began picking up speed. Seeing that it was useless, they dove into the river. With vigorous strokes they reached the bank and sat on the rocks, watching the raft disappear into the tumbling whitecaps of a rapids.

"We put a lot of work in the old girl," Lew said.

"It would have made no difference if we had landed it here," Charlie replied. "There would have been no way to portage a thousand pounds of logs. We were lucky that we made it as far as we did. Pierre's camp can't be that many miles ahead. Check your pockets," Charlie added, trying to suppress a note of worry. "I hope those two pistol shells aren't wet."

"They aren't," Lew grinned, "not after I smeared them with beeswax."

Charlie nodded his approval at that.

"We have passed six branches so far," Charlie said. "That means the next one marks the beginning of Pierre's trapping ground. I hope it isn't deep. One swim a day is all I care for."

They picked their way along the rocky bank past the rapids to where the river widened back into its natural channel. Lew in the lead suddenly stopped. "Listen," he said. "What's that noise?"

Ahead in a thick clump of lodgepole pine, they heard a grinding noise mingled with grunts. Running forward, they burst through the thicket and saw something incredible—and they had cause to be thankful for months afterwards.

Chapter 4 – Pocket Knife Deer Hunt

Peering through a thick tangle, Charlie and Lew watched two large buck deer fighting savagely, flanks wet with sweat as they thrust and parried with well-antlered heads. It already had been quite a battle, and the stumbling told of fatigue nigh on to exhaustion.

So absorbed were the bucks they did not see or scent the men watching a scant 40 yards away. "Oh, what wouldn't I give for a rifle!" breathed Lew, his eyes glistening with excitement.

His voice must have carried farther than he thought, either that or the animals caught first sight or scent of man, for they both jerked up. But something was wrong, and Charlie saw it at once.

"Their horns are locked, Lew. Give me that knife. Quick!"

Lew handed over an open pocketknife, and Charlie ran straight at the struggling deer. "Be careful!" warned Lew.

But Charlie did not hesitate. He crouched low to dodge the locked antlers, reached in, and slashed at the throat of the nearest animal. It was as though the deer went mad, struggling to break free with insane fury. Charlie fell back from the leaping, plunging whirlwind, but a flying hook still sliced his cheek. He dodged in again at every opening, slashing at the same hairy throat.

When the steel finally severed the windpipe, it whistled shrilly. He could only hope that more slashing would sever a vein large enough to bleed the deer down before the horns separated and both deer were free to escape. The blade was too short to reach the heart.

Lew hovered about, shouting encouragement. Finally, he could see Charlie was succeeding, and the deer sank back on its hindquarters, antlers still locked with the other.

"You've got him!" Lew whooped. "Give me the knife and I'll get the other."

But Charlie shook his head, and jumping forward, plunged the blade deep into the throat of the other buck, twisting the steel. The deer was held by the weight of his dying adversary yet still knocked Charlie sideways. Lew, fearing that the buck would break loose, picked up a heavy limb and struck the animal across the head with a thunderous blow. The buck stiffened and then slowly sank. Charlie was breathing hard, a primal glow lighting his normally calm eyes.

Lew was practically stammering. "We got two big mule deer —

with nothing more than a pocketknife and a tree branch!"

"I never expect to be so again lucky in all my life," Charlie replied. "But I'm winded. Take the knife and start working off those hides—carefully. We may need every inch."

Lew started cheerfully to work, visions of fried liver dancing in his brain.

"Skin as much of the fat off the hide as you can," advised Charlie. "The more you leave on, the harder it will be to flesh later. We are going to cure the raw skins and make buckskin the way Indian squaws do, though I will draw the line at chewing them soft."

Lew was skillful with a skinning knife and made splendid progress in spite of the short blade. "How can I split the heads to get the brains?" he asked. "We must have them for tanning. And I've got to separate the ribs from the backbone, somehow. We can't afford to take any chance chopping bone with the knife. It might break."

"Let me look about," offered Charlie, and a few minutes later he was back offering Lew a jagged chunk of flint. "Here is man's first hatchet. It will be clumsy and wasteful, but it will smash bone."

He directed Lew to carefully cut out the long strands of sinew along each side of the backbone. "Those make the best sort of cord, and when they dry, they tighten like iron bands."

Lew kept working at the deer, smashing ribs off with his crude ax. "It will be dark before we get this job finished," he finally said. "Suppose we camp right here?"

"Good idea," answered Charlie. "I'll take my turn with the knife. You start on a lean-to."

Lew dragged in several slender dead trees. Then he jabbed one into the ground about 8 feet to the side of a young pine, lashed another pole to it and tied that off to the tree, making a ridge pole. Then he leaned more long poles on this to form a roof with a sharp pitch. He used shorter branches of pine and spruce to thatch a roof.

"What about fire," he asked Charlie. "Shall I try to strike a spark from the flint with the knife blade?"

"Yes," Charlie replied. "But go easy with the blade."

Lew opened up the fired cartridge and shook out a small pinch of the powder on a slip of bark. Then, holding the knife in one hand and the rock in his other, he carefully brought them together. Nothing resulted, and he struck them harder at a better angle. Minutes later, their second campfire was going strong.

"I've simply got to have some liver," sighed Lew. "But burnt on the end of a stick over the fire it will taste like shoe leather."

"If you want to finish up these deer," Charlie offered. "I'll see what I can do."

"Willingly," agreed Lew.

Charlie found a thin slab of rock on the riverbank, carried it over and leaned it in the blazing campfire. While the rock was heating up, he used the knife to slice half a liver into thin strips. Then he raked the hot stone out of the coals, propped it up on four smaller rocks, pushed live coals underneath and heaped more around. He greased it well with fat from the deer intestines, and it sizzled with an aroma that made Lew's mouth water.

"That-a-boy," he cried. "It's a regular stone griddle. It won't cook as fast or quite as well as in cast iron, but I won't mind one bit."

"If you can eat with your fingers," Charlie said, "try this."

"I could eat it with my toes," Lew assured his partner, after slurping down the first delicious bite.

As fast as the liver cooked they ate it and piled more on the sizzling griddle stone. Finally, even Lew could hold no more, and they went back to finish the butchering.

"Let's string up the quarters," Charlie said, and Lew climbed into the tree supporting the end of the lean-to and Charlie hoisted them to him. Four was all they could load in the tree. The rest were tied in another close by the circle of light cast by the fire. That done, they sat down in the spruce shelter and watched the dancing flames.

"I'm tired," Lew sighed, "but mighty happy."

Charlie agreed. "We have 200 pounds of meat and fat, and two big hides to tan for winter clothes. We have sinew to sew garments together, and the deer hoofs can even be boiled down to make glue. The tips of those antlers will make deadly points for arrows, if we must resort to such."

"The deer is a great all-round animal," agreed Lew sleepily.

They heaped up pine and spruce boughs for beds and settled down to sleep.

A keen chill that penetrated to the bone awoke Charlie less than two hours later. Their fuel was all light limbs that did not make good coals, and the embers were dull when he piled on more wood. Charlie sat up by the blaze, his mind working on all of the various problems they faced.

A half-hour later, a rustle caught his ear, coming from where they had dressed the deer. Charlie stood and stared into the night, not really seeing anything. He checked the venison, and satisfied that the quarters were lashed firmly in place high enough to be out of reach of any camp robber, returned to the shelter and went back to sleep.

But the cold woke him again, and as he added wood to the fire, the pad of footfalls sent every nerve tingling. Then he caught the flash of two eyes glowing in the building blaze.

Then he remembered the two fresh deer hides. He had laid them at the cooler opposite end of the lean-to. And when he felt about with anxious fingers, he discovered one was gone.

The dull scraping noise of something heavy dragging over the ground brought him running. But when two eyes glowed in the dying firelight, Charlie stopped so abruptly he nearly skidded.

He could not run blindly in the dark at an unknown animal. Charlie shouted loudly, but the eyes held their ground, and a low-throated growl raised the hair on his head.

What sort of beast could this be? He seized two brands from the fire and waved them in the air until the rush of oxygen made them burst into flame. Charlie hurled one of the flaming brands at the eyes. They shifted a little, but their owner held his ground and growled again, this time with shriller menace.

That's when Lew stepped in, a burning brand in each hand. Charlie hurled his remaining brand at the eyes, and this time, the beast trotted off into the timber.

"What the devil is going on here?" asked Lew.

"Something stole one of the deer skins," Charlie answered. "Here, give me some light." When he found the hide, it was not damaged. "Our luck is holding," he said. "It isn't even chewed."

"What sort of beast was it?" asked Lew.

"I don't know, but we better post a guard," Charlie replied.

"I'll take over," Lew offered. "Let me sit up and watch."

When Charlie awoke a third time, to faint streaks of crimson shooting through the gray haze of morning, he found Lew dozing peacefully beside the fire and all well in camp. He woke Lew with the tantalizing smell of broiling venison.

Lew sat up, rubbing his eyes. "Have you looked for prints?"

"Found them," answered Charlie.

Lew followed him to a bare patch of earth and then broke out with a low whistle. "A wolf. And a big one!"

Chapter 5 – On Pierre's Trapline

I hope to sleep indoors tonight," Charlie declared. "As soon as we eat, we'll load up with one of the hides and a quarter of meat and then start looking for Pierre's cabin."

After breakfast, Charlie slung a rear quarter over his shoulders and Lew picked up the biggest of the raw hides. Then they swung along the river at a brisk gait. In less than an hour they came to a tributary that appeared to flow swift and deep.

"This is the seventh branch," Charlie said. "When we cross it, we should be in Pierre's trapping country, and his cabin can't be far away. Let's walk up the bank. Maybe there'll be a shallower place we can ford."

As they walked, Lew examined the ground. "There is a faint path. See how it leads between the biggest trees?" A hundred yards on they came to a woodsman's bridge across the river. The skillful ax man had felled two trees—one on either side—so cleverly their tops met in the center and overlapped. The branches had been trimmed off to make walking easy, and the trunks had been lashed together with wide bands of rawhide.

"Come on," Charlie called to Lew after crossing. "It's solid."

Lew joined him on the other side, but before they started again, his keen eye caught sight of a weathered wood stake in the bank. Seizing it, he pulled from the water a double-spring trap big enough for otter. They grinned at each other. Now here was a find.

"Try the springs," Charlie advised.

Lew set the trap with his feet and then sprung the pan with a finger from the underside. The jaws snapped together with a resounding click.

"Not as strong as new," Charlie observed. "But plenty strong enough for small stuff. That means we can start catching food, and it also means one less deadfall on the line."

"We sure have been fortunate," Lew added. "I'm starting to think maybe things have come too easy—that luck might turn the other way."

"You needn't worry," assured Charlie. "If we had sat beside the river feeling sorry for ourselves after the canoe went over the rapids, none of this would have come our way. The fellow who grins at hard luck and digs in a little harder always comes out with his head up."

They crested a low knoll and simultaneously caught sight of the log cabin. "Hurrah!" Lew shouted. "That's Pierre's cabin or I'm a mama's boy!"

There was a window on each side, and the entire rear wall was laid up of rough stone with the chimney in the center. The door was hand-hewed planks held with a big brass padlock.

"I don't want to break a window," Lew said. "Think we can we force this lock?"

"We can try," said Charlie, using the long spring of the otter trap as a lever, heaving and prying.

"It's coming," cried Lew and then added his strength to Charlie's. The clasp pulled out of the wood with a loud creak, and the lock fell to the ground. Charlie pushed the door open, and a damp, musty odor met them. But the inside was fairly clean, and the 8-inch logs were well chinked with a mixture of clay and ashes. Pierre had finished the room with a ceiling of narrow, straight poles to better hold the heat of the fireplace in winter.

A deep bunk was built against one wall, made of split poles with interwoven sides of willow and filled with dry river grass. A magnificent caribou head with full antlers hung over the stone fireplace, and on the hearth sat three small stones partly covered with ashes and bits of charred wood.

"This must be Marie's cooking stand," Charlie observed, "where she sets her kettle and rakes hot coals underneath."

A rack above the bunk made of forked limbs had probably held Pierre's guns, but it was empty. There were two rustic stools and a crude table. Otherwise, the place was bare—not a tool or implement.

"I thought sure there would at least be an ax," Lew said. "What do these Cannucks do? Take everything they own with them to the trading post?"

"They haven't much to take," said Charlie. "Pierre probably has a gun, an ax and a knife, and his wife a kettle and fry pan. That is about the size of their kit. And they need them on the trail, just as much as they do when at home."

"I wonder where Pierre stored his furs?" Lew said. "There's usually a shed or something, but I saw nothing of the kind outside."

After another cursory look, Charlie declared that they should head back for their meat and hides. "It will take two trips, and we can't take a chance on anything happening to it."

The shadows of late afternoon were creeping across the little clearing when they returned with the last load.

"I think I know where Pierre stores his fur," Charlie said as they entered the cabin. There must be at least four feet of space between the pole ceiling and the roof."

"A fellow would have to stand on something to reach it," reflected Lew. "I'd say the bunk would be most convenient."

He climbed up and pushed on the poles. "Half a dozen loose ones," he announced. "That's a trap door."

He pushed it up and then drew himself in the opening. "Traps!" he cried down to Charlie. "Dozens hanging from the rafters. And a big pile of stretcher boards. We're all fixed up for the trapline."

Charlie heard him rustling about some more. "Nothing else but dust. I thought sure I would find ... an ax head, Charlie! It's an old ax he must have tossed up here when he got a new one."

Lew dropped to the floor and eagerly held out his find. It was a light, double-bit head, ground back and worn short in the blade, but still capable of a lot of service.

"Just what we need to flesh those deer hides," Charlie observed. "And I'm going out right now for some handle stock. You drag in the firewood, and tonight, I'll sit up and whittle a handle by the light of the fire."

Charlie sat up until midnight shaping the handle with Lew's pocketknife. Finally, he passed it over to his partner. "All done but the wedge. I'll put that in tomorrow."

They slept soundly through the night—not the shivering sleep of the last few nights. As Lew rubbed his eyes open, he asked, "What's the program for today?"

"We must get after those deer. They have to soak about three days, and while they soak, we'll dry and smoke the meat into jerky."

There are three stages to making buckskin. First the raw hides are soaked and grained, which means removing the hair and the grain or black epidermis. Then they are softened by manipulation; and finally, they are smoked, which closes the pores, making them practically waterproof. The smoking also toughens them and gives the rich color.

Charlie laid the hides in the river, weighing them down with heavy rocks. Then Lew started in on the venison, carefully slicing just lean meat into strips a half-inch thick. Charlie built a drying rack of wood poles, spread the meat on these, and started a slow fire of black birch.

"The black birch will give it a pleasant taste," he said, "which we'll appreciate since we haven't any salt. We must keep the fire low—drying, not cooking, and we'll have to turn the strips often. We'll have to sit up tonight and take turns. We dare not leave the meat outside unguarded from scavengers. And we've got an ax to use if any bold wolves try anything."

When night came, he let Lew sleep and took the first turn. Lew took his place when the night was half gone, as near as either of them could guess.

The smoking fire required little attention, and Charlie had built another brighter blaze out beside the rack to keep away night prowlers. Lew sat before this, half dozing, when suddenly he found himself alert and listening intently. Was that faint "tunk-tunk" drifting across the river the sound of a canoe paddle?

Then he heard it so plainly there could be no doubt a canoeist was drifting by, using his blade just to keep the craft straight. Lew peered out into the blackness but he could see nothing. The noise was not repeated, and after a half-hour of tense listening, Lew resumed his place by the blaze, waiting for dawn to break.

He told Charlie in the morning and then added, "I'm going to scout around a bit, if you don't object. I'll start after lunch and see what I find."

"Go ahead," agreed Charlie. "I'll finish drying the meat while you're gone."

At noon they chewed a few strips of venison, and then Lew slung the ax over his shoulder and started down the riverbank.

Charlie decided to store the jerked meat up in the pole ceiling. It would be safe there for a few days, but within the week they must devise a means of protecting it from the mice that would be attracted by the smell.

As the afternoon wore on he began to wonder if perhaps it had been unwise to let his partner go exploring. Lew had a bent for getting into scrapes. The meat now was dry, and as he was stacking the last load up in the loft, he made another discovery. A tin canister fell out from behind one of the rafters, and opening the lid, he saw it was a third full of tea. Charlie searched carefully behind each rafter, but found nothing more.

As he searched around for something in which he could boil

tea, he realized again that he had never been in a cabin so bare—not even a tin can.

When it was nearly dark, he walked down to the riverbank. There was no sign of Lew, and Charlie was debating whether he should start searching for him when he heard someone paddling a canoe up the river. Then he made out the outline of a single occupant rowing a canoe doggedly against the current, head and shoulders bent low. There was something familiar about the form—could it be?

"Stand by, old-timer!" Lew hailed from the canoe.

"Lew! What the devil have you been up to? Where did you get a canoe?"

"That's quite a tale," answered Lew in jaunty tones. "Guess it takes old Lew to bring home the bacon."

Charlie looked down in the canoe and whistled low in astonishment. "I'll say it does!"

Chapter 6 – Lew's Big Coup

When Lew left the cabin he merely hoped to examine the country the best he could, not only to discover if there were other inhabitants but to roughly map out one of the loops they would string out as soon as furs were prime. From all indications, they were in the middle of a very rich fur section. It would be a serious challenge to follow the rough life of the fur seeker minus guns, snowshoes, blankets and outer clothing.

But Lew was cheerfully confident and a fast walker. Two hours put him about five miles below the cabin. Here, to his delight, he found a network of shallow creeks flowing into the river, a half-dozen within the short space of a quarter-mile. They flowed slowly, and the country back along their course looked low and marshy. Over each creek, Lew found a fallen tree which served as a bridge, and he guessed that Pierre had prepared and used this path.

Lew followed one of the small branches. It penetrated a wet valley, and the whole thing appeared to be one mammoth beaver colony. Lew counted four dams, and this was only the front end of the marsh. Miles of it stretched to the horizon.

Lew turned back to the big river and walked another half-mile before a wider branch barred his course, and he turned up it hoping there would be another woodsman's bridge. But he walked several hundred yards without finding one, and as he was miles from the cabin, he decided to turn back. And just as he began to retrace his steps, his keen nose picked up the faint smell of a smoking pipe. There was no doubting the rank odor of Trading Post tobacco.

Lew started eagerly forward but then halted. There was no way of knowing who this might be. It might even be a rival trapper who had jumped Pierre's rich fur claim. Lew decided it would be much better to approach noiselessly, without being seen. There would be plenty of time to introduce himself afterwards.

Testing his steps before trusting his weight to each, he stole forward from one clump of brush to the next. Tobacco smoke can drift for long distances, and he had no way of telling how far off the smoker might be. But as he approached an unusually thick growth of birch beside the water, he heard the faint murmur of voices. There was more than one of them, then.

The voices' steady tones reassured him. If he had been discovered, chances were the talking would have ceased. He crept in closer and recognized the familiar voice of Old Jean Labady!

Lew sneaked closer and saw that the man beside Old Jean appeared to be part French and part Cree. His face features had a twisted, squeezed appearance that was decidedly unsavory. His clothes resembled Jean's, only dirtier if that were possible.

"Who I think?" Old Jean spoke. "I think it those boys from the States who come down Big Beaver with canoe full of traps."

"An' if eet is—you do what?" asked his companion.

Old Jean scowled. Laying one hand on the short knife at his belt he drew the other across his throat.

"What you think Pierre say?" the half-breed asked. "He send them to work his line. Maybe he tell?"

"Bah!" Old Jean spat in disgust. "Pierre drunk most of the time. I tell you his foot it swell as beeg as his head. It is the whiskey in his blood. Before he come we take all the fur and we go. It will be easy. Didn't Jean cut the paddle and make them smash canoe on the big rocks? Everything they bring is gone, including their guns. Last night when we float by and see one awake by the fire, if both had been asleep, all would now be finished."

So it was Old Jean who had passed by the cabin in the night. Lew knew he had heard something.

"But ..." the half-breed began in reluctant tones.

Old Jean cut in angrily. "If you afraid ..." he said witheringly, but the other shrugged a denial. Evidently, Old Jean had not been exactly clear upon the murderous intent of this venture. But it was not the man's conscience that bothered him. One glance at his face told Lew that there was no such component in his make-up.

"I no afraid. But Pierre find out you gone. Then he hunt dees boys. We must fix him, too."

"Leave Pierre to me," said Jean.

"An' tonight, what we do?" asked the half-breed, as he pulled his pipe from a shirt pocket and proceeded to load it with tobacco.

"Paddle back to the cabin," said Old Jean tersely. "These boys up all last night. Now they sleep. If they bar door, we wait until daybreak. You make noise by door and I stand ready with noose of rawhide. We work it like we feex Joe Arndt up on Moccasin Creek. Just two boys found drowned in river."

The half-breed grunted in assent, and Lew's hair commenced

to rise on the back of his neck. Before him sat two well-armed men who had decided to murder him and Charlie. Old Jean was speaking again. "We paddle all night, now we rest. Then, when the sun goes down ..."

Jean knocked the ashes from his pipe and settled back against a tree. The other followed suit, and Lew could see that they were already half asleep, a trait common with woodsmen who have trained their faculties to rest upon short notice when the opportunity comes.

"Now is my time to make a getaway," Lew thought. Flattening himself to the ground, he squirmed backwards away from his hiding place. Although their eyes were closed, Lew knew they rested lightly, only a veritable catnap.

Inch by inch he crept backwards until he reached the shelter of the larger timber. Then he stood up and stole swiftly down to the river. He knew he must get back to the cabin in time to warn Charlie. They were unarmed and facing men undoubtedly well supplied with rifles, besides the pistol and knife he had seen on Jean's belt. It was lucky he had overheard their plot. If they had been caught unawares, they would have had no chance. If they only had guns ...

Then a thought struck Lew, and a plan so daring it literally took his breath away. Their rifles were probably still in the canoe, along with other much needed supplies. Was he enough of a woodsman to move in and take that canoe so quietly their woods-trained ears would not hear him?

"That would settle the whole business," he decided. "Charlie would try it if he were here."

He turned around and crept down to the riverbank. There, a hundred yards up the stream, was the canoe, half out of the water. Lew held the camp ax in his hand, resolved to throw it straight at Old Jean's head if he reached for that ugly pistol at his waist. He would trust to chance that the half-breed was unarmed.

The bank along the water's edge was soft, and Lew's feet made not a sound. He had to fight the urge to make a quick dash and end the suspense. The beached canoe was easily visible from where the two lay. If Old Jean opened an eye, he could not help but see him creeping towards the craft. There was scant chance of Jean missing even a pistol shot at that range.

As he stretched out an arm to grasp the gunwale, the half-breed snored. Lew froze rigid as ice, poised with extended arm. He turned his eyes—not his head—and saw Old Jean stir. Lew sucked in his breath slowly, nerving himself for swift action. Jean's eyelids flickered while Lew's hand closed over his ax, but they did not open.

Lew's other hand settled over the gunwale, and silently drawing it towards him, he laid the ax gently in the bottom and climbed—an inch at a time—over the side into the canoe. With a flash of satisfaction he saw two heavy packs weighing down the center space between the thwarts. A buckskin coat was spread out in the bow, two paddles leaned on the loaded packs, and grasping one, Lew pushed off with a strong but silent stroke.

His heart pounded as the canoe swung out, and then, freeing itself from the bank, responded to the current and went dancing down towards Big Beaver. Lew could scarcely restrain from shouting in triumph. With one stroke he had drawn the teeth of the two rattlesnakes sleeping back on the riverbank and had gained the things they needed so vitally for the winter trapping season. Wouldn't Charlie grin when he told this tale?

Lew glanced back over his shoulder for one last view of the place where he had turned such a neat coup. But his self-congratulations stopped as suddenly as they began. Old Jean was running down the riverbank, pistol in hand, and he ran as silently and swiftly as a coursing hound.

Lew drew his head down to present as small a target as possible. He expected any second to hear a pistol ball whistle past his head. Why didn't Jean shoot?

Crack!

The sound of the shot sent a cold chill up Lew's back, but the splash twenty yards downstream reassured him. Evidently, Jean was too angry to stop and steady his aim. When he glanced back, however, he saw Jean gaining on him, no more than a hundred yards back!

Lew's paddling lost its easy, powerful rhythm, and Old Jean settled into a dogged gait which slowly but surely would overhaul him. And then Lew saw the little beaver stream pouring into the bigger branch, and about its mouth a wide strip of soft marsh. Hope rose again; this surely would hold Jean back. But then Jean would surely steady his arm and take deliberate aim.

"Guess it's coming to this," Lew thought.

But then fate intervened again. The river turned abruptly in a sharp curve, and he passed out of Jean's sight. Lew caught one last fleeting glimpse of the man halted before the narrow marsh.

The chill of night was creeping up from the water, and Lew

shivered in spite of his hot, sweaty body. He reached forward and picked up the buckskin coat in the bow and uncovered two rifles lying side by side on the slatted bottom. They were the short repeaters used in northern brush country, showing years of use by the worn finish and bright edges of receiver and trigger guard, but also showing signs of care from the oil seeping out from bolt and hammer.

"Hot dog!" breathed Lew. "I wonder what caliber they are? Probably .30-30. I hope Old Jean was thoughtful enough to bring along plenty of shells."

But he restrained his curiosity and kept paddling.

As dusk deepened, Lew wondered had he really left Old Jean behind? And then he caught sight of a rosy glow flowing out of the open cabin door from the fire on the hearth. Charlie was standing on the bank, waiting for him. And for the moment, Lew forgot Old Jean, pistol in hand and blazing mad.

Chapter 7 – Return of the River Rat

Charlie took a swift inventory of the canoe's contents. "Rifles, packs, leather coat, canoe and paddles. All stuff we need, but who does all this stuff belong to?"

"Us," Lew replied. "I confiscated it under the law of the woods."

"Well, then, who did it belong to?" Charlie asked.

"Our kind friend Old Jean," Lew replied grimly. "He came to jump Pierre's claim, and when he saw us in the cabin last night, the plan expanded to include choking us with a noose and pitching our bodies in the river. And you should see the guy he brought to help. This bird makes Old Jean look as soft as a feather pillow."

And then Lew sat on the gunwale of the canoe and told him the whole story. When he reached the chase down the river with Jean running after the speeding canoe, pistol in hand, his face beamed with the humor of the situation. But Charlie jumped to his feet, anxiously peering back into the darkening night.

"I guess you were justified, all right, in taking the canoe. Old Jean deserves all you gave him—and more. Only it looks to me like you've started something that will be hard to finish. Why, we won't be able to step outside the cabin without expecting an ambush. Old Jean isn't the type to lie down and let you get away with this stuff."

Lew's chest gradually shrank and the confident grin vanished from his face as Charlie spoke. "Gosh," he replied. "I never thought of that. All I could see was a loaded canoe and how badly we needed it. Of course Old Jean will be laying for us. He may even be creeping up behind us now. That thought makes me shiver. Let's get inside and barricade the cabin, quick!"

He picked up one of the rifles and a pack. Charlie followed suit, and they carried the stuff in the cabin. Then Charlie returned to the river, swung the light canoe over his head and carried that to the cabin. There was not room for its length inside, so he laid it close against the wall under the eaves.

"Now we'll look over the swag," he grinned. "Cheer up, old man! I didn't intend to dishearten you. We'll show Old Jean that we are more than a match for him. I'm darned glad you took that little stroll down the river today. If you hadn't, things would have gone bad for us. Let's see what these packs contain."

Lew picked up a rifle, first. "This one is a .30-30," he said and then pumped the shell from its chamber and looked down the bore. "Far as I can see by this light, she's in good shape. Old Jean may be a scoundrel but a good woodsman. This other, though, is a .25-35. Pretty small for the Northwoods. I hope they brought plenty of shells for both."

"The .25-35 makes a dandy trapline gun," Charlie replied. "Jean probably doesn't shoot a lot of big game, and he is woodsman enough to stalk within close range. See how many shells you can find in the packs. They'll probably be inside the blankets."

Opening the packs, they found closely woven Hudson Bay blankets of the finest wool, a little soiled and smelling strongly of stale tobacco, but nevertheless thick, heavy and warm. They found two in each pack, and unrolling them, shook out boxes of cartridges, small canisters of tea and salt, and a pouch of tobacco. A bundle of heavy Scotch wool socks, two pairs of moccasins tanned of soft moose hide with the hair on, and a small kettle rested in the bottoms of the packs.

"These boys travel light," grumbled Lew. "Only three boxes of shells for each gun. That means we'll have to use them carefully this winter, Charlie. We can't afford to take any pot shots that miss."

"They probably expected to make another trip back for the rest of their stuff," Charlie said. "But think, Lew, this is just the stuff we needed in the worst way, things that we would find it hardest to make ourselves. But only one coat. I sort of wish we had brought Marie with us now. I'll bet she could sew up another coat in a hurry."

"So, what kind of trouble is ahead of us—trouble with Old Jean?" asked Lew, his mind returning to this vital issue.

"Well, put yourself in his place," replied Charlie. "What would you do if someone had sneaked away with your canoe and outfit? Would you let him get away with it? From now on, no one leaves the cabin without a loaded rifle."

Charlie grilled more venison steaks for dinner, only this time seasoned properly with salt. Lew ate heartily and then shook out a pair of blankets and spread them in the bunk. Charlie barred the cabin door with a heavy timber.

"A regular bed," Lew sighed with satisfaction. "How long has it been since we slept in one? And we won't have to keep up a fire all night. These blankets will sure save a lot of wood."

And so, by the dim light of the hardwood burning down to coals in the fireplace, Lew and Charlie rolled up in Old Jean's blankets and dropped asleep. Would the state of siege that Lew predicted come with the break of tomorrow's dawn? Or did the forest surrounding the cabin already harbor danger in its black shadows?

Charlie awoke hours later, choking. The cabin was filled with smoke, and the thought flashed through his brain that Jean had crept up and started the cabin burning. He threw off the blanket and leaped from the bunk. Then, as he gasped for breath in the swimming smoke, he saw there was no blaze; even the fire on the hearth was dull. The heavy vapor had a curiously sickening smell, not like the odor of burning wood, and he reached over to shake Lew to awaken him.

"What is it?" gasped Lew. "Did a skunk fall in the fire?"

"The chimney is clogged," answered Charlie. "Let's get out in the air while we still can."

He dashed to the door, unbarred it and inhaled deeply as it swung open and cold night air met his face.

As he turned to peer back to see why Lew had not followed, he felt the cold nose of a pistol jammed into his side and heard the husky voice of Old Jean.

"Jean feex you, boy!"

In the fraction of a second before the tightening of Jean's finger discharged the gun, Charlie's brain clicked with lightning speed and hit upon his only possible chance. He remembered a peculiar trait of the automatic pistol, and pressing forward, he jammed the ugly muzzle of the gun even closer into his body to keep the barrel in forcible contact. This pressure forced back the slide of the gun only a fraction of an inch, but this was sufficient to act as a lock on the firing mechanism. As long as he could maintain this, Jean could not fire—the bolt slide would not fully close and consequently lock. The manufacturer had provided this safety to prevent accidental premature discharge, and it was a lifesaver for Charlie.

Jean grunted in surprise when the gun refused to fire, and Charlie gained enough time to twist his arms back, grasp the pistol with one hand and Jean's wrist with the other, keeping the muzzle pressed into his side.

At that instant, Lew sprang through the door, rifle in hand. His burning eyes took in the scene in one glance, and he used the short rifle to club the pistol jammed against Charlie's side. Charlie held on as long as he dared to prevent the pistol firing, for Jean still pulled at the trigger. Then, just as the blow landed, he twisted away.

The rifle landed before the handgun fired, and with a gasp of pain, Jean let the pistol fall from his hand. His fingers were stinging from the jolt, and he stood snarling, working them much as a man does when he finds a limb asleep.

Lew put the rifle muzzle in his face. Charlie stooped and gathered up the pistol with a sweep of his arm. One glance told him the slide was broken, so he tossed it inside the cabin.

"So, you greasy old devil," Lew began. Then a sharp warning from Charlie cut short his speech.

"The other one's on the roof. Watch out, Lew!"

Shooting a glance up at the top of the cabin, Lew saw a dark figure crouching beside the chimney. He saw an arm shoot forward and a bright flash marked the course of a knife flying straight at his face. Lew instinctively flung up the rifle, and the keen blade deflected off the walnut stock and stuck in the ground 20 feet away. As it glanced, the tip of the blade caught a finger on the hand that held the stock and slashed a gash from knuckle to end.

But Lew never heeded the bleeding hand. He jumped back to a position from where he could cover both Jean and the man on the roof and commanded, "Get down here before I shoot you off the roof!"

The fellow lightly dropped to his feet.

"Now get over there beside Jean," commanded Lew. The half-breed slouched up to where his partner stood, watching Jean as though waiting for some cue.

"What have you got to say for yourselves before I send you to the devil?" Lew demanded, raising the rifle.

Until now, Jean's face had been twisted with rage, but now the lines of anger faded and were replaced with a look of eager surprise.

"By Gar! It is my fren's who stay with Pierre and Jean! What you do here? Me and Chenau think you drown in river. That what Big Tom and his brother who live below rapids tell us. Didn't they, Chenau?" And Jean looked over at his partner for confirmation.

Jean's words were the last thing Lew or Charlie expected. Did he really think they would believe this? Then Lew laughed derisively. "I'll say you've got nerve to try that."

But Jean continued volubly, using his hands to emphasize his words. "Chenau and I think you 'Jibway poachers who steal Pierre's fur. The last thing Pierre say—he say, 'Jean, you go and watch my land; keep the fur thieves out until my foot well.' This is what we do, Chenau and I. When we see light in cabin, we think it thieves."

"Listen, you lying scoundrel," Lew replied quietly. "Before I got your canoe, I lay twenty feet away on the riverbank, listening to you plan our murders."

Charlie already had hit upon the only feasible plan for getting them out of the way, and now he stepped forward to give Lew a chance to cool down and collect himself. "What was that stuff you threw down the chimney to smoke us out?"

"Wet duck feather," Jean replied with a nasty chuckle.

"By all rights we should shoot both of you and roll you in the river," Charlie replied. "But I'm going to give you two minutes to clear out. Next time, we shoot on sight. You can take the canoe."

Jean shrugged his shoulders, and with a glance at Chenau, walked over to the canoe. "Here are the paddles," Charlie added, and they carried the craft down to the river. As they paddled out of sight, Charlie followed along the riverbank with rifle ready, to make sure they knew he meant what he had said.

When he returned, Lew demanded, "What did you give him the canoe for? The walk back would have been good for them."

"With the canoe," Charlie explained, "they are much likelier to really leave. Otherwise, they might hang around here trying to steal it. Of course, we don't know when they'll come tearing back on the warpath, but I'd say we'll have at least a week's peace."

"Say," said Lew, "I believe that bird left his coat over the top of the chimney. I'm going up and see." A minute later he was holding out another buckskin coat for Charlie. "Now we've each got one. Gosh, doesn't luck break our way?"

"There's a good knife lying over there on the ground, too," replied Charlie. "Better get it. I'm going to air out the cabin."

He threw up a window and let the night air clear out the smoke. On the coals in the fireplace lay the smoldering remains of the wet feathers that had so nearly suffocated them. Charlie raked them out on a flat piece of bark and carried the mess outdoors. Then he kindled up a small fire to start a draft up the flue.

"The cabin will smell for a week," grumbled Lew. "But it was worth it: another leather coat and a hunting knife. Every scrape we get into leaves us just that much better off. I wonder what Old Jean will bring for us when he pays his next visit?"

"Trouble!" declared Charlie bluntly. "I'm afraid he is going to keep on until we are forced to kill him or he kills us. The odds will be on his side—he'll have the advantage of surprise, you know."

"Well, I'm going back to sleep," said Lew. "Things should stay quiet at least until daybreak. Tomorrow morning, we'll organize our lines of defense."

In the morning, Charlie carried a rifle when he went down to the river and pulled out the two deer skins which had been soaking there. Although the immediate need for coats had been relieved, he still planned to tan the hides and lay them away for future use. A trapper wears out clothing quickly.

Lew met him at the cabin door. "That looks like a lot of work," he grinned. "Let me at them. The back of Chenau's knife has a long straight edge that will scrape dandy."

"I'll fix up a log to throw the hide over," Charlie offered.

And as they worked, Lew remarked, "Wonder who'll be our next caller? I hope whoever it is, they come in peace."

But as fate would have it, they did not.

Chapter 8 – The Crees' Warning

While Lew worked on the deerskins, Charlie checked the traps he had set the afternoon before for small game. One held a rabbit, and he reset the trap then carried his catch back to the cabin.

The skins had not soaked quite long enough for the hair to slip easily, and Lew was rubbing ashes into the spots that offered the most resistance. After the hair and grain were removed, Lew would turn the hide and flesh it carefully with the keen edge of the knife, working the skin down to an even thickness. After this, the hides would be ready for working until they would remain soft and pliable wet or dry.

Charlie dressed the rabbit and then spoke. "It's my turn to take a stroll in the woods, Lew. This dried venison is good, but my stomach craves fresh fried liver, and I hate to use up all of our dried meat in this nice weather, when the timber is full of game. We will need it later when we may go weeks without seeing a deer."

He walked inside the cabin, picked up the .30-30 rifle, and then went straight back into the timber directly away from the river. It was a wonderful day for a jaunt through the trees. The sun was halfway up and the air cold and fresh. At the edge of the clearing, Charlie saw two lines of tracks strung over water-logged ground. A small deer—a doe likely—had run across the clearing a short time before, for the tracks were still cleanly cut in the damp earth.

A little to one side ran a row of wide paw marks, and Charlie felt a thrill shoot up his spine as he recognized the track of a wolf, and a big one, maybe the same beast that had raided their camp beside the river and tried to drag away one of the deer skins. Charlie whistled softly. "Evidently, that fellow is still hanging around."

He followed the tracks across the marsh into the timber. Perhaps if he stalked carefully, he might get a shot at the wolf. It was hot on the trail of the deer, and Charlie could picture the beast in his mind, swift as a shadow following the fleeing deer.

A quarter of a mile on, he came to the end of the trail—the final act in this drama of the Great Northwoods. The half-eaten carcass of the deer was sprawled on the ground.

Charlie stopped before he came to the place and stood looking from a distance. Here was an excellent place to set traps, and he determined to bring several of the big double-spring traps from the cabin that evening and set them. Until then, he would keep back to leave as little man-scent as possible around the carcass.

From the encounter that night at their river camp, he suspected the wolf was a dangerous brute, as it had displayed no fear of man and a disposition that was foreign to the nature of ordinary wolves in this season. It would be better not to have such a beast around their cabin when winter came and brought a scarcity of food for man and beast. When faced with extreme hunger, the wolf might even prove as dangerous as Old Jean.

Charlie proceeded carefully now. He was far enough from the cabin to expect to have opportunity to use the rifle he carried over his arm. A twig snapped out in the forest ahead. It sounded like a .22 pistol shot in the still woods, and Charlie searched for some sign of movement or a patch of color among the trees.

Five minutes passed, but still he did not move. He knew he was all but invisible as long as he held his rigid pose, and he determined to wait patiently. Minutes more passed, and he had just about decided to give up and move on when a buck deer stepped noiselessly out into an opening a hundred yards ahead.

Charlie threw up the rifle and fired. He heard the bullet thud against animal flesh. The buck jumped straight into the air, and turning as it leaped, wheeled and disappeared through the timber. Charlie searched the ground for blood, a little chagrined for not dropping the deer in its tracks.

He knew the bullet had struck the base of the buck's neck, for he had formed the habit of calling his shots whether directed at target or game.

Charlie found a single drop of blood on the pine needles, but finding no others which would testify to a freely bleeding wound, he sat down to wait until the running buck would lie down and bleed out. If he followed now, it would hear him coming and keep up its desperate gait, leading him on a day-long chase.

So he rested, squatting on the ground for a full half-hour, and then arose to track down the wounded game. The deer had left a trail that could be followed even by a novice in woodcraft, and Charlie swung along at a fast pace, now and then marking blood.

Glancing again at the ground, he made a surprising discovery. Plainly impressed over a bloody spot was the paw print of a wolf of unusual size.

"That fellow sure is something," thought Charlie as he pressed forward at a faster rate. With the wolf on his trail, the buck would not lie down. He paused a moment to consider this, but the lure of the chase was hot within him, and he pressed ahead.

When he judged he had come some eight miles from the cabin, he decided it was foolish to keep on. When he did overtake the deer, it would be a half-eaten carcass. He hated to give up on game, but at least the wolf would see that its end was sure and swift.

He decided it was time to retrace his steps when he emerged into a small clearing made by the recent cutting of several dozen small trees. Indeed, the ax marks on the stumps were quite fresh. And straight on ran a narrow trail, made, he decided, by someone dragging the sapling trunks. Without doubt, somebody was camped close by.

Remembering Lew's adventure of yesterday, Charlie walked slowly and watched the path ahead, determined that if it were at all possible, he would look over the strangers before they saw him.

He stopped now and listened—sure that the sound of voices was coming back through the timber. Then a pack of mongrel dogs rushed down the path, surrounding him and snapping at his heels until he was forced to kick out to keep them from tearing his clothing.

Charlie knew an Indian village lay ahead, and since it was of no use to attempt any unannounced approach now, he walked boldly forward. A minute later he found himself before a dozen tepees spread out over the banks of another river about half the size of the Big Beaver.

He was surprised to find a stream as large as this and a camp so close to Pierre's cabin. And then he caught sight of the drying racks with fish curing over smudge fires of damp bark and birch wood. The Indians were only here for a winter's supply of river fish, which also explained the temporary nature of their lodges.

A swarm of children scampered into the nearest of these shelters, and lying flat, peeped out under the raised bottom edge at the stranger who had appeared. Women busy at the drying racks glanced curiously at the white man, and a dozen swarthy, thickset men advanced slowly to meet him.

Charlie held up his right hand with the open palm of friendship extended. "How!"

One of the men repeated the greeting. Then he spoke sharply to the dogs, and they retreated, growling and sullen, back behind the tepees. But he did not, as Charlie noticed, raise his hand in the universal sign of friendship and peaceable intentions. There was nothing hostile in their demeanor; it was more a pose of watching and waiting for him to explain his presence in their village.

And, he found it difficult to think of something to say. "Do the fish run good today?" he finally asked.

The Cree before him grunted but did not answer. Instead, he turned to a tepee and called a sharp command. A lad of maybe 15 years stepped out and stood between them.

"He no speak English," the boy said in the slow, precise tones of one who has learned a tongue one word at a time. "I work Fur Post three years. I speak for him. Where do you come from, and what do you want?"

Charlie explained, first telling how he had followed the trail of the wounded deer to their camp. Then he told of coming down the river, of Pierre cutting his foot with the ax so badly he was laid up and how Pierre had asked Lew and himself to take his place and gather the beaver pelts until he was able to follow.

The lad followed his words with interest while the men behind shuffled impatiently. When Charlie finished, he turned and repeated what he had said only in Cree, using many gestures.

They all listened attentively, and at the end broke into excited jabbering. Charlie could hear the hostile tone in their voices, and he gripped the short rifle firmly in his hands, ready to dash back into the forest when the storm broke.

The lad turned back to Charlie when the men finished talking.

"They no like you in Pierre's cabin," he said. "Pierre's Marie— she belong to our tribe. They think maybe you rob Pierre. They think maybe you lie. White men make much trouble."

Charlie considered this and then spoke in a loud, clear voice. "Tell them to send a man up the river to Jean's camp. He will find Pierre there, and Pierre will tell him the same."

Once more the boy translated Charlie's words into his native tongue. The group of men spoke among themselves again, this time in more subdued tones.

"Jean a bad man," began the interpreter. "Pierre and Marie should not be there. They will send a man as you say. You no trap until Pierre say OK."

"Fair enough," agreed Charlie. "And tell them I don't like Old Jean any better than they do. He tried to kill us last night. I'll go back to the cabin and wait until you let us know what Pierre says."

Charlie raised his empty hand again, turned and left the village. "Here's another mess," he thought as he walked through the woods. "Suppose something has happened to Pierre at Jean's camp? These Cree will blame us. The beaver are about ready to trap. But we might as well move out if we're going to have Old Jean and a tribe of Cree after our scalps."

The return trail after the excitement of the chase is always longer and Charlie was fairly tired when he entered the little clearing about the cabin. Lew was still working over the deer hides and he straightened up with an effort when he heard Charlie whistle. Charlie noticed with a grin that the other short rifle was standing beside him within easy reach.

"Where's that fresh venison you promised," Lew said. "I heard the shot hours ago and I've kept the fry pan hot for liver ever since." Charlie sat down and told the story of his day's journey. Lew shook his head when he heard how the Crees had warned Charlie not to touch a single pelt until they got the OK from Pierre.

"Gosh," he cried. "What will happen next? I can't say that the future looks so promising or profitable for us, Charlie."

"Things are piling up," Charlie agreed. "But I believe Pierre will tell them not to interfere with us. The real danger still comes from Old Jean. That reptile is positively deadly."

"I'll have both hides ready to go by night," said Lew. "What then for the morning?"

"Well, seeing as how we won't be trapping for at least a week," answered Charlie, "we can soften and smoke these skins. And we can get in a nice pile of wood for winter. A stone fireplace is different from a sheet iron stove. We'll be feeding it pretty heavy this winter."

"Anything for a change," agreed Lew. "I don't want to see a deer hide again this month. I'm darned glad I wasn't raised a squaw. If Marie came along about now and repeated her offer, I do believe I'd take her up on it. I'll welcome some real work with an ax."

Charlie's plan for bringing in wood from the upstream deadfalls worked flawlessly the following morning. They cut the deadfalls, trimmed the trunks, rolled them into the river and tethered them with rope braided from strips of the rawhide. One man could tow two logs at a time, pulling them up on the bank by the cabin. Later they rolled them up close to the cabin and stood them on end. There would be plenty of time later to chop them down to proper size for the fireplace.

The need was to get a supply of burnable fuel close to the cabin, and the seasoned deadfall logs were ideal.

It took three days to bring in the logs. Then they gathered resinous pine knots and roots for starting fires and also to produce quick heat in emergencies.

Next they turned to the buckskins. Charlie decided to employ the softening method used by Lake Superior Indians, which does the trick with a minimum of labor. The skins were soaked soft and then looped over a stout limb. The ends were then twisted until the entire hide was pulled up into a hard knot and left to dry. This was repeated until, after the final drying, the hide remained as pliable as chamois.

The final treatment was the smoking. They dug a small hole in the ground and started a smudge in it, using the half-rotted dead wood commonly called "dozy" by woodsmen. Sticks were stood up over the hole, and the skins draped over them. The low fire was kept going until the skins were light brown. Then they were laid away to season several days with the smoke side folded in to set the color permanently. All in all, Charlie and Lew were pleased with the buckskin they produced and considered the hours of hard labor justified by the finished product.

"It is about time we heard from the Crees," said Charlie as they sat before the fireplace that night. "They have had plenty of time to make the trip and see Pierre."

"If we don't hear from them tomorrow," answered Lew, "I'm going over to their camp for the lowdown. We've got to start trapping soon. The water is ice-cold. What's that?" he asked suddenly.

"I don't hear anything," said Charlie. "What was it?"

"Sounded like a footstep outside the cabin," answered Lew.

Before he reached the cabin door, it flew open and a crowd of Cree warriors sprang upon them. They were overpowered and pinned to the floor before they could offer any real resistance.

"What the ..." began Lew, but a rough slap silenced his lips. They were bound, dragged over and set up against a wall.

"What just happened?" Lew whispered to Charlie.

"Lord only knows," answered Charlie. "Something must have gone wrong with Pierre. Wait—here is the interpreter. He can tell us."

The lad approached calmly. "Pierre is dead," he announced. "Our messenger brought word today. Marie is gone. You killed Pierre, maybe killed both—and tomorrow you die."

Chapter 9 – Foxes and Wolves

Charlie and Lew sat speechless upon the floor of the cabin as the Cree lad who acted as interpreter for his tribe told them this terrible news. Pierre, their lighthearted trapper friend, was dead. Marie, his young wife, had disappeared, and these men of her tribe, believing them guilty, had vowed revenge.

"But," cried Charlie, "Pierre was all right when we left him, all except his foot. We haven't seen him since. How could we have killed him from out here?"

The boy shrugged. "Our messenger says you did it," was all the answer he returned.

"Jean killed Pierre, if he is really dead!" exclaimed Lew. "Jean and his half-breed partner. They are the men you want, not us."

"You try to steal Pierre's wife when he was hurt," the boy replied. "Now you take the fur from his land. That is enough."

Before they could deny either of these charges, a sharp command from one of the men drew the interpreter away. Evidently, he had been ordered to cut off conversation with the captives.

"Do you think they really mean to kill us?" Lew asked.

"I don't know what they'll do," answered Charlie. "There is no law or anything else to stop them. Even if they gave us some sort of a tribal trial, I don't know how we could prove we didn't kill Pierre. Old Jean must be at the bottom of this. If he is—I guess things are going to work out pretty well for him."

"Don't say that," begged Lew.

"We're in a desperate place," Charlie replied. "But we have pulled out of others about as bad. I wish I could understand their lingo. All we can do is to talk through that boy who knows English, and he doesn't act any too friendly toward us, either. In fact, he acts like he is enjoying this business immensely. I wish I knew what they were saying among themselves right now."

His voice had risen a little higher than he intended, and the men turned about from the hearth and scowled at him. One stood and shuffled over to them with a sharp command, and although they did not understand a word of Cree, they could not fail to know he was ordering them to keep quiet. There was no sign of mercy in his eyes.

The hide thongs that bound their hands and feet had been drawn painfully tight. Now their arms and legs were growing numb, and Charlie knew that in an hour more, their muscles would be so cramped and devoid of feeling they would be unable to take advantage of any chance to escape that might occur.

The cabin floor was hard, and never had the minutes passed so slowly. But long and terrible as they knew the night might be, the morning promised worse things—things they dared not let their minds dwell upon.

Charlie wriggled the ends of his fingers constantly to keep the circulation flowing through wrists. If he could only stretch the thongs a bit.

He leaned towards Lew, and placing his lips close to his partner's ear, whispered, "I've got an idea. Work about until your back is against mine. Do it an inch at a time."

Lew obeyed, shifting his legs an inch or so every minute, and Charlie did likewise until they were sitting practically back to back. Charlie located the knot at Lew's wrist and began to pick at it. There was little strength left in his fingers, and the knot was so tight it pressed into Lew's flesh until it was nearly inaccessible. Still, he knew the northern Indians favored a simple knot that could be loosened by pulling on one of the free ends, and he was hoping that they had used such a knot, knowing they would not be able to reach their own hands tied behind their backs.

When steady pulling made no headway, he jerked sharply on the bindings. His muscles throbbed, and he was forced to stop to rest at intervals. Whenever a Cree looked their way, they feigned sleep.

Charlie decided it was of no use, but he determined to give one more hard jerk before calling it quits. Accordingly, he rested several minutes, and then, putting forth all the strength left in his numb fingers, he gave a jerk so sharp it pulled Lew over against him. But he thought something else had given, too. A quick movement of Lew's hands told him it had. With renewed strength, he picked away until the knot was loose. Then he tied a fake knot to deceive any Cree who might decide to examine their bonds.

Lew then went to work on the knot that held his partner. With more freedom of movement and strength returning to his fingers, in a short time the knot was loosened, slipped, and then a fake tied in its place. Hope came back with a rush.

"Shall we work on the knots holding our feet?" asked Lew.

"No," whispered Charlie. "They'd see us."

"They may go to sleep," said Lew. "Then we could untie our feet and slip out of the cabin."

"No chance," answered Charlie. "These fellows sleep lighter than cats. We had better stop whispering now. See if you can sleep. We'll need all of our strength in the morning."

Charlie leaned back against the wall and dozed off. But he awoke at short intervals in spite of his fatigue, at times wondering if their plight was nothing more than a bad dream.

Lew was sleeping soundly, and Charlie was thankful his partner was not awake and worrying. He decided that if any sort of a chance came, they would put up as good a fight as they could.

The men squatting before the fire were mostly young, vigorous braves just grown to manhood. Perhaps they had started off in the impatience of youth to settle this matter in their own way.

The more he thought of the recent happenings, the more Charlie believed the theory correct. But it did not help them any. And then Charlie awoke from a longer period of sleep, and glancing at the cabin window saw the light of day approaching. Lew still slept, and Charlie decided to let him sleep as long as he could.

The Crees were standing, and Charlie studied them carefully, making an important discovery, so important that he pushed against Lew until he awoke with a start.

"Why the ..." began Lew as he opened his eyes.

Then he remembered where he was, and Charlie whispered for him to be silent. The Crees shuffled about, none paying much attention to their captives.

Bringing his lips close to Lew's ear, Charlie whispered. "None of them have guns, and our rifles are right above our heads, both with loaded magazines. Let's untie each other's hands and jump for them. If we get them, we'll have a fair chance. At least we can die fighting, and I know you'd prefer that the same as I."

Once more they swung gradually about until they were sitting back to back. Lew made short work of the loose knot at Charlie's wrists. It was his turn to free Lew, but just as he seized a thong, one of the Crees started towards them. Charlie dropped it and leaned back from Lew, yawning like he had just awoke from sleep.

Something had aroused the Cree's suspicions. He quickly pulled Lew over on his face and felt his tied wrists. Lew strained them to make the strings appear as tight as ever. The Cree grunted, and dropping Lew back against the wall, turned to Charlie.

It was now or never.

Quick as a cat, Lew rolled into the Cree's legs, tripping him to the cabin floor. "Get the guns," he cried, but Charlie was already on his feet, swaying on numb legs. His knees sagged as his hands clutched the air over his head. Where were those guns, anyway?

As more Cree sprang towards Charlie, Lew rolled into them like a bowling ball causing the first to sprawl out in the path of the others. This gave Charlie his chance, and with a final effort, he straightened his legs, pulled the rifle from its pegs on the wall, and cocking it, held the stock to his right shoulder.

"Stand back!" he cried in a stern voice that rang through the cabin. The standing Crees halted. Those on the floor arose slowly but held their distance.

Lew rolled over to where Charlie stood at bay.

Charlie did not dare take the time to free Lew's hands. He kept his eyes and the rifle straight on the group before him. He really didn't want to shoot any of them, and there would only be time to drop two, possibly three, before the rest overwhelmed him.

The door was at his left, only a few feet away, but he was so absorbed in covering the men before him he did not see it swing open, nor did he see the tall form that filled the opening. Then something crashed against the side of his head, and he fell to the floor. He remembered nothing later but a flash of light as he fell.

When he opened his eyes again he was sitting with his back against the cabin wall beside Lew. His wrists were tightly bound as before. The room was empty save for a single Cree who leaned against the opposite wall watching them sharply.

Lew breathed a sigh of relief. "Thank God!" he exclaimed. "I thought they had finished you that time."

"What happened?" asked Charlie.

"A Cree opened the door and threw his knife at you," explained Lew. "The heavy butt struck you behind the ear."

"Well, old-timer," said Charlie. "We did our best. Whatever comes we'll face it like men."

Before Lew could answer, the Indian boy stood before them, explaining the way they would die. The tribe had decided to give them a sporting chance. They would be given a minute head start to run for their lives, "Like foxes chased by wolves."

They welcomed even this slim chance. But they knew the game was being played to furnish sport for the young Crees, that was all.

The man guarding them cut the thongs from their wrists but left their feet bound. Then he jerked them to their feet, and they hobbled out of the cabin, knife-wielding guard at their backs.

As Charlie studied the powerful, agile men around the fire, he was struck by the accuracy of the boy's simple explanation of the deadly game they were about to play. Truly, these were wolves of the birch woods, if men could be likened to such beasts.

The boy brought them broiled fish and they ate heartily. After they had eaten, they were given cups of hot tea.

Several of the Crees had stripped off their buckskin shirts and stood naked from the waist up. Some were limbering up their muscles, others whetted the keen knives that swung from their belts.

Finally, one cut the thongs that tied the ankles of Charlie and Lew. The moment had arrived for them to run for their lives. But their numbed feet, heavy as clogs, would not obey their will, and after a few clumsy steps they fell back on the ground.

Sharp grunts of anger came from the crowd behind them. Several flashed threatening knives, and Charlie said, "They think we are too cowardly to run, Lew. They don't realize we can't." He pointed to his feet and then rubbed his ankles briskly.

The cries of rage ceased, and the boy was pushed forward.

"They say you wait until you run good."

After five minutes of massaging his legs and feet, Charlie turned to Lew and asked, "Ready?"

Lew nodded, and they both stood up. The Crees behind were shifting impatiently, eager for the kill. Then a voice called loudly in Cree and then English, "Stop!"

Chapter 10 – Marie to the Rescue

Charlie and Lew whirled about and saw three figures coming around the corner of the cabin. Two were Cree men of mature years with grizzled hair and weather-beaten faces, but the third—the one whose voice had commanded a stop to the deadly Cree game of Foxes and Wolves—was Marie!

Probably the only person who could save them had arrived in the nick of time. Lew fell flat upon the ground, spent. "It's all right now, Charlie," he said in a tone of measureless relief.

It didn't take Marie long to straighten out the situation. Under her lashing tongue, the young braves who had been so eager for this deadly game began to slink away one at a time, looking more like coyotes that wolves.

"Listen to her," cried Lew joyfully.

"She just saved our lives today," Charlie replied. "From now on, what she says goes with me, too."

Marie was still scolding the men who had appointed themselves executioners to avenge the murder of her husband, following the last to leave the scene, scolding him at every step.

"She has it particularly in for that fellow," said Lew. "He must have been the ring leader of this killing party."

"Why, that's the messenger who went to Old Jean's cabin to find out about us," answered Charlie. "But he got the wrong dope, somehow. Maybe he lied about us purposely. We'll know now. Here comes Marie."

She stood before them, her eyes searching their faces.

"They did not hurt you?" she asked.

When they both shook their heads no, she continued, "The messenger sent to find us spoke only with Old Jean. Pierre is dead. Jean killed him in the river, and then I ran to save myself."

"We're terribly sorry," Charlie began. "And I guess in a way we are to blame. We chased Jean away mad as a hornet, and he took his revenge on you and Pierre. You saved our lives this morning—we will never forget that, and we will help you however we can."

Lew could restrain his curiosity no longer. "But why did that messenger fellow lie about us?" he asked. "We never did anything to him—never even saw him before."

"Joe Beaver wanted to marry me when I was still a girl in the village," she explained, "and he always wanted Pierre's land. Maybe Jean put him up to it, but I have marked him for a liar and a thief. To my tribe, he will be like the dogs about the lodges. Even the children will mock him."

"You are sure about Pierre?" Charlie asked gently. He hated to ask, but he needed to know if there could be any mistake.

Marie nodded. "I saw he blow that knocked him senseless in the river. He was still sick and he could not swim. I waited a minute and he did not come to the top. Then I ran before Jean came after me."

"What are you going to do now?" asked Charlie. "This is your home. We will move out at once."

"No," Marie answered. "I will go with my tribe when they return to their trapping country. I want you to stay here and trap as Pierre asked you. Then in the spring, you can give me part to pay Pierre's debt at the Post. I know you are good men—that you will do this and I can trust you."

"Why?" Lew asked. "You have only known us a short time."

Marie smiled. "After Pierre cut his foot, did you really think I would leave my man? I got in your canoe that morning to see what kind of men you were, and I saw I could trust you."

"And all this time you've been thinking it was your good looks that made her jump into the canoe," Charlie grinned.

"Shut up," Lew growled.

"I almost forgot," Charlie said to Marie. "Where is Old Jean and his partner? Are they hanging around looking for a chance to knock us in the river, too?"

"They will not bother you," Marie assured him. "Jean knew my tribe eventually would learn the truth and take revenge, so after lying about you to buy time, I think they head north into the frozen swamps. But he would never dare come here, and in the spring, when we are done tending our traplines, we will hunt down like a dog."

"Well, that's good," said Lew. "We can trap now without worrying about being knifed in the back."

Just to change the subject, Charlie asked Marie about the big wolf that had raided their camp and whose footprints he had followed to the village of her people. He was curious to know if the Cree hunted the beast.

Marie turned to the men, and as she spoke, Charlie saw their faces settle into grave lines. They answered, shrugging their shoulders like Frenchmen.

"They know him," Marie translated. "But no hunter can kill him. They think he is a spirit—a ghost of the birch woods. Twice he has slashed the throats of men. You were in much danger when you followed this beast."

A shiver chased up Charlie's spine as he recalled the dark night when he faced the unknown beast with only a burning branch for defense, but all he said was, "I'm going to nail his hide up with the rest of the furs we get."

"Be careful," warned Marie. "He laughs at traps and turns them upside down."

"Not our traps," Lew replied with his usual confidence.

"We will go now," Marie continued. "All of the Cree in this country will know you are helping me. If you need help, they will give it. Good luck to you."

Walking beside her companions, she paused at the edge of the timber to wave and then disappeared into the shadows.

"That's that," said Lew. "Let's hope the monkeyshines are all over. I want to start trapping as soon as possible now."

"It's time to start trapping," agreed Charlie. "We are well fixed, certainly considering what we had two weeks ago. Tomorrow, we'll look over the beaver prospects. From what you told me, the big marsh sounds like a beaver trapper's paradise."

"I hope so," returned Lew. "It cost us some dough to get up here, and we lost several hundred dollars when our canoe and outfit went down the rapids. A bale of two hundred nice beaver hides would go a long ways towards refreshing the cash box."

* * *

That night the weather changed abruptly, with swift clouds of a dull hue flying overhead. When Lew filled the kettle at the river's edge, he saw tiny slivers of ice close to the bank.

"Time for us to get to work," he shouted briskly as he entered the cabin. "Let's take a couple of beaver traps with us and set them today. That's the best way to find out if the fur is prime—catch a sample and know for sure."

They felt safe now leaving the cabin unguarded. So they shouldered their guns, the ax and two big double-spring traps then started downstream together, toward the open marsh where Lew had seen so many signs of beaver.

"We need a canoe," Lew grumbled as they tramped along. "I wonder if I could make one from birch bark?"

"I doubt it," Charlie answered. "But we might buy one from the Crees, if any are still camping over on the other river. They might sell us a sack of flour, too. We're going to get tired of meat before spring. I'm hungry for biscuits right now."

Charlie's eyes glistened when he saw the beaver marsh. Lew had not exaggerated a bit in his description.

At the first beaver dam they saw that dozens of poplars had been cut down within the last few days and buried in the bottom of the dam for winter food. The stream was a small one, some ten feet across, but the dam had backed it up over an acre of land.

Charlie used the ax to carefully cut a small section of the dam down to the waterline. Then he set the two traps just below the surface, exactly where a beaver would step when repairing the break in the dam. Lew suggested they place one trap at two different sets, but Charlie vetoed this.

"We are only after a sample," he said. "We must leave as little sign of man here as possible. Beaver are not hard to catch, unless the trapper gets careless and messes things up. If the fur isn't yet prime, we don't want to waste even one pelt."

"Then suppose we head back into the timber and look for deer?" Lew suggested.

Charlie agreed, and a half-dozen plump grouse flew up from their feet as they entered the timber. Lew raised his rifle as the plump birds landed in a tree.

"Careful," warned Charlie. "We have only about fifty loads for each rifle, and they must last all winter."

"You're right," agreed Lew. "But my mouth is watering for fried grouse breast."

"Look there," whispered Charlie. "See that bush move? There is something in it."

Lew jerked the rifle to his shoulder and fired. A heavy body burst through the undergrowth, and Lew called, "I got him!"

"You got him going," answered Charlie, "that's all. And I would remark you shot on pretty short notice."

"I had a better angle and saw the bear clearly," replied Lew as they reached the brush. "See the blood? Let's follow. I'm sure I hit him right in the shoulder. It should have knocked him flat at this range. Come on."

They followed slowly along the trail of the wounded animal, now and then noting a track, then a broken bush or a spot of blood on the pine needles. But after a hundred yards, they had lost the trail completely.

Lew sat upon a fallen log to think. "Of course, bears are fast on their feet and as silent as any big game, but I don't figure out how this fellow disappeared so quickly. Maybe ..." his voice arose in a sudden yell as a muffled groan sounded behind.

Charlie jumped to his side in alarm, but when he glanced down behind the log he laughed aloud. "No wonder you couldn't find the bear, you were sitting on him," he cried.

Lew scrambled to his feet and looked. Sure enough, there lay the bear, feet just stiffening into the rigors of death. Lew stepped down, and calling for Charlie's knife, proposed to bleed the bear.

"An animal shot with a soft-point, high-power bullet doesn't need bleeding, Lew. He has been bleeding out ever since he was hit. But he does need skinning, though."

* * *

The first beaver was prime, and the heavy snows held off. Light flurries whisked through the timber as they tramped each morning to the beaver flat to gather another harvest of pelts.

They worked hard, early and late, and the pile of round, stretched beaver skins built up in the loft of the cabin. The traps were moved from stream to stream, for Charlie and Lew followed Pierre's wise policy of trapping only a few of the inhabitants of each colony.

"You run the traps today," Charlie said one morning. "I'm going into the hills and prospect for fox and marten."

Fine snow bit into his face as he returned home that evening. Charlie wondered if the snow was finally coming—the heavy fall that announced the earnest beginning of winter. He had worked hard locating sets for a long line of marten and fox traps, and he was looking forward to a roaring fire in the cabin and hot food upon the rough table.

Charlie halted suddenly to examine footprints in the light snow. They were partially filled, but the outline struck him as strange. He had grown so accustomed to the footprints of Lew and himself that he could tell at a glance whose moccasins had made which impressions. Were strangers about?

Charlie walked faster in spite of his aching muscles. Topping the hill, he saw the cabin before him. It was dark—no rosy glare from the window facing him—and he broke into a run. It was probably all right. Lew might be late like himself.

Flinging open the door, he saw the cabin was empty. The ashes on the hearth were warm and he raked them aside, uncovering live coals. Soon, the fire was blazing, and Charlie looked about. He saw a note on the table, scrawled hurriedly in Lew's handwriting. It read:

"Old Jean stole most of our beaver skins today. I'm going to get them back if I have to follow him to the Arctic Circle. Keep the traps busy until I get back. Lew."

Chapter 11 – Chasing Fur Thieves

A good catch awaited Lew—four blanket beavers. He reset the traps, and carried 100-plus pounds a quarter of a mile back from the nearest dam and skinned them. None were ever pelted close to the beaver streams, and they never built a fire or ate their lunch close enough to give the animals cause for alarm. As a result of this carefulness, the beaver were still easily caught.

Lew reached home early in mid-afternoon. The cabin door opened when he leaned against it, and he called out, "Here's four more, Charlie."

He dropped the load and looked around for his partner. Charlie would never go far and leave the door unfastened. Then Lew glanced up at the wall and saw his partner's gun gone. A feeling of apprehension seized him. Lew sprang to the door and examined the lock. It had been forced open.

Lew looked about the cabin again. Everything seemed to be as they had left it, and, he reflected, their belongings were so few one swift glance could inventory them. Then he thought of the furs in the loft over the cabin. He jumped upon the double bunk, pushed up the poles that formed the trapdoor, and climbed into the attic.

The piles of beaver pelts were severely depleted; only small hides of poor quality and little value remained. The thief knew fur and had taken the best.

Lew was fighting mad when he dropped back upon the cabin floor. He ran outside and found the prints of broad, soft moccasins leading from the cabin out towards the timber. The marks were fresh, for Lew remembered that the snow had just started to accumulate enough to hold footprints when he was half a mile from home. The thief was only a few minutes ahead, and Lew determined to follow and recover the stolen fur. He ran inside and stuffed several pieces of dried venison in his pocket. Sweeping up two boxes of shells from the shelf under the gun rack, he made for the door. Then, on second thought, he added the birch bark box of tinder Charlie had prepared for emergencies. It held finely shaved pine mixed with gunpowder and would catch and hold the feeble sparks struck from flint and the blade of his knife. Deciding to leave a note, he scribbled a few lines.

Lew was running true to form—acting on impulse in the heat of the moment. He believed he could overtake the thief within an hour, possibly less if he hurried, and he was sure it had to be Old Jean. No other person in the country would try such a stunt.

If Lew had overtaken the man ahead within a few minutes while the first heat of anger possessed him, there might have been shooting. But when he passed out of the clearing into the forest he suddenly halted, sobered and cooled by what he saw. The snow had gathered a little thicker among the trees, and he saw a second trail join the one he followed. There were two ahead of him now—one had evidently stood guard while the other raided their fur cache.

It was probably the half-breed Chenau, and this changed the situation. One man would have been badly overloaded with the weight of the furs and could have made only slow headway. With the pack divided between two, they would move more swiftly. As he followed the trail the seriousness of the situation slowly dawned upon Lew. He was tracking two desperate men. What would prevent one of them dropping behind a log or a bush to await his coming? He would make a very easy ambush target.

Lew slackened his pace and considered returning to the cabin and waiting for Charlie. But Charlie was not the man to sit there and wait. He would be on the trail himself just as quickly as he could.

Smoldering ashes dumped from a pipe in the trail spurred him on. The ashes were warm; they could hardly be a mile ahead. Knowing the ways of the trapper, Old Jean would not expect somebody on his trail so soon. Trappers come in from their lines late in the evening, as a rule. The tobacco ashes proved they were making no effort to hide their trail. And they might be counting on the snow to cover tracks.

Wise in the ways of northern winters, Jean had timed his raid for just before a fall of snow heavy enough to cover tracks. Further, Lew realized that if he failed to follow close upon their heels, he might lose the trail. He could not take the chance of going back or of waiting for Charlie. He must keep going or lose them entirely.

When Lew left the cabin he had blazed his trail in the manner he and Charlie always employed, cutting and bending low bushes close to the path with their tops pointing in the direction he traveled. He was mighty thankful he had, for he realized his own footsteps might be snowed in before Charlie caught up with him.

The hours passed, and the light of day started to merge into the shadow-streaked gray of dusk. Lew climbed a low knob covered with stunted pine and paused on the crest to look ahead. Less than two hundred yards away on an open flat, he saw two moving figures bent under the heavy loads on their shoulders.

Lew's arms trembled until he thought he was suffering an attack of buck fever. He threw up the rifle to shoot—not at them, but ahead and close enough to stop and turn them back. There was no heavy timber near to serve them as cover. Things couldn't be arranged better.

He pulled back the hammer of the gun and then remembered that the magazine was only partly full. He hurriedly tore open a box of shells, still keeping his eyes glued on the figures ahead. He started to stuff a shell through the loading gate, but it did not enter like it should, and glancing down he saw to his horror that he had picked up the wrong box of loads. These were for Charlie's rifle—those for his own still lay on the rough shelf back in the cabin.

Desperately, he worked the lever, holding his hand to catch the ejected cartridge. He must know how many were in the gun. One ... and then an empty click. He stuffed it back in the gun but he did not raise the muzzle. Instead, he stood silently staring at the men ahead. While he watched, they tramped into the thicker timber beyond and out of sight.

He could do nothing else. One shell—two men. Should he return to the cabin for the right loads? Lew stood watching the snow settle among the trees. In a few hours there would be no trail to follow.

Lew resolved to keep on. But he must walk slowly; he dared not press too close. As the dusk deepened Lew wondered if the men ahead would press on through the night or would they make camp until morning? He saw that it would soon be too dark to follow the path. Apprehension filled him again. If they knew the country well enough to pick their way in the dark, he might as well turn back now. He would either have to do this or make his own camp soon. There was nothing to gain by walking blindly on.

One point, he reflected, was in his favor. The men ahead were packing heavy loads, and he felt sure they would have to rest soon.

He climbed a low ridge and saw a tiny point of light. It was a campfire. They had stopped for the night. With a feeling of thankfulness, Lew backed down the ridge. Then, blazing bushes as he went, he backtracked his trail as nearly as he could until he crossed a second ridge. Behind this, he could camp in comparative safety. Jean might climb the first ridge to look for sign of pursuit, but the chances of his continuing back to the second were small. Lew worked fast, dragging up saplings and branches to shape a rough lean-to.

With flint and knife he struck a fire, and shielding it carefully with chunks of rotting wood, kept the blaze down as low as he could.

Then he lay back in his lean-to and chewed on a chunk of dried venison. Lew could hardly feel the heat of the tiny fire. It looked, too, as if he would have to sit up most of the night in order to keep it going at a low level.

Dried venison is only a fair meal. The ground under him was hard and cold, and he bunched more spruce branches up to conserve his body warmth.

Lew wondered if he would have any luck if he tried to rush the camp of Old Jean but gave up the idea as too risky. The lack of ammunition for his rifle meant he had to play a watching, following game until Charlie appeared.

It was a long night. Lew could only snatch short periods of sleep between the dozens of times he fed the fire. In the morning, his limbs ached from the hard ground, his eyes gummed shut with smoke and grime, and thirst raged through his body. The snow had ceased, but a three-inch fall had completely filled in his tracks.

He walked carefully up towards the camp of Old Jean and Chenau. Doubtless they had already gone, but he decided to take no chances. He climbed the second ridge and peered over its edge. The camp lay somewhere ahead, but just how far he did not know. He decided to walk on and saw a wisp of smoke hanging over the trees.

Guided by the smoke, Lew circled and approached from the other side. Pursued men seldom look ahead—their gaze is invariably directed back over their own trail. Coming in from the front, Lew saw a lean-to much like his own. A few steps more brought him to a wide trail freshly made in the soft snow. It was the outgoing trail; they had broken camp and left.

Scraps of food scattered about the ashes of the fire indicated that they had eaten heartily of deer steak, bannock bread and tea. Lew's anger arose as he pictured them well fed and sleeping comfortably on piles of stolen beaver pelts.

He strode after them, not forgetting to leave his blaze of lopped bushes. He devoutly wished Charlie would hurry.

Where a small creek crossed his path he drank heartily. A thin layer of ice covered the water, and Lew realized the weather would soon be bitter cold. The skies might open any hour and hurl down one, two or three feet of snow. Lew settled into a dogged gait.

More smoldering ashes from a pipe lay in the trail. They were not far ahead and leaving a broad trail in the snow. Charlie could swing along over it at top speed, but this was not what caused Lew to draw in his breath and freeze in his tracks like a crouching rabbit. Back on the crest of the hill a huge, dark wolf sat in the path, its nose pointed towards him.

It was the ghost wolf of the Crees—the beast that feared no man—and Lew involuntarily clutched his rifle. Thank God he had a gun, but he remembered even as he started to raise the barrel that there was only one load left.

The beast had shown it was unafraid of fire, too, and Lew shivered as he thought of the risk he had run last night. Perhaps it had been on his trail just as he dogged the steps of Jean and Chenau.

When Charlie came they would have it sandwiched between them, and he could not afford to risk his single shell until then. Neither dared he alarm the men ahead. So he turned and carried on. Looking back, he caught sight of a whisking shape. The wolf was dogging his steps. There was no danger so long as daylight filtered through the trees, but when night fell ...

* * *

Charlie stared at Lew's note. Here was a situation that he had not anticipated. Old Jean had not been a hundred miles north; Marie had been wrong about that. He had returned to play this last trick, to rob them of the furs they worked hard to gather. It was like Old Jean to wait for them to do the work and then step in and lift the reward.

Charlie jumped up on the bunk as Lew had and looked in the little loft. Then he dropped back on the cabin floor and reread Lew's note. Lew would need help when this trail ended. Charlie searched outside for Lew's trail. He could just see the outline of footprints, but then the snow swept over them, blotting out all traces. Then he stumbled on until he saw a bush with a bent top. A feeling of satisfaction filled him—Lew had left a plain trail he could follow in the daylight.

But Charlie saw nothing would be gained by attempting to follow now. He would only flounder about in the brush and probably end up lost. The better way was to pack carefully and take up the trail in the morning. Jean and Lew both would have to camp sometime. They would not get so very many miles ahead of him.

Then he discovered the mistake Lew had made with the cartridges. What if Lew was carrying an empty rifle and two boxes of misfit shells? He would be the same as weaponless.

Charlie was up several hours before daybreak, but he sat in the cabin until he could see to travel. Then he shouldered his pack and started. He knew the chase might stretch out over several days, and he did not waste his strength at the start. He made the distance to Lew's night camp an hour sooner than it had taken his partner to cover the same distance. He picked up the fresh snow trail there and decided Lew could not be too far ahead. Then, planted squarely over the mark of Lew's moccasin, was the track of a huge wolf—the ghost wolf of the birch woods was stalking Lew!

The grim irony of the chase struck him. Lew on the heels of Old Jean, the fur thief, the big wolf stalking Lew, and finally himself pursuing them all. Charlie settled down to a shuffling run, a gait he could maintain for several hours.

A fallen tree lay across the trail. Lengthening his stride a bit, Charlie leaped for its top. But he did not gauge the distance right and landed a few inches short. His foot slipped, and he felt a sharp pain shoot through his ankle.

Carefully, he tested the foot with his weight. The pain warned him it would not bear the pressure. He sat down upon the trunk, staring at the trail ahead. Just when Lew needed him the most, he had crippled his foot with that foolish leap. Why hadn't he slowed down and stepped over the log?

A rifle shot rang out in the timber. He jumped to his feet, but the pain of the wrenched ankle brought him back down.

Chapter 12 – The Nick of Time

After that single rifle shot, everything was quiet. Charlie wondered if Old Jean had laid in ambush and shot Lew, but all he could do was sit there with a wrenched ankle and grit his teeth. Charlie removed his moccasin and rubbed snow over the ankle. It had not started to swell, and this encouraged him. If he could remain still for several hours, the pain might subside so he could hobble on. But he must be careful about putting weight on the ankle. Otherwise, he might make it worse and be crippled for a week.

He built a fire, made tea and chewed dried venison. He had a blanket and enough food to last several days and wasn't worrying about himself a bit. But Lew needed his help. Somehow, he must travel on, if only slowly, and overtake his partner on this trail of peril.

Meantime, Lew was back on the trail of Old Jean and Chenau. As the hours passed, he began to wonder why Charlie had not caught up. A rifle shot halted those thoughts, and he jumped behind a bush. It sounded just a few rods ahead in the frosty air, but he heard no bullet whine and assumed it had not been fired at him.

He had no idea Charlie was waiting as anxiously only two hundred yards away in the timber. Nothing was visible but snow-laden trees, and after a tense wait, he started on again, picking his way with extreme caution. He knew somebody, very probably Jean or Chenau, had fired the rifle. But, as he reflected, it likely had been a shot at game.

When he came upon the half-skinned carcass of a small deer in the snow, he knew that assumption had been correct. With much satisfaction, Lew helped himself to a front shoulder. This was all he cared to carry and enough for a couple of days.

He thanked his lucky star for another break, and as he started on again, he reflected that what meat he had left would make a good meal for the wolf. He was beginning to fear the approach of night and hoped the wolf would gorge itself on the fresh meat.

By the freshness of the trail, he knew Old Jean could not be over a mile ahead. He judged it was nearly noon, and following the custom of Northern woodsmen, he knew the pair would stop soon to boil tea and rest. He slowed even more, not wanting to stumble upon them with but one bullet and no plan of attack.

So he made a fire and broiled a slice of venison. Then he sat with his back against a tree, eating and resting. Lew was feeling drained, for he had passed through a very hard two days. He anticipated another cold camp that night, if Charlie did not appear soon.

Lew continued on, hoping to see the remains of a fire where Jean and Chenau had eaten and rested as he had done. Glancing back, he caught a glimpse of the wolf on his trail, less than a hundred and fifty yards back. It would soon be dusk, and Lew wondered what it might do then.

Lew considered spending his single cartridge on the wolf. A hundred yards was point-blank range a rested rifle. Of course, then he would have to wait for Charlie to continue his pursuit of the men ahead. But just as he had about decided to do this, a large snowflake bit his cheek. Lew knew snow would mean a lost trail if he hesitated now. The thieves would escape with their beaver pelts. No, he had come too far and risked too much to give up now.

When it was time to camp, Lew turned a little way off the trail and started to gather wood. He set his rifle against the trunk of a tree and laid the joint of meat beside it while he searched for dead limbs partway up on the trunks of the pines.

Lew never could explain his carelessness in leaving the rifle, but suddenly he was startled by a swift rush through the brush, and he whirled to see the dark shape of the wolf running past. Instinctively, he jumped for a tree thinking the beast meant to attack him. But the wolf vanished in the timber, and when Lew returned to where he had laid the venison, he saw it was gone.

He only had that small chunk of dried venison left.

He was more alarmed at the boldness of the wolf. Maybe that night, it would grab Lew himself from his pile of spruce. He built a rough lean-to, using the trunk of a broad tree for the back. This would protect him from the rear. With a fire in front and rifle in hand, he might be safe in the night.

Lew ate his last jerked meat soberly. Now he was more afraid of the wolf than of the men ahead. He had almost forgotten them.

Darkness fell and he increased the size of his fire. An owl boomed from a nearby tree, and Lew welcomed it as something companionable. Holding his rifle across his knee, Lew sat and dozed. The owl hooted at regular intervals, and its call awoke Lew with a start, thankful for an alarm that kept him alert every few minutes.

Come morning, Lew was hungry and thirsty, and required hard

effort to arouse his fatigued body. He rubbed a handful of snow over his face. He must get food. He looked for rabbit tracks but found none. But a little farther on he saw much larger tracks—the paw prints of the wolf.

Lew pressed on desperately, caring less if he did stumble upon Old Jean and Chenau. He could shoot one of them and bluff the other with an empty rifle—and they would have food. A mile and a half on he found their camp deserted. Lew glanced back. Yes, the wolf was even closer than before, and no longer did the beast jump nervously or hide when he looked over his shoulder.

As he walked, Lew grew discouraged. Turning to dart nervous glances over his shoulder, he caught himself talking aloud. He decided to catch up and settle this thing once and for all. But by the appearance of the trail, they were pulling away.

This country was vastly different from that bordering the river. The ridges were sharp, and stunted timber ran in belts between stately aisles of huge pines. Lew still broke brush tops to mark his path. These blazes would be his only salvation when he turned back to find his way home.

The wolf stalked steadily along behind him now. It was heavier than the average timber wolf, with thicker limbs. "I believe you're part dog," Lew spoke to the canine, "with a streak of mastiff."

When he paused to rest, his breath was in gasps. The wolf also halted, eyeing him. Then it lifted its head, the ears cocked forward like a dog's, and trotting out in a wide circle, ran past him and into the timber ahead.

Then a sudden crashing startled Lew, and five caribou burst out of the brush dashing straight towards him. They swerved as they saw him and crashed off to one side. Lew watched in amazement, and he did not remember the rifle in his hands until the last one disappeared. Was he losing all of the woodcraft he had worked so hard to acquire?

This was what had drawn the wolf ahead, and Lew backtracked the trail of the caribou to a strange sight, an opening trampled by many hooves, and in its center lay a half-grown caribou with the wolf tearing out its throat.

He aimed at the wolf and pressed the trigger. But the beast saw the movement, and as the hammer fell, jumped. Lew's bullet kick up a spurt of snow just below the wolf.

"Put down that rifle," a voice spoke behind him, and wheeling with lowered gun, he stared into the eyes of Old Jean, who held a gun leveled at his head. Chenau stood beside him, a wide grin creasing the sordid face.

"Good day, my fren'," Jean spoke. Now you must throw down the rifle. Here!" pointing to the ground at his feet.

The man raised his weapon, and Lew pitched the gun over. It was useless, anyway. He had shot his lone cartridge.

"We sorry, but we cannot take you. But we leave you in good company. You stay with the beeg wolf. When he get hungry—then maybe you make good meal."

"You ..." Lew started, but Jean cut him short.

"You bother me," he growled. "Shut up or I finish you now."

When he and Chenau tramped away, Lew did not attempt to follow. He realized he was no worse off than before—he already had spent the single load before Jean carried off the rifle.

And then a sharp command in French rang out, and Jean and Chenau halted in their tracks. The voice snapped with cold fury, and a figure stepped out from behind a tree with leveled rifle, covering the pair. With a cry of recognition, Lew sprang forward.

"Pierre!" he cried. "I thought you were dead!"

Pierre did not turn his eyes from the men cowering before him. "No, Pierre did not drown in the river. We can talk after. Now take a rifle, and keep them standing there."

With keen satisfaction, Lew took Jean's rifle, and cocking it, jammed the barrel into his side.

"Put your hands back," Pierre commanded.

They obeyed, and Lew heard two clicks followed by squeals from both. Pierre had caught their hands in the jaws of fox traps.

"Now they follow like dogs," Pierre grinned.

"For a week I wait for these devils. They think me dead in the river. But I know where they are going. When I hear shot, I creep up and take them. I guess I come in, what you call, nick of the day?"

"Nick of time," corrected Lew. "And I don't know when I was any gladder to see anyone. What are you going to do with Jean?"

Pierre's face sobered. "Take them to the tribe of my wife, Marie. Maybe they kill her. I know not. But the Crees will punish."

"Marie is safe," Lew told him, and Pierre cried joyfully as he told of her rescuing them, and then all of their adventures since they had left him crippled at Jean's cabin.

"How glad I am that you happen along in canoe to be my fren'. Now take Jean's gun and go back to the cabin. I will handle these rascals. You trap more furs. I make Jean and Chenau pack out what they steal. We sell in the spring, and you get half. You know that you can trust Pierre."

Lew nodded his assent. Things were working out fine.

Backing Jean and Chenau up against a tree, Pierre lashed their ankles, hobbling them much as a wrangler hobbles a mustang. There was hardly a chance of their working their wrists out of the strong jaws of the traps.

Then Lew cooked big slices of fresh caribou steak, and Pierre joined him in a hearty meal. Lew felt his strength returning even as he ate. Then Pierre told his own tale, how he had narrowly escaped drowning when Jean knocked him in the river, and how he had trailed the murderous pair, biding his time.

"What will the Crees do with them?" Lew asked.

"Not kill them, I think," answered Pierre. "But they get plenty hard time. I think we never see fren' Jean again."

Pierre herded his captives off into the timber, and Lew started back on his own trail. Now that he had plenty of cartridges, he hoped the wolf would pick up his trail again.

* * *

Night found Charlie still sitting helplessly against the log on which he had slipped and wrenched his ankle. He hopped out on his sound foot and gathered more wood for the fire and also built a rough lean-to against the log. He made tea and ate sparingly of his dried meat. Then, wrapping himself in his blanket, he slept.

When morning came, he struggled to his feet and found the injured ankle could bear nearly his entire weight.

A twig snapped behind him, and turning, Charlie caught a glimpse of a dark shape dashing toward him through the trees. He stood motionless, rifle out of reach, when a rifle exploded so close he jumped in his tracks, and then a familiar voice whooped, "Got him! I've laid low the ghost wolf of the birch woods!"

Then Lew burst out of the timber, and seeing Charlie standing there, halted in amazement. "Where have you been, old-timer? I've been watching and waiting for you for two days."

They sat on the log swapping experiences.

"Well," Lew finally concluded, "Now that we know the monkey business is finally over, let's go back and pound that old trapline!"

The End

Tamarack Trail

Chapter 1 – The Devil Bird

Tamarack Trail! A pathway of mystery through an unbroken wilderness of pine and willow, whitewood and tamarack—the ghost tree of the woods Indian. Paths that exist only in the muscles and brain of the hardy timber cruiser and prospector and in the keen edge of his blazing hatchet. Trails that are invisible to the layman—nonexistent to his untrained eye and clumsy pavement-trained foot. They are the roadways to adventure and danger, paths that beckon the woods-dweller ever deeper into the maze of virgin forest.

The trail opens ahead—let us shoulder our packs and follow.

* * *

Lew stopped at the end of the log which served as a footbridge across the stream. Loosening the Poirer pack from his shoulders, he wriggled his arms out of the soft broad straps but slipped the tumpline across his forehead. This was a precaution Charlie and he always took when they crossed these rude bridges of log or crossings of rock stepping stones, or at any spot where the going might prove uncertain and dangerous.

In the case of a slip or misstep, a quick twist of the head would free him entirely of the pack and leave him unhampered by its weight and bulk, able to make the best of any precarious position. Many of the streams in the North Country are swift and deep, and the weight of one's blankets, food and ammunition contained in a waterproof pack of brown canvas could easily drag him down to the bottom, with perhaps fatal consequences.

"Come on, Charlie," Lew urged. "I know you are supposed to be leading, but I can't wait for you all day. I'm getting hungry, and I'm crossing on over to find a camping place for tonight."

Lew started across the slender log that bridged the tumbling stream. Charlie, on the other hand, stopped to leisurely adjust his pack and take a few deep breaths. He possessed the temperament of a true woods cruiser and pursued his way in a calm, unhurried manner, which, while deceiving to the eye of a casual observer, nevertheless enabled him to cover an astonishing distance on the foot trail between the rising and setting of the sun, and furthermore, with a minimum of fatigue.

"Go ahead, Lew," he agreed. "Don't wait for me. I'll catch you at the finish, as I always do. Hullo! What's that?"

He craned his neck to see around Lew and better observe the animal that had ambled out upon the other end of the bridge, and which, after a second's hesitation, advanced to meet Lew in the middle. It was a large, bushy skunk, with a small white star upon its head. The skunk halted, eyeing Lew as he continued to approach.

"Look out, Lew!" cried Charlie in warning, and Lew, realizing the predicament of his position, halted. The skunk waited, possibly to see if Lew was going to back away, as Charlie suggested later. Then, as the man did not move, it turned and raised its tail in a threatening manner. Lew realized he had no time to lose if he wanted to avoid the obnoxious deluge which would surely follow. He leaped from the log into the icy stream.

The water was shallow and he stood submerged only to his hips, holding his rifle and pack above the water, cursing fluently this particular skunk and all of its relations and friends. The skunk peered down over the edge of the log at Lew with its beady eyes. Then, apparently satisfied that this noisy intruder down in the water was unworthy of any more attention, lowered its back, and turning slowly about, walked back to the side from which it had come.

"Well, I'll be jiggered!" Lew declared.

Charlie exploded with laughter. "I've been waiting for something like this to happen ever since we started. Something that would teach you the foolishness of hurry and impatience in the woods, especially when you are trailing. How often have I told you, my boy, that it is the easy, steady gait of the woodsman that gets him where he is going? You saved nearly half a minute when you busted in ahead of me, and now you'll waste half an hour drying yourself out. Here, hand me your gun and pack. You might as well wade on across. You won't get any wetter."

Lew scrambled out on the opposite bank. He was grinning now, the first flush of chagrin having already passed. "It's a lucky thing for that blamed skunk that his hide isn't prime. If this were fall now instead of spring, I'd already have him stretched over a green bow of moosewood. But I guess I do prefer a soaking to getting scented up."

"So do I," chuckled Charlie. "That would mean making two camps tonight with yours on down the wind. Much as I enjoy your company, Lew, I draw the line at skunk smell. Did you get any water in your rifle? Never mind, I'll look. Strip off those wet clothes."

Lew hurriedly removed trousers, moccasins, socks and underwear. Wringing them out as best he could, he redressed. Charlie was squinting down the barrel of the gun.

"Hardly any water in it," he observed. "Just a few drops. If it was really wet, I'd say shoot off a load to dry the bore, but we haven't any shells to waste, and we'll need them all for shooting some meat."

Lew started walking briskly. The weather was warming, but still a trace of winter frost remained in the keen air, and Lew did not care to run any chance of catching cold. Charlie had suggested that they camp at once at Skunk Crossing, as he named the spot, but Lew protested. "I'll walk on until these clothes dry a bit more," he said. "Then we can camp and I'll finish drying out before the fire."

Charlie did not insist, for he knew that exercise could be just as warming in such emergencies as a campfire. There was an abundance of water in the country through which they were trailing, and it was not difficult to find a good, dry campsite close to spring or stream. An hour later, with the sun setting fast, they camped on a rather prominent knoll.

Charlie opened his pack and took from it their shelter tent. It was simply a waterproof sheet of light canvas which they pitched with poles and stakes to form a shed-like lean-to. With a fire in front and the open ends blocked with brush, it made a comfortable camp.

Lew worked briskly dragging in wood, and when the fire was burning merrily, he stripped again to his waist and sat on a log close to the heat to "bake," as he put it. His moccasins and socks were propped close by on short stakes. Charlie started preparing their evening meal.

"How long has it been since we left Pierre's cabin?" Lew asked.

"Just three days."

"Gosh, it seems like a week since that trader came down the river in his big boat and bought all of our furs," Lew answered. "We did well, too, didn't we?"

"We sure did," agreed Charlie. "And that was the best way to handle it. We had no way to get the stuff out except packing it on our backs, and that would have taken two trips. He gave us about as much money for the entire lot as it would have brought at the trading post. He was an independent buyer, I think. You remember he acted real anxious to get our fur aboard and then be off down the river."

"And when he told us about these thousand square miles of timber south of the cabin, I felt the same desire to hit the trail and be on our way," said Lew. "The land route he suggested was directly on our way and a whole lot shorter than following the river as we had on the way in. We should be through by next week, don't you think?"

"About that," conceded Charlie. "But I want to look around as we go. We might find some good hunting grounds that we could come back to some winter, or even another place to trap."

"I wonder how so much tall timber has escaped the lumberman?" Lew replied, looking around at the stately pines.

"There must not be a good way to get it out," said Charlie as he mixed a batch of camp biscuit in the end of the flour sack, adding water until the dough lifted out in a solid ball.

"None of these streams we have crossed has been big enough to float down log rafts, and there isn't a railroad within a hundred miles. It may be another year or two before one pushes up into this wilderness. But it'll be here someday, and then the timber will go. You can bank on that. I'll bet some logging outfit already has an option on these very trees. Sooner rather than later, the ring of the ax will sound through this forest, and then goodbye virgin woodland. What with the forest fires that follow the logging, it will soon look like a mangy pup that has lost all of its hair."

"Well, I for one hope that day never comes," remarked Lew as he looked in admiration down the natural aisles of tall, straight timber that seemed to radiate from their elevated camp on all sides.

He slipped on his trousers and announced, "No mosquitoes, yet. If there had been one in this entire woods, it would have found my bare legs by now. Just the same, I expect to run into them any night. Funny how they spring up in millions while there is still frost in the low places. Too bad that fur trader didn't have a nice screened cruiser tent with him. This pup affair is all right until mosquito time; then, it'll be the dickens."

"We can avoid the buzzers by camping in high, exposed places where the wind will blow them away," remarked Charlie. "We about cleaned out the trader as it was," and he grinned as he recalled how the voluble Frenchman had protested against selling the shelter tent, compass and other necessities from his own outfit, only agreeing when Charlie refused point-blank to part with a single piece of fur under any other conditions.

"While the biscuits are baking, why don't you make yourself

useful and clean one of those grouse?" he resumed. "I'll make the tea, and as soon as the biscuits and bird are done, we'll eat. This backpacking doesn't appear to weaken your appetite any, does it, Lew?"

His partner grinned at that but did not reply. He already was busy cleaning both of the plump grouse they had surprised early that morning. He used the rough but effective method employed by woodsmen who dislike to waste any more time than is absolutely necessary to prepare game for the pan. After a couple of cuts, the entrails were flung out with a couple of vigorous shakes; then the wings and neck were cut off and the rest roughly skinned.

"Slip both of these in that frying pan," he said, handing them to Charlie. "No holding out one of them for breakfast. I'll shoot some more in the morning."

Charlie started to protest, but he was nearly as famished as Lew, if that was even possible, and squatting beside the fire, they attacked the food with the hearty appetites that only an all-day tramp through the wilderness can produce. Lew set his cup of tea on the ground beside his knee and waved a broiled leg of grouse expressively.

"This is the life! Oh, boy!"

"Yes," Charlie grinned, "as long as the grub holds out, I can count on your enthusiastic support."

"Well, I haven't noticed you turning your back on a square meal yet," Lew retorted. "I wouldn't ..." he stopped and listened. Then he exclaimed, "What's that noise?"

A low, droning hum slowly filled the evening air, and as they listened intently, it grew steadily in volume and tone until it throbbed like a swarm of locusts.

"It's an airplane," exclaimed Charlie as he settled back down. "I wonder what the deuce an airplane is doing up here?"

"Can't be bootleggers," remarked Lew. "We aren't near enough to the border for that. But he sure is moving along."

When it sounded like it was about to pass overhead, they gazed up into the night sky. "Look!" cried Lew. "There she goes!"

A bright light shot past them with the speed of a comet and then was hidden behind the trees. "Must be making two miles a minute, easy," Lew added as the sound of the motor faded away. But before the faint roar ceased altogether, they heard a short sputter of explosions. Then all was still.

"What the dickens just happened?" asked Lew.

"I don't know," returned Charlie. "But if something did go

wrong, I pity the pilot. There's no place to make an emergency landing in these woods."

For a full minute they stood like statues, straining their ears to catch any faint noise. But nothing was audible save the usual sounds of the forest. "That's a real puzzler," said Charlie finally.

"I'll bet within ten miles of here," said Lew, pointing in the direction of their own course through the woods, "we find the plane smashed to bits. Shall we start looking, now?"

"No use in this darkness," said Charlie. "I hate to think of someone lying out there half dead, but we don't know for sure that he did crash. All we can do is keep a watch out as we travel tomorrow."

Then they rolled themselves in their blankets and slipped into the light but restful sleep of the outdoorsman who awakens at sunrise as fresh and vigorous as ever.

When Lew opened his eyes in the early morning, Charlie already was bending over the remains of the evening fire, fanning the coals back to life. "If you are going to get grouse for breakfast, I suggest you start now," he said as Lew sat staring at him.

"Gosh, it's wet. I'll get soaked out by the dew."

"It won't kill you," grinned Charlie. "And after this, don't eat enough for two and we'll have meat left in the morning."

But Lew already had slipped on his moccasins and was picking up his rifle. As he strode into the timber, Charlie built up the fire with an armful of dry wood he had stored under the tent. When it was blazing well, he propped up the dew-soaked blankets to dry.

As he worked, a rifle cracked out in the forest. "Lew gets lucky again," he thought as he made more biscuits and heated the fry pan.

But it was not Lew's rifle that had fired.

* * *

Lew stalked cautiously, looking for roosting grouse in every tree he passed until he was several hundred yards from camp. Then, just as he had decided to circle about and return from another quarter, a rifle shot rang out so close that for a moment he thought someone had shot at him. Then he remembered that if that had been the case, he surely would have heard the bullet whine past.

Still, the shooter could not have been over three hundred feet from where he stood. Filled with curiosity, Lew started off in the direction from which the shot had sounded.

As he walked, an uneasy feeling stole over him, and he about had decided to turn and beat it back to camp when the reason for the shot lay before him—a buck deer sprawled on the ground. Lew's keen eye noted the bullet hole through a shoulder, just high enough and far enough back to be an instantly fatal spine hit. And then, as he stooped over examining the animal, an aged Indian stepped out from behind a broad tree. Looking directly at Lew, he pointed with a steady finger and said, "My deer."

He was a little old and bent but still formidable in buckskin shirt, trading post overalls and handmade moccasins. He carried a single-shot trade musket, and Lew noted with a glance that the piece had been reloaded with a fresh cap under the hammer.

"Sure," Lew agreed instantly, "and a darned good shot, too."

Lew stepped aside and the Indian stooped over his deer. Pulling a thong from his pocket, he started to tie the four feet together, preparatory to slinging it over his back.

Then a thought struck Lew. Venison would be a fine change from the grouse they had been eating every meal. True, deer hunting season had closed months before, but he knew the woods Indian hunted year-round, needing the meat and regarding the game as rightfully theirs. He also wasted nothing and in the end had less of an impact on game populations than the white hunters who came north once a year to shoot everything in sight.

"Say," Lew finally broke the silence. "Will you sell me a piece of that deer? We haven't eaten anything but grouse for three days."

The man nodded, drew his hunting knife and looked at Lew, his silent gaze asking, "How much?" as plainly as if he had spoken.

"Enough for today," answered Lew. "Say, five or eight pounds."

The Indian sliced a chunk from a rear quarter with a few skillful passes of the blade. Lew drew out some silver coins. But the old man shook his head. "The deer belong to all," he said. "Who am I to sell the gifts of the Great Spirit?"

Lew thanked him heartily, already tasting the juicy broiled steak which would start them out over the day's trail. The old man didn't seem interested in conversation, but he still asked, "Say, did you hear that airplane go over last night?"

The Indian just looked at him, and Lew realized that the term "airplane" might be foreign to him. So, he made a noise similar to a plane motor and waved a hand across the sky, portraying as clearly as he could by sign the passing of an airship.

The face of the old man lit up with the light of comprehension. "Ho!" he exclaimed. "Devil Bird!"

Then his face clouded. "It come to bring trouble for my people. But the Great Spirit is watching," he resumed. "I see Devil Bird. And I see ..." he hesitated and then looked craftily at Lew. "Maybe you find Devil Bird—maybe in top of tamarack?"

Lew started in surprise at the last words. The first part of the speech he had attributed to the supernatural beliefs of a woods Indian, but the last part was so concise he had to wonder. Did the man know more about the plane than he cared to tell?

But the man went back to tying the deer feet together, and with a quick movement, slipped his head through the loop and slung the heavy carcass across his shoulders with practiced ease. Turning without another word, he tramped back into the woods.

Charlie was waiting for him with fry pan in hand. "Where have you been?" he asked. "The biscuits are almost burned. I heard you shoot a half-hour ago. Where's the grouse?"

"Here's something better," said Lew as he handed over the thick slice of venison.

Charlie looked at the still-steaming meat and then aghast at Lew. "You didn't shoot a deer out of season, did you?"

"Hardly," came the answer, "but I begged this steak off the hind leg of one which was shot this morning, and what's more, you're going to help me eat it. Whether this is going to make us accessories after the fact or not, I don't care. Now, get that skillet sizzling."

And while Charlie fried a thick steak, he told of his encounter with the old Indian and of the stranger conversation and prophesy.

"He might have been stringing me a bit," Lew concluded.

"Looks like it," answered Charlie thoughtfully, "except the northern Indians, as a rule, don't string folks. I wonder what sort of trouble the plane was bringing to his people?"

"Hard to tell," Lew replied. "Maybe he is just a bit goofy. Still, you know I'm going to look in the top of every big tree we pass."

"You'll get a stiff neck if you do that," Charlie answered after swallowing a big bite of venison. "Now, when you've eaten enough for two, let's pack up and hit the trail."

After making sure there was nothing left within reach that was edible, Lew complied. Ten minutes later, Charlie covered the remains of their fire with damp earth and then shouldered his pack.

While there was no defined trail, Charlie picked their course through the timber by compass. At times, they would happen upon trails made by men or deer, pathways that coincided a distance with their course. But most of the time they blazed their own way.

Lew happened to be in the lead on a deer trail when he suddenly stopped to examine something on the ground before him. When Charlie pressed to his side, he saw his partner turning a charred object over with the toe of his moccasin.

"What's this?" Lew asked.

"That's the stub of a signal flare," Charlie said. "Say, I'll bet that plane pilot dropped it last night, looking for a place to land. It's a wonder it didn't set the whole forest afire."

"We're hot on the trail," Lew replied in a satisfied tone.

Both saw it at the same time, and it stopped them in their tracks. There sat the airplane—lodged high in the top of a giant tamarack! One wing dangled like the broken wing of a goose, but the machine had settled in the branches in such a way it looked like it was poised to resume flight, "Like a big hawk on its nest," Lew put it.

How had the old Indian been able to prophesy it so well, down to the variety of the tree?

After the first shock of discover, they ran to the base of the tree. First they searched the area in vain for a pilot. Then they turned back to the plane in the tree. It was fairly small, but the engine appeared large, and although both were novices in the matter of aircraft, they guessed—and rightly, too—that this plane was built for top speed.

"Look!" exclaimed Lew, pointing to the front of the plane. "That's a machine gun mounted behind the prop." Following his finger, Charlie saw the nose of a Browning automatic.

"That's funny," he said. "Civilian planes don't ordinarily carry machine guns in times of peace."

"Where do you think the pilot is?" asked Lew. And then, without waiting for an answer, he added, "I'm going to climb the tree and see if he is in the cockpit."

"Go easy," warned Charlie. "That plane isn't any too secure."

Lew jumped for a knot on the trunk that projected several feet above his head. Grasping it, he started to "shin" his way up the bare trunk. But then a sharp command in a harsh, unknown voice caused him to relax his hold and slide slowly back to the ground.

Wheeling, he saw Charlie staring into the business end of a blunt automatic pistol. Behind the gun's sights, which weaved a trifle as if the holder was nervous, was a pair of about the nastiest looking eyes either of them had ever seen.

"You heard me. Get away from that tree, big boy!"

Chapter 2 – An Odd Job Indeed

Charlie and Lew both backed away from the tamarack. "I was just climbing up to see if you were lying there with a broken neck, and right now, I wouldn't care if you were," Lew said.

At Lew's last words, a spasm of rage contorted the pale face. "Don't get smart!" the fellow snarled. "I feel rotten, and I'd just as soon start the day off by pluggin' the both of you."

Lew started to edge away from Charlie, thinking that in the event of trouble they would be able to attack the man from two sides.

"No you don't!" the man snapped, waving the gun menacingly. "Now get back there together!"

For a second they both feared he would shoot. His hand trembled so it was a wonder the gun did not discharge just from the twitching of the finger on the trigger. And while they stood there, a tense tableau of three actors, another man stepped into view. This man was dressed in riding breeches and laced boots. His lean face was clean shaven, and his eyes snapped as they quickly took in the situation.

"What's the trouble here, Dutch?" he asked.

"These guys was goin' to climb up there and nose around the plane. I ordered 'em down and then they gets fresh with me."

Charlie spoke quickly, hoping to head off Lew before he could say something to further agitate the pistol-packing menace.

"We were simply checking to see if someone in the plane needed help," he said. "We couldn't find a pilot on the ground and thought he might still be up there."

"Put the gun away, Dutch," the taller man ordered. Then, turning to Charlie, he asked, "Are you timber cruisers?"

The question seemed a bit incongruous considering the situation, and Charlie thought he could detect a note of sharp interest.

"No," broke in Lew. "We're trappers on our way home, just cutting across the woods to reach the first railroad south of here."

"I see," said the man. "Can you tell me anything about the lay of the land, the shortest route to the mouth of the Big Beaver?"

"We trapped on the Big Beaver this winter," said Charlie. "But we stuck pretty close to our lines. We do have a fair map of the country that we got from the man who bought our furs. He said he knew it like a book, and so far his directions have worked out OK. With this map and a compass, I am sure we could find our way there."

"I can use you two" the man replied quickly, already having settled the matter in his own mind. "I represent the International Timber Company. Blake is my name, and I'm a field engineer. We were on our way to the settlement where Big Beaver joins the lake when the oil pressure dropped and our pilot cracked up attempting to land. He did his best, poor devil."

Charlie caught the significance of the last words. "Hurt bad?"

"Neck broken," was the rather short answer. "Dutch and I just finished the job of burying him when you came along. No sense in carrying out a dead man."

For a moment nobody spoke. Charlie and Lew were thinking of the tragic death of the pilot, and also of the indifferent manner in which the engineer had spoken of that death. Didn't the man have relatives back home? And then, as though he sensed the thoughts which ran through their minds, the engineer spoke quickly.

"We are here on a very important job. It means about a million dollars to the company, and we have the strictest orders not to let anything, not even death, delay us. We must reach Yelping Dog—that is the settlement—at once. We should have been there this morning. If you guide us there, I'll give you each ten dollars a day, and I'll pay your expenses back to your homes. It will only be a few days, not over a week at the most. What do you say?"

"We were counting on getting home as soon as we could," Lew replied. "What do we say, Charlie?"

"We'll take you there," Charlie decided, "with pay in full when we reach the settlement."

"Fine!" said Blake, and the feigned friendly interest fell from his face. Turning to Lew, he ordered, "Go up that tamarack to the wrecked plane. In the rear cockpit, you will find two leather cases. Lower them carefully with the rope that is coiled on the side of the plane. We brought our personal stuff down this morning—it was light enough to carry while we climbed—but we forgot the cases."

Without any further attention to Lew, Blake turned to Charlie. "You look like the brains in your outfit, and I'm appointing you leader of this expedition. Dutch and I know nothing of woodcraft, and I'm putting the responsibility on you. We have no food or blankets. That will be up to you, too. We can endure some hardship, but I hope a good woodsman can live off the land and also make us fairly comfortable in camp. Show that ability, and earn your pay."

"Quite an order," answered Charlie, "but I'll handle it."

Meanwhile, Lew was climbing steadily, working his way from knot to knot on the tamarack. Presently, he was directly below the plane. It looked like it would be difficult to climb up and inside the ship. But a rope dangling down on the opposite side provided a way. It was the rope the men below had no doubt used to make their descent, and Lew figured if it had held them, it should hold him.

The airship rocked and trembled as Lew swung his weight out on the rope, and for a moment he feared the plane would turn over on him. But the sound wing was lodged firmly among the limbs, and soon he stood upon the fuselage and then lowered himself inside.

A dark stain had spread across the floor near the pilot's seat, and Lew shuddered as he realized the source. He stepped gingerly over it into the passenger compartment. Here were the two cases Blake had described. Lifting one, Lew grunted at the weight.

"Must be instruments of some sort," he said as he reached for the rope. Dutch was on hand to catch the case and untie the rope, and Lew sent down the other case in the same easy manner. As he turned to go he paused to look longingly at the machine gun.

"I'd love to shoot this baby," Lew thought as he squinted along the jacketed barrel. It was one of the latest models, shooting the Government rifle load and cooled by air. Lew resolved that if the timber company who owned the plane abandoned it, he would return to salvage such a superb firearm.

As he finally turned to leave, his toe kicked a small object on the floor. Stooping over, Lew picked up a glass phial filled with white pills. Someone had forgotten his medicine. Lew thrust it in his pocket, intending to ask those below if it belonged to them.

Then he climbed out, steadied himself with the rope and swung down into the limbs of the tamarack. He breathed a deep sigh of relief when he was on solid ground again, rubbing the bark from his clothes and soothing a blister raised upon the inside of one leg by that first hasty downward slide.

The engineer divided the load. He took a square, heavy case and gave Dutch the lighter, longer one. Blake and Charlie carefully calculated their position on the map and then laid off a compass course towards Yelping Dog, the picturesquely named Indian settlement at the mouth of the Big Beaver River. Lew and Charlie picked up their own packs and rifles, and the strange procession started off.

Dutch grumbled over his load, light as it was, while Blake pressed close on Charlie's heels, shifting his feet impatiently whenever Charlie stopped to study the trail ahead and pick out the best way through brush. Blake's load was heavy—Lew knew exactly how weighty it was—but he carried it without visible effort, shielding it carefully from the sweeping branches as they penetrated every patch of brush. Lew decided the man's strength came as much from his determined will as from the actual muscle on his frame.

It must be a surveying expedition that had brought these men up to the Northwoods, Charlie decided, and they were in an urgent hurry to reach the settlement. The fact they had chartered an airplane proved that. Indeed, the mission had pushed all other thoughts and consideration from their minds. Even the death of their pilot had passed unheeded and apparently forgotten.

They tramped half a mile before Dutch suddenly stopped, dropped his load and began to slap his pockets and search through his clothes in a manner that speedily grew frantic.

"What the devil is it now, Dutch?" asked Blake irritably.

"I gotta go back," cried Dutch. "I left something back in the plane, something I gotta have." His face was working, and his hands shook as if he had the ague.

"We can't wait for you to go back," Blake replied sharply. "We haven't a minute to spare. Harris may beat us yet. Pick up that case, and let's go. That's an order."

But Dutch refused. In fact, he turned and started to run back down the trail. In a minute more he would have passed from sight. Then, for some reason Lew suddenly remembered the glass bottle he had picked up in the plane.

"Here!" he called. "Is this it?"

Dutch turned, and seeing the bottle in Lew's hand, burst out with a cry of relief. Leaping upon Lew, he snatched the bottle from his outstretched hand. They watched in astonishment, except for Blake, who, with a disgusted curse, turned ahead on the trail.

Dutch's face twisted in an ugly grin. "Thanks, young fellow," he said in a half-grudging tone. "I was dreadin' to climb that tree. But I gotta have my medicine. I'd die in these woods without it."

With a quick jerk of his head, he swallowed one of the pills without waiting for water. Shortly, he broke into a whistle, and Lew eyed this sudden transition into good humor with frank curiosity. Certainly, they were cruising with strange companions.

Charlie took the lead from Blake, keeping his eyes open for any sign of game. There were four mouths to feed now, and he knew Blake would protest any delay to hunt. He must do the best he could and rustle all the grub possible while on the trail. He and Lew also carried fishhooks and a line. If they camped close to a stream, they could fish for trout.

At noon they halted and finished the rest of the venison Lew had brought in that morning. Blake ate hurriedly and then fretted when Charlie insisted they rest half an hour before hitting the trail again. "We'll make better time in the end by resting now," Charlie assured him. "Lew and I can push as we've been walking the line all winter. But your muscles and feet are unaccustomed to this."

Blake, whose common sense saw the wisdom in these words, assented reluctantly. The afternoon passed with little conversation as they held doggedly to the pace set by Charlie. And, as the hours wore on, Charlie found himself liking their new job less and less. There was something about these men—Blake and the fellow he called Dutch—that gave him a bad feeling.

The offer of ten dollars each per day and expenses back home from the settlement had been too good to turn down, though. It would allow them to save nearly every dollar they had received for their winter's worth of prime northern fur. They had spent the long winter nights in the cabin talking over their plans for the coming season and had agreed to buy an automobile and head south through the mountain states, looking for sport and recreation. Ever since they had left their trapline on the Big Thunder River, they had felt a desire to return to the blue skies and purple peaks of the southern range.

Besides, they would reach the settlement soon, and then they would leave these men and make their way back home. He held onto that thought, that the job ended when they arrived at Yelping Dog.

They pitched camp an hour before sunset beside a small brook that tumbled over granite ledges. Charlie asked Lew to try his luck with hook and line, and to Lew's dislike, Dutch offered to accompany him and would not take no for an answer.

They walked up the edge of the stream until they found a deeper hole that looked promising. Leaning over, Lew saw the shapes of swimming fish. As he unwound his line, Dutch spoke up.

"Lemme show you how to get them babies. You head up there and herd them back to me."

When Dutch pulled the automatic from his pocket, Lew started to protest the shooting of fish but decided it would be better to mind his own business and say nothing. Dutch seemed possessed of a very short temper. Besides, they were after food, not sport, and it mattered little how food fish were taken. Dutch fired twice into the water, and four nice trout floated to the surface.

"That's enough," Lew said. "All we can eat before they spoil."

But Dutch only laughed and kept shooting until the clip in the gun was empty. "Pick 'em up, boy," he ordered with his ugly grin. "I guess Old Dutch hasn't forgot how to use a rod."

Lew collected the fish in silence. This wanton destruction angered him, but he kept his counsel. The fellow was reloading his hot pistol when he asked, "Want to see a little fancy stuff?"

"I don't care," Lew answered shortly.

Dutch shoved the pistol back in his hip pocket and pointed to a white birch across the pool. "See that tree?" he said. "Well, that's a guy who's sore on Old Dutch. Now watch!"

His hand whipped back to his hip, and with a swing of the wrist he drew and fired in one motion. The bullet struck the birch in the center, shoulder high from the ground. Dutch grinned a supercilious flash of teeth. "That's the way we do it in the big city, kid."

"Not bad," Lew admitted. "Now, let me see that gun a minute."

Dutch hesitated but passed the weapon over with reluctance. Lew shoved it into his own hip pocket and pointed in a different direction where the trees stood farther away. "See those two birch trees on the bank? They are bad men who have just committed a terrible breach of etiquette."

Then with a move too rapid to be followed with the eye, he drew and fired twice, the shots sounding so close together they nearly blended into a single report. The second might have been mistaken as an echo of the first. Dutch stood staring at the trees. There was a neat round hole drilled dead center in each, heart high.

Lew handed the gun back and picked up the fish he had laid down to take the gun. "I never shoot less than doubles," he remarked dryly. "If a single fresh guy shows up, I let my partner clip his wings. Now we better get going back to camp. The fellows will be hungry."

Dutch swallowed hard a couple of times before he spoke.

"I gotta hand it to you, kid. That was red-hot shootin'. Say, you otta come back with me. I could get you in the big stuff, real money. You know, the big town could use a kid like you."

Just how his ability to shoot quick and straight was going to ease him into city life, Lew did not ask. A suspicion that had been forming in his mind about Dutch now took on definite significance. But he only grinned at Dutch by way of reply.

When they reached camp, they found the shelter up and a fire going. Blake was lying on the ground pretty well winded from their strenuous hike. Charlie was thatching browse for beds. There was a supply of fir close to the campsite he had chosen.

"If you two men are not used to sleeping out of doors," Charlie offered, "you can take the tent and use our blankets. We will doze by the fire. It won't be the first time, will it, Lew?"

But before Lew could answer, Blake cut in. "I already counted on that," he said. "Fact is, that's why I am paying you twenty dollars a day. I figured rent for your gear as part of the wages."

It was a rather cool way of putting the matter, Charlie thought, but he let it go and began preparing supper.

After a hearty meal, Charlie and Lew went to gather bigger wood for the night fire. They met fifty yards away in the timber, out of earshot of Blake and Dutch back in camp.

"The more I see of these birds, the better I like mangy dogs," Lew said.

"I'm thinking the same," agreed Charlie.

"That Dutch, now isn't he a nice little playfellow?"

"I've got him spotted as a hoodlum," said Charlie. "Blake brought him along as sort of a bodyguard. Why he needs such a fellow in the woods, though, beats me. And he's a drug addict, too. Did you notice the way he grabbed that bottle out of your hand?"

"I'll say I did."

"Well, I guarantee that stuff is dope, probably morphine, although I didn't know it came in pills. He is just plain bad medicine, Dutch is, the kind to get all doped up and then they start shooting. That's the way punks get up their nerve, out of a bottle. Take away their dope, and they go to pieces. Watch out for him, Lew. I'd rather be camping with a rattlesnake."

"Well, what do you want to do?" asked Lew. "See it through, or dig out? We can leave them easy after they fall asleep."

"No, I signed us up for this," said Charlie, "and you know I never go back on my word. Besides, I see no reason for quitting now. It won't last long, and they don't dare get hostile with us for they need us too badly for guides.

"But whatever their business might be, I'll wager it's shady.

Blake seems like a professional man—he is certainly smart enough—but there is something wrong with his eyes. Did you notice how he looks right through you, like you aren't even there?"

"Sure, I noticed those lamps of his. They give me the creeps," said Lew. "And if that bird Dutch wants to go around braggin' on his gun play. I'll call him on it again."

"Was he boasting?" asked Charlie.

"You bet," answered Lew. "I got his number, though. He was soaring high on the pills and did some fancy shooting, but my gun work got his feet planted back on solid earth in a hurry."

Then he told Charlie about the birch tree shooting. "I'm glad you showed him up," Charlie chuckled. "These sidewalk gun-toters tend to forget that a backwoodsman lives by the gun. Well, we better go back or they'll think we're the ones up to something."

They lounged comfortably before the campfire. Blake and Dutch were plainly all in and fell asleep almost immediately. Charlie knew their pace would be slower on the morrow because of sore joints and stiff muscles. Still, they had covered many miles at a faster pace than Charlie liked when trailing. While he was nominally in charge, he had felt the continual urging of Blake's impatience behind him and had quickened his step in consequence.

Lew raised himself up and sat listening intently, head cocked like a hound. "Somebody coming down the trail," he said. Lew had exceptional hearing, and Charlie had never known him to be fooled.

"Two, no three," continued Lew in a whisper. Why he dropped his voice he could not say, but there was something stealthy in the way the party approached in the night. Glancing across the circle of light, Charlie saw that Blake was awake, face set. Dutch also was awake, and his hand strayed back to his ever-ready gun.

Chapter 3 – Harris Comes Calling

Charlie nodded to Blake and then he and Lew edged back away from the fire until they were in the shadows beyond its bright glow. Naturally, they were first to see the figures walking towards them, three dim forms coming Indian-style one behind the other. When the little group was twenty yards away, they stopped.

"Howdy!" the leader cried and then advanced alone into the circle of light. His empty hand was raised in the universal sign of peace, used and recognized by all races of man who inhabit the wilderness regions of the earth.

Charlie's ear caught a tense whisper as Blake leaned towards Dutch. "It's Harris!"

Lew answered the hail from his spot out of the light. "Howdy, yourself, stranger. Come on in and join us by the fire."

But Charlie and Lew remained back in the shadows, realizing here was a scene in which they would be mere spectators—an audience to whatever might follow. Dutch started to draw the gun from his holster, but Blake pushed his hand away with a whispered command. "Wait until I give the orders."

The spokesman of the trio of strangers walked closer, and stooping, looked directly into Blake's face. The engineer returned this scrutiny quietly, but Dutch snarled a hostile exclamation.

"So, it is you, Blake," the stranger finally said. "Tatuma told me you had come, but I hoped he was wrong."

Then two Indians stepped out from behind the speaker up into the firelight. One was a mere youth of stripling build, the other an older man of many winters. They squatted on their heels and stared impassively into the fire.

Lew poked his partner in the ribs. "See the old fellow?" he whispered excitedly. "He's the one who gave me the deer meat. The same man, I swear. Remember he also told me about the airplane, said I would find it wrecked in a tamarack?"

"Yes, it's me, Harris," Blake said evenly. "You shouldn't be surprised. You knew I was coming."

"I didn't count on you getting here so soon," answered the man he called Harris.

"Modern industry moves fast," Blake replied with a half-smile.

"And with devilish treachery," added Harris in flat tones.

"Come on," there was a trace of impatience in the engineer's voice. "No use in us quarreling again."

"We won't," was the short answer. "I knew the crooked outfit you represent would jump at another chance to strip the timber from my Indians' land. But I hoped we had you headed off for good when your last bid was turned down because of faulty descriptions."

"There was nothing wrong with *my* numbers," Blake replied testily. "The fools back at the office bungled the calculations. Besides, I never give up on a project—at least not one as profitable as this promises to be."

Charlie thought the words were calculated to stir the other to anger, but Harris did not take the bait.

"No," he spoke calmly, with perhaps a note of suppressed anger under his voice. "You just got busy again, pulling strings and bribing the politicians like you always do. And you got one more hearing from the Land Office. And this hearing comes May first. That gives you nine days from tonight to get the boundaries surveyed and return with accurate figures—if you can get it right *this* time."

Clearly, Harris had returned the dig, and he continued, "Did you really think I'd stand idle and see this land stripped bare? I've fought the timber trusts all my career, Blake, and I'll keep on. My duty is to my wards, the three tribes of the tamarack."

The engineer laughed softly but offered no answer to that.

"I've stood off the likes of you for twenty years," Harris went on. "This woods must stay virgin. My Indians must keep their homes, where they can hunt and trap like the Creator intended. I'll never let these people go to ruin through the chopper's ax and the poison trade whiskey that always follows the likes of you."

"Let me plug him and stop his racket," muttered Dutch, his hand again straying back to the holstered gun.

"Shut up!" snapped Blake.

"So, you brought a gunman?" Harris noted. "Just like you, Blake. A bully always needs a gang to do his bidding."

Then Harris looked pointedly to Lew and Charlie, sitting back in the shadows. Lew started to protest, but Charlie silenced him with a light poke in the ribs.

"Listen," Harris continued. "And listen good. If anything happens to me tonight, there'll be five hundred Indians on your tail—bloodhounds that can track a man across bare rock. These people believe in me, and they will stand by me to the limit."

"I'm a businessman, not a murderer," sneered Blake. "That north line must be rechecked, that's all, and I'm going to do the job and take the figures back in time for the hearing. And, since you started this talk of trouble, mind telling me how you plan to stop me?"

"I don't know," confessed Harris.

"No, you don't," Blake said. "And I don't think you will resort to criminal force. You know it would cost you your cushy government job. I'm here within my rights as a citizen conducting private business. And I'm not scared of your dirty half-breeds. My company will ship in a regiment of armed militia, if they have to. You know us, Harris. We'll go any length to get what we want."

"I know you only too well," replied Harris. "And I also know that this is your last chance at these woods. Word on the grapevine is that you have gone too far with the bribes, that high-ranking officials are scared to let this continue. If you fail, I will have you blocked for years. That's why I'm going to keep on fighting to the last minute!"

"You're talk makes me tired," yawned Blake. "Why don't you roll up in your blankets by my fire? Maybe we can continue our discussion in the morning."

"I should," was the answer. "I should keep an eye on you every second, looking for your trademark underhanded dealing. But I can't spare the time. We must go."

Then he stood and addressed the Indians, "Let's go, Tatuma."

Tatuma glanced across the fire at Lew, whom he affected to now see for the first time. Then he spoke too softly for anyone else to hear, but the words were clear to Lew's keen ears. "You find Devil Bird. Find Devil Man, too."

Then Tatuma took his place in the lead and the little party faded back into the black timber. As their footsteps died away, Blake turned immediately to Lew and demanded. "What did the Indian say? How you know him?"

"I met the old codger this morning, when I was hunting breakfast," explained Lew. "He gave me the venison we cleaned up for lunch. I also think he saw or heard your plane last night—he called it 'Devil Bird.' Told me I might find it wrecked in the top of a tree—a tamarack tree. Pretty good guesser, that old boy. Darned if I know how he hit it so straight—unless maybe the woods Indians were expecting you and sent someone to keep an eye on you."

Blake glanced apprehensively out into the darkness that ringed the campfire. It was not a pleasant thought—hostile eyes peering from the cover of the tamaracks, and Charlie could see that it effected the man more than he wanted to let on.

"I'm not worried any about Harris' Indians," Blake finally blustered. "You needn't, either. I would have come up here alone—it is perfectly safe—only my boss suggested I bring Dutch. He can handle a transit rod as well as a gun, you see. Now you boys only have to follow my orders, and I'll see that you are paid off well."

He waited for an answer. It came from Charlie. "We hired on to get you to Yelping Dog as soon as possible, so I suggest we turn in now. We must get an early start to make time on the trail."

Satisfied with these words, Blake rolled under the shelter and stretched himself out on the thick bed of fir tips.

Charlie replenished the fire and then they took to their own beds under the sky. Lew opened his mouth to speak, but Charlie stopped him with a warning frown. They lay back and settled under their own loose evergreen beds as best they could. Charlie anticipated a chilly night minus shelter and blankets, with only the fire for warmth.

Several hours later he awoke. The fire was low and he kindled it up with quick-burning wood until the welcome heat drove off the chill which had settled over him. Turning back to his bed, he found Lew staring at him with open eyes.

"All right," Charlie whispered, "out with it."

"I'm ashamed of you," Lew began, after a cautious glance at the shelter where Blake and Dutch apparently lay sound asleep. "You've tied up with a timber trust, to drive the Indians from their land; regular old home-breaker you are. The poor devils' timber will be cut, and then fire will kill what the loggers leave. In two years, this will be a desert, not a tamarack forest."

"That ten dollars per day doesn't sound quite so good now, I admit," Charlie replied. "I am not going back on my word to guide Blake safely to Yelping Dog, but that doesn't mean we have to help him steal the Indian's timber, and he still has to get the surveying done and the straight dope home in time."

"I'll say," Lew agreed so heartily Charlie immediately wondered what his partner might be planning. But Lew just closed his eyes and turned over.

In the morning, Blake called for Charlie's map. He studied it closely, comparing it with his own notes and then, after the fish were fried and eaten, he announced, "I've changed my plans. I believe I can cut straight to the river from here and pick up this end of the north line which has to be resurveyed. That will save the time of doubling back from the settlement. I'm taking a big chance. It has been five years since I laid that stone, but I'm going to locate it by compass. If I can do this, we'll already have the figures when we reach Yelping Dog. It may puzzle Harris, too, if we don't come straight in and start to work from that end."

He glanced first at Lew and then Charlie, as if to read their thoughts. He was feeling them out to see where their sympathies lie in this contest between his timber trust and Harris the Indian Agent, a contest with a vast and valuable tract of tamarack as the prize.

"I call that a good plan," agreed Lew. Then he went back to scouring the fish smell from the fry pan with wet moss and sand from the spring. Charlie looked at Lew but said nothing.

They had eaten the last of the trout for breakfast, and Charlie knew he would be up against it trying to feed four hungry men from the limited supplies in the pack sacks and what game they could secure on the trail.

The sun was just breaking over the tamaracks when they started. Dutch and Blake walked painfully the first few miles until their aching joints and sore muscles loosened. Then Blake pressed as close as ever to Charlie's heels. Dutch followed well enough, but he grumbled at intervals, complaining about the pace. Lew, walking in the rear, seemed to derive much satisfaction watching the engineer and his gunman grumble at each other. It was a queer combination, he reflected, and a stranger mission on which they had come.

In the middle of the morning, they began to see evidence that the woods were inhabited. Trees had been cut, and the freshly chopped stumps revealed recent activity. Then a barking dog ahead told them they were likely approaching a hut or perhaps a village.

They walked slowly now, Charlie making more noise than he usually did. He preferred not to burst in upon an Indian encampment too abruptly. The half-starved curs about the lodges would no doubt give warning of their coming, but Charlie was not one to count on such happenstance.

Presently, he saw through the thinned timber a line of tepees, summer homes of the woods Indians. Charlie walked straight towards them, thinking it a lucky encounter because they could likely buy food from these people. They would have bear or deer meat, and perhaps bacon and flour, too.

Copper-skinned children scampered inside the skin tents as the strangers approached. Women bearing loads of wood hastened their steps to avoid meeting the four men in the narrow lane between tepees. Charlie walked straight to the largest tepee, decorated with signs and simple images that indicated the home of the chief or head man. Beside the big tepee stood a rack of poles—a meat rack Charlie saw with satisfaction. Three quarters of meat hung on it.

Six Indian braves were sitting before the door, seemingly indifferent to his approach. But Charlie knew they were watching with keen eyes under a mask of abstraction. He halted at the proper distance and saluted with upraised palm.

An Indian stood and answered. His dress individualized him as holding an important position in his tribe, and Charlie wasted no time parleying for food, using signs to carry his meaning. Charlie pointed to the meat poles, and holding up a single finger indicated the amount he wished. Then, pulling plenty of money from his pocket, displayed the silver coins and his willingness to pay.

The Indian nodded and turned to the quarters of fresh venison. But then another tribesman walked quickly to the group and spoke a single word. The others wheeled towards him, and gathering together, they conversed in low tones.

Then they all faced Charlie, and he saw the abrupt change in their bearing. Before, they had been mildly curious, to all appearances indifferent to the strangers in their village. Now, they were positively hostile. Scowls met them from every side, and the spokesman with whom Charlie had parleyed shook his head vehemently. Then he laid his hand on the short knife at his waist and waved them away from his lodge.

It was not hard for Charlie to guess what had happened. Harris had sent messengers warning every village about Blake and his purpose. No wonder these people had turned so hostile, and every woods Indian in the region would show bitter enmity as soon as they received the word.

Charlie's mouth watered for the fresh venison hanging from the pole, but he understood the Indian mind well enough to not attempt to argue or coax. The sooner they left the better, so, calling to the others behind him, he marched briskly back towards the timber.

Blake and Dutch protested as they followed, but Charlie said, "These Indians have been warned against you. You couldn't buy food from them at any price. We are lucky they did nothing more than order us to go."

"Watsa matter with you, chicken?" Dutch asked testily. "You ain't scared of those birds, are you? Why, I could give the whole bunch the works by myself."

"I wouldn't try it," advised Charlie. "I know these people. Lew and I had some experience with them last winter, maybe not this tribe, but another across the river, and I tell you they can turn deadly when they want to. Did you see the other men watching from inside the tepees? If you had made a wrong move, they would have riddled you with bullets before you knew the war had even started."

Dutch pondered this in silence. Blake only scowled, anger breaking through the calm that usually masked his true feelings.

"We needed that meat pretty bad," Black snapped. "It would have saved time wasted hunting. I'll remember that when I'm running this timber, and I'll bum rush those pompous half-breeds out of there before they know what hit 'em."

They walked on in silence after that, until Lew offered, "I guess we'll have to fall back on our old reliable—the porcupine." Then he pointed into the top of a nearby tree. Charlie wrinkled up his nose, but Lew dropped his pack and climbed up to shake the animal out.

Dutch could not believe what he was seeing. "I ain't eating that stinking thing," he sputtered.

"It's either that or we take half a day off to stalk grouse or kick out some rabbits," Lew called down from the tree.

"We eat porcupine, then," Blake stated. "We can't waste time unless it is absolutely necessary to hunt." Then he sat down to rest, watching Lew skin the bristly little beast.

"There won't be much left when he's done," Dutch grumbled.

"Don't worry," retorted Lew. "You eat your one-fourth, old sock, and you'll be doing well."

Charlie estimated they covered a good twenty miles that day. Two and a half miles an hour for eight walking hours was a good daily average for such a party.

They could not find a trout stream to camp beside that night. They did locate water, a sluggish spring draining out from under the upraised roots of a toppled tree. Another porcupine provided their meat. The animals were thick along the trail, and they could have secured as many as they wished, but, as Lew stated, "One quill-pig goes a long ways."

Lew choked down a few mouthfuls, drank his cup of tea, and

seizing his gun, started out to find something more palatable. Dutch complained louder than ever, and Blake's temper showed signs of cracking wide open from fatigue, lousy food and his gunman's grumbling. Of the trio in camp, only Charlie worked calmly, thatching beds of browse for the party.

As the twilight deepened, Lew returned empty-handed. He sat down his rifle and said to Charlie, "In the morning, you and I have to hunt for grub before time to hit the trail. If we don't find anything, we'll keep on looking until we do. A fellow can only last so long eating porcupine meat."

A hand tugging at his shoulder awoke Charlie in the night. He sat up and found Blake beside his bed. He could not tell how long he had been asleep. The fire was shooting up with fresh fuel supplied by the engineer.

"What's the matter?" Charlie asked.

"There's somebody in the timber back of my tent," whispered Blake. "Twice I heard a noise. Take your gun and look."

Charlie noticed Blake was carrying a heavy service revolver with a swivel in the stock fastened to his wrist with a leather strap.

Charlie made a swing through the timber back of camp but found nothing. He expected this. An intruder would be safely away by that time, or else well hidden in the brush. But to satisfy Blake, he walked several hundred yards through the trees before returning.

Dutch still snored throatily. Charlie had noticed him reach for his dope bottle more often that day. Now he appeared so dead to the world he might as well have been in a stupor. Charlie stopped behind the shelter tent and examined the ground carefully.

"See anyone?" Blake asked.

"No," replied Charlie. "Are you sure you heard a man? It could have been a porcupine sneaking in to gnaw on our boot leather."

"Don't mention those animals again," groaned Lew from beside the fire. "I was having a nightmare just now—a whole roasted porcupine on the Thanksgiving table!"

Blake shook his head, pointedly dismissing Lew. "No, it was a man. I clearly heard the sound of someone brushing against the tent. It was too real for any mistake."

"Whoever it was is gone now," assured Charlie.

"I have been thinking that some of Harris' Indians might try to steal my transit," continued Blake. "That would be a sure way to stop me. I could never get another up here in time to finish the job."

"Your gunman slept pretty soundly through all of this," Lew observed, and Blake shot a quick glance at him.

"Dutch is worn out with all the walking," he excused. "Usually he is alert enough, and he can shoot."

Lew grinned at this last remark but did not offer any opinion he might have about the gun work of Dutch.

"It's strange you heard nothing," continued Blake. "I thought woodsmen slept lightly?"

"Not after they've eaten porcupine," Lew yawned.

"We will start out very early to hunt," said Charlie, "so if you find us gone when you awake, you'll know where we are."

"Good luck to you," answered Blake shortly. "And get back to camp as soon as you can. I expect to start surveying tomorrow."

Charlie and Lew set out before sunrise in search of game. They stalked noiselessly over dew-soaked ground, watching for roosted grouse, their best chance of securing food without breaking any game laws, something they already had told Blake they would not do.

"Blake getting jumpy?" Lew asked when they were out of earshot of camp. "Was he hearing things last night?"

"He may be getting a little paranoid," Charlie replied. "But his hearing seems to be good. There was somebody back of the tent."

Lew looked at him in surprise. "How do you know that?"

"I examined the ground," Charlie informed him. "Of course, I saw no tracks; I couldn't have seen them in that dim light if there had been any. But the stake I had driven to hold the tent corner by Blake's head was pulled up just enough to notice. Apparently, whoever was snooping back there caught his foot momentarily, likely the very noise that awoke Blake."

Lew whistled in amazement. "One of Harris' Indians sneaking in to stick a knife in the engineer?" he suggested.

"Harris would not stand for that," Charlie replied. "He looks to me like a square shooter. No, I think Blake hit on the answer to that one. They were trying to steal or damage his transit. That would be the easiest and surest way to stop this survey."

"I wish they had," Lew said. "Harris has his hands pretty well tied, and Blake knows it. He can't use force—that would put him in bad with the Government, maybe even jail. If I was Harris, I'd drop a few hints around the Indians, like scalping or some such thing. I sure wish we could help him."

"You had better follow my usual advice in such situations,"

Charlie grinned. "And you know what I mean."

"Sure," Lew affirmed. "Attend strictly to my own business. But a fellow should interfere in a case of this kind. You know the tamarack should stay just as it is: a home for the Indians. Blake's getting it by a crooked deal. He won't admit it, but I feel that it is so."

"I do, too," Charlie agreed. "But I won't go back on my word to guide him to Yelping Dog, and I am not sure it would do much good if I did. Then he would have a real case to make, that we had sided with Harris and sabotaged him. And unless we were willing to commit libel before a legal hearing, we would have to admit it, and that would be enough to get him all the extension he needs to come back up here and get the figures right.

"We should find grouse in this timber," he added, deftly changing the subject as the morning light grew stronger until they could look up thirty to forty feet in the trees.

"There they are," whispered Lew a minute later, pointing to a row of dark humps on a branch. Charlie swung up his rifle.

"We must get at least four," he said. "Take the first bird with a headshot and the next wherever you can hit him. Hurry, they see us and are getting ready to fly!"

"Let her go," answered Lew. Two reports rang out, and a pair of grouse tumbled. But before they could work the levers of their rifles for follow-up shots, a louder crashing in the brush drew their attention away from the birds.

"It's a bear!" yelled Lew. "Get him, Charlie!"

Charlie covered the dark form scurrying off with the speed of a startled rabbit and shot as fast as he could work the repeater.

"He's down!" Lew cried. "Come on, old sport. Let's go collect meat in a big package!"

Lew was right that it was bear, but a skinny little one perhaps starved early out of hibernation. "Poor as a crow," Lew said in disgust, after rolling it over for dressing.

"What are you grumbling about?" inquired Charlie. "This might not be a trophy bear, but it beats porcupine and it ends our need to hunt early every morning. Sure, spring bear meat can be stringy. But you didn't expect to shoot prime beef in the timber, did you? Now help me cut a pole, and then we'll pack him back to camp."

"I can't wait to see Dutch's face," chuckled Lew, "when I tell him he must lug a quarter of bear meat besides that little case he makes so much fuss about."

"That sure was luck," Charlie reflected as they tied the bear's feet together and slipped a stout pole through them. "I don't understand how we got so close before he spooked."

"He must have been rooting around in the ground, looking for grubs," Lew answered. "Pretty good shooting, too."

Even Dutch grinned widely when they walked into camp with that load of meat. The grouse were cooked for breakfast, and then they skinned the bear and hung up the best of it to cool until they were ready for the trail.

Blake was even more impatient than ever. "I know I can pick up my starting point at the river today. There is a natural marker I can't miss." It looked to Charlie as though last night's prowler may have struck a nerve, even though Blake didn't mention it again.

High sun found them on the bank of the Big Beaver. "Just like home," said Lew when he caught first sight of the bright water.

Blake immediately sat down and started figuring. Then he measured carefully over his own map. "We'll soon see how close you estimated our daily travel," he told Charlie. "The directions were right—I checked them with my own compass. If we averaged twenty miles a day, then we are less than a mile from the point I need to locate. It is opposite the mouth of a branch nearly as big as the Big Beaver itself. We split up and two go each way, following the bank. Whoever finds the branch, fire a shot to alert the others."

Lew turned downstream and Dutch automatically fell in beside him. Charlie realized by this trivial circumstance that Blake no longer trusted Lew and himself alone for any length of time.

He and Blake went in the opposite direction. They walked briskly along the bank until Blake paused, sniffing the air. "Smells like wood smoke. Can you smell it, too?"

Charlie nodded. He had noticed the odor for some time but had decided not to say anything until he had a better idea what it might mean. While he was considering what to say, a pistol shot echoed through the forest.

"Dutch has found it!" Blake cried in triumph.

Chapter 4 – Gunman Goes Missing

Hurrying back along the river, they found Lew and Dutch standing close to the water, opposite a wide branch coming in from the other side.

"This looks like the place," Blake declared. "I remember my guide was half-drunk when we crossed over from that side and he nearly spilled us out of the canoe. My benchmark should be thirty feet back from the river's edge and in line with the center of the opposite stream. It is a stone, flat on top with figures chiseled in it. It will be buried, but no more than three or four inches deep."

He stepped back and carefully estimated the point. "Dig here!"

Charlie and Lew drew their sheath knives and probed about in the topsoil. "Just like looking for pirate treasure," Lew grinned. Blake stood directly over them, watching every thrust they made.

The ground was free of gravel, and they rapidly explored it, adding square yard after yard to the search area without result. Blake grew impatient. He consulted his notes once more. "This must be the place," he urged. "The next branch of the river on that side is over seven miles from here."

"I've found something," Charlie called. Then digging deeper with his blade, he speedily uncovered a buried rock. When he brushed off the dirt they saw figures in the flat side of the stone. Blake examined them.

"OK," he confirmed. "This is our starting point. Now, instead of following down the river as I did before, we will run back into the forest five miles at a thirty-five-degree angle. This is necessary to miss five small land grants the Department made to settlers."

"I should think the Department would have its own survey description of land grants," said Lew.

"Apparently, the Indian Agent was unable to locate them," said Blake dryly. "That's why I now must get the straight dope myself on the ground. If I don't, they will pick another flaw in the authenticity."

As he spoke, he was unboxing the transit he had carried so carefully the last three days. Dutch opened his own case and drew out a tripod, several parts from the head which had been removed to lighten Blake's load, and a telescoping target rod.

"Now," Blake spoke crisply to Lew and Charlie, "your jobs are this. Charlie will carry the pole. Dutch and Lew will chain the line behind as we go. I realize you two boys know nothing about surveying, but you'll pick up enough to be able to handle that small task. I know you didn't hire out to work on a survey crew, and I'm going to double your pay starting this noon."

"Hooray!" cried Lew, drawing another speculative glance from Charlie. But Blake just looked disapproving and then began giving each of them concise instructions. They started at once to lay off a five-mile line leading back from the river.

Five miles of timber line is a considerable challenge for the average transit man, but Blake proved adept at his work. He ran along with the heavy transit over his shoulder at a half trot, and with sharp commands kept the rest of them snapping to the job. His eyes were remarkably keen, and he made long shots through the timber and brush. Fortunately for him, the woods here was fairly open with only a small number of tamarack clumps, the balance being stately spruce and pine—the prized timber his company desired.

As they worked, Charlie noticed the smell of smoke more than ever. The ground ahead broke into several steep ridges, and when they climbed to the top of the first they finally saw the source of the smoke-tainted wind.

Looking down and ahead, they saw a long line of smoke edged at intervals with shooting flame. Blake set his transit down. "Harris has fired the timber to stop me," he growled. "That fire line will be directly in our path when we turn the angle and begin our long line into Yelping Dog."

"That's a dirty shame," Lew declared as he watched the fire. Blake glanced at him so sharply Charlie knew the look carried a fresh tinge of suspicion. Lew slipped his loaded pack to the ground and rested while the engineer once more studied his book of field notes.

"We can finish this line before night," he asserted as he consulted his watch. "We won't worry about the fire until morning."

On they worked, Charlie and Blake blazing a trail for the two chainmen who pressed close upon their heels. It was hard, hot work, and Charlie and Lew were handicapped by loaded packs. Fortunately, both were as hard as iron from their winter on the northern trapline. Otherwise, they would have had difficulty keeping up with Blake, a hard task-master.

Late in the afternoon, they drove a stake at the five-mile mark. Blake had just been able to sight his last shot through the forest before night settled over them with uncanny speed. Tomorrow, he explained, the job would be to turn a right angle at this point and project a line straight for the settlement of Yelping Dog. Any slight error here would not matter, because if they missed the village by a few hundred feet, the only loss would be a few acres of surveyed timber.

And this meant nothing to the company, Blake explained with a nasty laugh, because the logging crews weren't fussy about such things after they arrived. They cut whatever they wanted.

Because the woods were damp and the timber green with swelling sap, the wildfire made only slight headway. In fact, it seemed to be confined to a narrow valley running at right angles to their proposed course. The glow of the distant fire seemed to fascinate Lew. At every opportunity, he stood watching the light in the sky, perhaps gauging its position.

The fire presented a serious barrier to surveying. The heat and smoke arising from burned-over ground would make transit work practically impossible. Charlie thought it strange that Blake did not show more sign of being worried. He decided the engineer was tired like they all were and had probably forced thoughts of the fire from his mind, preferring to wait until he was actually confronted with it the next morning. They ate a hearty meal of bear steak. And all were thankful to be eating anything other than more porcupine.

Charlie noted the care Blake took to protect his transit that night. The instrument was buried in the bed between the engineer and Dutch, and both men slept with their guns close to hand.

In the morning, an unexpected change in Blake's demeanor surprised Lew and Charlie as they started the camp work.

He was no longer impatient to start. Indeed, he sat beside the fire sipping tea and consulting his notes in an almost leisurely fashion. And after the meager outfit was packed and ready to be shouldered for the trail, he told them to wait until the sun was high enough to drive off the mist and haze that hung about the treetops.

Had Blake given up? Was the fire burning in the valley below causing him to abandon the survey? Blake finally stood, and walking to the high point of the ridge, carefully scanned the forest in all directions. Then he came to them with a look of satisfaction.

"It will be easy," he said. "I will beat Harris' juvenile prank with simple mathematics. I'm surprised he didn't think of something better than that. You won't understand, of course, but I'll try to explain what I'm going to do.

"First, you mark this corner so I can see it from a distance. Then I double back over the line we ran yesterday a given distance. That will give me two angles and one side of a triangle. With a little figuring, I can estimate how far we must chain to cut our line again on the other side of the forest fire!"

No matter where their sympathies lie in the matter, Lew and Charlie both had to admit to themselves that Blake was plenty sharp. His air of leisure vanished as he urged them to action.

To mark the corner, he substituted a twenty-foot peeled pole for the stake. Then he blazed a long, wide surface on a tree standing beside the pole, and as a further aid, ordered Charlie to build a smudge fire of smoking wood a few yards from the corner. With so many marking signals, he expected no difficulty picking up this location from a distance. Then Blake shouldered his transit and plunged off into the timber.

That day lingered in memory as a nightmare of feverish activity. Charlie and Lew both declared they had walked at least one hundred miles over the two sides of this gigantic triangle before they made camp at night.

"Whew!" Lew breathed as he lifted his face from his teacup. "If this is a sample of a white collar job, give me good old skunk trapping every time!"

Blake was tired, too, but highly pleased with himself. Indeed, in his pleasure he had grown even more arrogant, a mood irritating to the others. Still, it had been quite a coup, detouring about the fire barrier with only a small loss of time.

Later, Lew watched over Blake's shoulder as he jotted down rows of figures. "That's a mighty lot of numbers," he said slowly.

Blake glanced up from the page. "Yes, it will take two men and a calculating machine five hours to work all of this out," he replied. "I've allowed a day in my schedule for that."

"You won't have any time to spare, either," asserted Lew. "After we reach the settlement, you will still be a long ways from home."

"I don't know what kind of transportation they have now," Blake replied. "And I had counted on the plane for my return trip, of course. I will have to hike or canoe as far as the first telegraph to transmit my figures back to the home office."

Lew set out to drag in firewood for the night, and Charlie joined him. Apparently, Dutch was too tired to keep an eye on Lew this time. "That blamed engineer thinks of everything," Lew began. "I was counting on a couple of days of rest when I saw that timber burning in front of us."

"Yes, I suppose a chance to rest was all you had in mind," his partner replied. "Now drop the act. I can tell by every move you make, Lew, how badly you want to see this job fail. Better be careful. Blake is starting to notice, too."

"Well, what if he does?"

"Nothing, only he might have Dutch put a bullet in you some dark night. Or he might fire you off the job. Then you couldn't work whatever scheme I believe you are trying to hatch."

Charlie said all of this in a joking way, but he noted a change in Lew's manner when they resumed work the next morning. Lew bent every effort to push the job without exhibiting a suspicious amount of overt enthusiasm. He was the first man loaded with pack and ready for the trail.

As the hours passed, Charlie noticed that Lew seemed to be working to get on friendlier terms with Dutch. At one point, he saw Lew carrying part of the gunman's load besides his own.

They made good headway that day. The line they were running was straight, and the timber opened up in large tracts of brush-free expanse. Several times during the day they passed close to small clearings, those land grants to settlers that were making this second survey necessary. At one of the cabins, they purchased five pounds of flour from a French trapper. Bear meat was certainly better than porcupine, but a straight diet of any meat grows tiresome, and camp bread was welcomed by all.

For three straight days they cruised the timber, staking and blazing the line. Once Lew asked, "Aren't you afraid the Indians will just pull your stakes and hack away the blazes?"

Blake answered with a crooked smile. "It won't do them any good if they do. The line merely establishes an accurate location for review by the Land Commission. When the logging crews come in, they won't pay any attention to the lines, anyway."

The evening of the third day, Blake was first to see water through the trees ahead and became jubilant. "It's the lake," he called back. "My schedule has worked out to the very hour. Yelping Dog is probably only a hundred yards to our left. We'll stake this last corner and then camp in the timber. Don't make any more noise than necessary. We don't want to announce our arrival."

Then he sighted the last shot and watched with keen satisfaction as Charlie drove the last stake.

Charlie looked down the lakeshore through the dusk and saw a dozen scattered cabins. That must be the settlement, and it had the quiet, deserted look most such settlements assume at the end of the day. Smoke arose from two of the chimneys. The shoreline was covered with willow and cottonwood. The lake itself was vast, and he could not see across to the opposite shore.

Blake made a few entries in his notebook and then directed them back into the trees to pitch camp. As he kindled the fire, Charlie glanced at Dutch and noticed another change in the gunman. His face was pinched and colored putty gray, and his hands twitched as he stood talking to the engineer.

Blake turned away in disgust and approached the fire. Noting Charlie's look, he explained, "The fool has lost his dope again. He told me about it in the middle of the afternoon, but I forced him to carry on. I'm afraid he'll crack wide open if he can't get more of the stuff. There may be a doctor at the settlement who can help him out."

"What'll you do if he does go loco?" asked Charlie, visions of a wild-eyed Dutch shooting up camp filling his mind.

"I've got a pint of whiskey in my pack. I think that will quiet him. If he can't get any dope tomorrow, I may have to keep him drunk until we get home. If I had known he was an addict, I never would have brought him along. But I didn't find it out until the night the plane crashed."

Charlie had finished cooking when he noticed Lew was missing. He stood and looked towards the lake. Lew might be washing up or he might be in the forest gathering firewood.

"Grub's ready!" Charlie finally called. Blake looked up from his notebook and asked, "Where's Dutch?"

Charlie stood waiting for any answer to his call. But the woods were silent. Neither Lew nor Dutch appeared to eat, an unusual thing for both of them. Blake grew suspicious and then angry. "I bet the fool started back in the dark to look for his pills! He would spoil everything for me at the last minute. If he does …" he left the threat unsaid, but Charlie noted the frank menace in his voice.

"That's where he went, alright," guessed Charlie. "But I don't understand why Lew doesn't come."

"He probably went with Dutch to make sure he doesn't get lost," Blake replied. "I don't know why, but they have become the best of buddies."

He shot an inquiring look at Charlie but got no response.

"It's lucky the surveying is done," Blake continued. "I really don't need him anymore, you know. Wait a second. I think I hear them coming now."

Steps sounded in the gloom beyond camp, and Blake turned back to his notes.

"If you fellows want to eat …" began Charlie, but the words suddenly changed to a cry of sharp surprise. A dozen dark figures were running towards him through the trees. Blake reached for his revolver, but before he could grasp the butt, both he and Charlie were pinned to the ground by wiry woods Indians.

Their hands were tied, and then they were pulled roughly to their feet. Blake started to curse, yet Charlie made no resistance. He stood quietly awaiting whatever might happen next.

He had not cried out in fright. He simply had been startled by the sudden rush of Indians. But he did not think they would harm him. They were after Blake and not him, reasoned Charlie.

Not a word was spoken by the Indians. They herded the two captives together and then pushed them along to the lakeshore. In the light of a quarter-moon, Charlie saw three canoes drawn up at the edge of the water. He was bundled in one, Blake in another, and then the flotilla pushed off.

The paddlers worked noiselessly, and the light craft shot across the water. Charlie lay on his side under a canoe thwart. He wondered where they were going, but he was more worried for Lew.

If the Indians found them, Dutch might be foolish enough to draw his gun. In doing so, he might get himself killed, and Lew might share that fate. What could have sent him off with Dutch? Charlie was thinking all of this over when the canoe beached. He was surprised, as they could not have covered more than half a mile.

He was lifted out to see the dim outline of an Indian encampment. Light gleamed through the doorways of the skin tepees from the fires burning within. Shadow silhouettes moved like ghosts across the translucent tepee walls.

More men met the party who had captured them, and with low murmuring, Blake and Charlie were pushed into a tepee and then down on a bundle of skins. Strong hands tied their feet.

Charlie looked up at the faces that filled the lodge and saw Tatuma, the old Indian who had met Lew in the forest and later guided Harris to their camp. He made a quiet but stern motion warning him not to talk, and then pointed to the knife on his belt as the possible consequence of disobedience.

Charlie immediately decided he would be glum as an owl. This was not his fight, after all. He simply worked for the man the Indians had kidnapped, although he realized that they might not distinguish as finely between employer and employee should things take an ugly turn for the worse.

Tatuma bent over Blake. With a quick move, he jerked open the engineer's coat, reached inside and drew out the book of field notes. With a grunt of satisfaction, he thumbed the pages. Blake strained at the thongs that held his hands, cursing until his voice trailed off incoherently with the intensity of his rage.

Tatuma merely grunted again. Then he turned to Charlie. "Lay still, no talk. We no hurt."

Then he leaned over and loosened the thongs until Charlie could relax with a fair amount of comfort. Charlie was exceedingly grateful for this kindness, remembering the terrible night when Lew and he had lain tightly trussed on their own cabin floor while a darker crowd eagerly planned the death race they were to run the next morning.

Tatuma vanished with the book of notes, and Charlie speculated on the next move. No doubt they already had destroyed Blake's transit. It might even be possible they would be released in the morning. With no instrument and the notes gone, Blake simply had no chance of duplicating the data and getting it home by the first of May, only four days hence.

Charlie slept comfortably through the night, thoroughly exhausted from the past days of work. With his usual equanimity, he didn't let the unusual situation prevent him from getting a good night's rest. Morning arrived, but it brought no freedom. An old squaw did enter with a pot of boiled meat, cooked with water like soup. She sat down and started to feed Charlie with a wide horn spoon. He was warmly grateful for this attention, and the meat broth was quite tasty.

Blake jerked away from the proffered spoon and refused to eat. The squaw turned back to Charlie with perfect indifference and fed him until he shook his head with a smile. He was surprised by Blake's foolish act. The engineer was only starving himself. Charlie always believed in making the best of a bad situation, and he knew a sulky prisoner never got favorable treatment.

The squaw waddled out, leaving them alone in the tent. But just outside the door, Charlie could see the legs and feet of their no-doubt armed guard. Blake had apparently lost all restraint and was giving his temper free reign. "Harris is back of this," he growled vindictively. "He will lose his job when I get home. I'll sue him for damages, ruin him and see him in prison for kidnapping."

"I'm worried about Lew … and Dutch," Charlie broke in, although he could not work up much feeling over the fate of the sourtempered gunman.

"They had no business leaving us," growled Blake. "I hope they get what they deserve. I'll stick Dutch in a sanatorium when I get him home, someplace where they will knock that dope appetite out of him with a week of cold turkey."

Charlie did not answer. The more Blake talked, the louder he got. One of the guards had poked his head inside and scowled at the last outburst from Blake. Charlie figured a gag would be next, and he didn't want a gag thrust in his own mouth.

It was a long day that dragged by with weary monotony. The old squaw fed them again at noon. This time Blake gladly swallowed his share of the food. Charlie was pleased at the treatment they had received so far. Evening brought more boiled meat, and he decided this indicated they would be well fed during their imprisonment.

Looking out past the woman, he could see the night shadows dropping across the lake. The engineer lay on the skin bed, scowling up at the cluster of poles that supported the tepee.

Then there was a commotion outside: voices and the padding of many moccasined feet past their lodge. Blake raised himself on one elbow, looking eagerly for rescue in some form.

Then the hanging curtains were thrust aside—and Lew stumbled in! His hands were tied, and after he was pushed over on the floor beside them, two Indians bound his feet. When Lew grinned at him, Charlie knew that he was unharmed. As soon the Indians left, Blake shot an angry question at Lew, "Where the devil is Dutch?"

Chapter 5 – Timing Is Everything

Dutch is out in the woods somewhere," Lew informed them. "I followed him last night. I was afraid he would get lost. Dutch isn't much of a woodsman, you know. When I saw him leave camp, I went along. He found his bottle of pills about four miles back on the line. He was pretty jumpy by that time. I never saw a man so crazy glad to find something as he was."

"Go on!" Blake snapped. "Get to the point!"

"When he found his bottle," Lew continued, "he took such a big dose it knocked him cold and I couldn't arouse him."

That brought another outburst from Blake. In a shrill voice he heaped such a variety of curses on the unlucky Dutch Charlie began to fear for the man's sanity.

When he had a chance to resume, Lew said, "I covered Dutch up with brush and started back for help, got a little lost myself, and it was way past midnight before I found camp. It was empty. I waited until morning, and when I saw footprints in the sand and the marks of canoes at the water's edge, I figured the Indians had carried you off.

"First I walked down to the settlement, but I found nobody there who could understand what I said. So I went back in the woods and looked around, trying to find you. Several times I hid from parties of men who appeared to be searching for somebody. Then I decided they were probably looking for me, and that the easiest way to find you was to be captured. So, I walked into a bunch and they tied me up and ran me down here."

"They should find Dutch soon," commented Charlie.

"They can't until he comes to," said Lew. "I covered him up good. I was afraid he would take cold from exposure."

"You needn't have bothered," growled Blake. "When he's doped up, an ax wouldn't hurt him. I'd like to use one on him, though."

Charlie had been watching Lew's face. Something in his half smile said he wasn't telling all he knew. He might be mistaken, but something in his partner's expression reminded him of a small boy who had been up to mischief.

"What are the Indians going to do with us?" asked Lew. "They treated me well enough. Nothing rough, just real firm. I didn't struggle, either. I didn't want to give them any reason to get angry."

"They will let us go in a couple of days," Blake snarled, "when it is too late for me to finish my work." Then he sank into silence.

"I'm half starved," Lew complained. "Do they feed us?"

"Sure," Charlie informed him. "Like clockwork. Good grub regularly three times a day."

"Well, I'm ready for three meals right now," said Lew, raising his voice in a shout.

Two Indians ran inside, threatening him with their knives.

"The only way to keep me quiet is with food," he told them with a grin. Then he wagged his jaws vigorously, imitating the motions of chewing food.

The men backed out, and presently, the squaw came back with her full pot and big spoon. "Reminds me of a time I was laid up in the hospital and had to be fed," Lew said between mouthfuls. "But I had a much prettier nurse then."

Another day passed quietly in the tepee. Charlie and Lew talked in low tones, for they soon discovered their guards did not object to conversation as long as it occurred in half-whispers. Blake sulked in anger most of the time. Regularly, at two-hour intervals, one or two of the Indians guarding them came and looked keenly at the knots on their tied ankles and wrists. Lew suggested they work on these knots and untie themselves as they had that dark night in the cabin, but Charlie firmly vetoed this suggestion.

"They have treated us well," he said. "In a day or two we will be set free. Why make them angry? They might pitch us in the lake."

Morning came after a weary night. At first, the inaction had been welcome. Now, as Lew put it, they were "fed up with loafing."

Only two more days remained for Blake to close the tamarack timber deal for his company, and Lew took a chance with Blake's irritable mood by reminding him of the fact. Blake snarled so savagely Lew also began to wonder about the man's sanity.

The skins over the doorway moved.

"Here comes breakfast," said Lew.

But Harris entered instead of the squaw.

Blake struggled to his knees at the sight of the Indian agent. If he had raged before, now he went totally mad. But Harris stopped the torrent of abuse with a terse, "Shut up, Blake, and let me talk."

The engineer sank back on the skins.

"I know you blame me," Harris began. "But the absolute truth is I didn't know you were being held here until half an hour ago. I just now got back to the settlement and Tatuma met me with the news. He said he was holding you in his lodge as a prisoner of the Cree people. I ordered him to release you immediately, and I came along to see that the order was obeyed."

"You're lying!" cried Blake. "Now that it is too late ..."

"I never lie," Harris interrupted matter-of-factly. "And you know that. I don't fight dirty, either. I will oppose you, but only by legal means. Tatuma took things into his own hands, and he will admit as much in a court of law. He fired the forest himself, and then he led the raid on your camp when you were captured."

"It won't make any difference who ordered it," Blake stormed. "I have been kidnapped and held by force. My field notes were stolen. You will pay for this, Harris!"

The Indian agent saw the futility of talking with the man. So he turned to Charlie. "I'm very sorry you were mixed up in this. I realize you were merely working for Harris, but I don't mind telling you you were tied up with a sorry outfit."

Then he called and Tatuma entered and carefully loosened their bound ankles and wrists. They stood and rubbed their joints, for while the thongs had not been tight, their legs and arms still were stiff and cramped from inactivity. Blake stumbled out the door.

"Come to the settlement," invited Harris. "I'll find a cabin for you to use."

"You're generous now that you think I'm beaten," sneered Blake. "But I'm not through yet, Harris."

Harris ignored this and again turned back to Lew and Charlie. "You will find your camping outfit all together and undamaged. Tatuma took good care of it all."

"Where's my transit?" Blake demanded.

"Tatuma told me to say he is sorry, but it fell out of the canoe when they were carrying you across the lake.

This started the engineer raging again. Paying no attention to anyone, he strode down the lakeshore to Yelping Dog, and the rest followed, Lew whistling a cheerful tune. Charlie wondered if the engineer would get violent in the depths of his despair.

At the settlement, Harris pointed out an empty cabin. Charlie looked inside and saw their camp duffle piled on the floor and their rifles standing in a corner. But Blake did not even glance in the cabin. He was examining his watch with a frown.

His anger seemed to have cooled, or else he had regained some of his usual composure. He called to Harris. "I must find Dutch. He may be hurt or sick in the woods. Can I get half a dozen Indians to help us hunt for him?"

Harris assented heartily. Then he dispatched an Indian boy back to the camp with word to bring six of the best forest runners in the tribe. "I can show you where I left him asleep," Lew offered, "but I'm afraid he probably has started to wander around, and he may be miles from there by now."

Blake fretted impatiently while they waited for the Indian search party. "Why don't they hurry?" he kept asking. Charlie thought this strange, the sudden concern for Dutch and also the constant looking at his watch. The man clearly despised Dutch, and why was he counting the minutes?

"You won't need a search party," Lew announced. "Look there!" Through the half-cleared area surrounding the settlement, they saw a figure stumbling towards them. It was a man who appeared badly exhausted. He staggered and fell, but recovering his feet, pushed on with grim determination. It was Dutch, his face streaked with blood from a scratch over one temple, his clothing torn and soiled.

Blake ran to meet him, grabbed the weakened gunman by the arm and shook him violently. "Have you got it?" he cried. "Speak up, man! Tell me!"

Dutch shook off the hand. "Give me a drink!" he snarled.

Blake pulled the flask from his pocket, and Dutch swallowed whiskey in eager gulps. "That's better," he said as he dropped the empty bottle to the ground. "I had a heckuva time in the woods, but I hung on to it. Here," and he passed Blake a sheaf of papers.

Blake uttered a cry of triumph. "You went to all of your trouble for nothing, Harris," he sneered. "I beat you in spite of your cowardly tricks. I was wise enough to make two copies of my field notes. The night we finished, I gave Dutch a copy to keep."

He held up the packet. "Here it is: the boundaries of the tamarack timber. You can expect the logging crews early this fall."

With this parting shot, he turned his back on them.

Dutch winked at them with derision.

Harris looked crushed, and as his shoulders sagged, Charlie realized how keenly the man felt for the Indian tribes. Harris had not been responsible for their capture—Charlie believed that—although it had worked to his advantage and almost produced the end to which he had worked so earnestly.

"Listen," said Charlie, "you're not beaten. That copy of field notes won't help. Blake can't get them to a telegraph or a telephone in time to do any good. Tomorrow is the last day, and there is no way to reach a line by then."

The disappointment cleared from Harris' face. "That's right! We still have him blocked. I know for a fact it will take Blake two days or more to reach the nearest telegraph."

The engineer was stuffing the papers back in his pocket.

"Now, Dutch," they heard him say, "watch this bunch. I don't trust any of them. Use your gun on the first fellow who interferes."

The gunman drew his pistol and held it poised in his hand. Charlie noticed his grip was steady now. A doped-up Dutch was a dangerous factor to be feared. But, Charlie thought, what was Blake driving at? Nobody was going to interfere. He was beaten already.

Blake again consulted his watch, and Charlie turned his head towards the south as a familiar if strange sound for the northwoods reached his ear, one he had heard recently, could it be …?

The others had caught it now, and Blake paced back and forth with barely contained excitement. There was no doubt now; it was the monotonous drone of an airplane motor.

"Keep your eyes on them, Dutch," Blake cried. "Don't let anything slip now!" He was drawing his own gun.

A thrill of premonition—a foreboding of sorts—seized Charlie. Blake was wearing a look of supreme confidence as he watched the speck in the sky grow in size, not the look of a man who had failed. Dutch was not watching the plane; his eyes were fixed with dangerous intent on him and the others.

The plane hovered over the settlement, flying low, just clearing the tops of the tallest trees and moving at a fair speed. Blake took off his hat and waved it vigorously.

It was a seaplane with pontoons, and the pilot cut the motor preparing to land. It banked and then slid easily upon the surface of the lake with a soft splash. As the plane turned and taxied towards shore, Blake and Dutch ran to meet it, wading out into knee-deep water.

A heavyset man leaned out over the edge of the cockpit. "Are we in time?" he shouted.

"Just!" Blake answered. "But watch out. I've had a narrow shave. They may try to stop us yet."

With a quick movement, the man picked up something from the floor and swung out on the wing. It was a shoulder-mounted machine gun, and he held it with the easy manner of great familiarity, keeping the muzzle trained upon the little group on shore.

Blake reached the plane first. He turned and boasted, "I win again, Harris! This is my last card, and I played it to win. When our plane started to go bad I radioed back to headquarters for another. My orders were to meet here today at 10 a.m. I had the time figured down to the hour, and my figures, as always, have proved correct."

He glanced at his watch and then turned to the man with the gun. "Actually, you're six minutes late, Louis. But I forgive that."

The pilot had not completely cut the motor, and the propeller was still turning slowly. Now he leaned his goggled face out and called, "One of you grab a wing and turn her around."

Dutch seized the end of a wing and pushed until the plane was pointing out into the lake. As he jumped up on the pontoon and then climbed inside with the others, the pilot gave the motor the gun. With a roar, the plane began skimming out across the water.

Blake leaned out and waved sardonically. Then, gracefully as a gull, the seaplane lifted into the air and was quickly lost from sight in the clouds.

It had all happened so quickly, the group on the shore still watched in stunned silence minutes after the noise of the motor had died away. "Fast work," Lew finally said, breaking the spell.

"Blake wins, after all," Harris spoke heavily.

"You know his outfit is just stealing this timber, getting it for less than a fourth of the actual value. Bribery did that, and Blake will come back to direct the logging and make sure more of the same keeps the skids greased until every tree is cut. He is a vindictive man, and he will do all he can to hurt me and the Indians who fought him. It is his personal evil I fear most. He will make sure whiskey gets the Indians. Then he will hire them for next to nothing, and then cheat them out of that."

"Say," Lew cried. "That reminds me. Blake went off without paying us. He owes us real money—twenty dollars a day for the first part of the week and forty dollars for each of the last three days."

"You'll never see it," said Harris wearily. "That's just his way of doing business."

"The son-of-a-gun," Lew muttered.

"Looks like we wasted a week for nothing," Charlie spoke soberly. "And helped a crook get what he came after. That's the part I hate the most."

"Actually, this is just what I hoped would happen," Lew spoke up cheerfully. "Now my conscience is clear."

"What do you mean?" asked Charlie and Harris in unison.

Lew grinned like the cat that ate the canary and said, "Mr. Engineer is going to be the most dumbfounded man in the country when they try to figure out the notes Dutch just handed over."

"Go on," they begged.

"Well, I'll begin at the start. I noticed on the first day that Blake was putting down figures twice. He would write on first one page and then turn to another. So I knew he was making a duplicate set of data and would probably give it to somebody else to keep. That somebody, of course, had to be Dutch."

"So, that's why you suddenly became so attached to him?" asked Charlie.

"Not at all," contradicted Lew. "It was his genial disposition."

When Lew paused too long for effect, Charlie gave him a punch to the shoulder and he continued the story, also rubbing the shoulder. "Remember how Blake kept implying we weren't bright enough to understand surveying? That was sure annoying, at first. But then it gave me an idea. You remember, Charlie, that winter I took a correspondence course in land surveying?"

"Sure," affirmed Charlie. "I wondered why you took all of that guff from Blake."

"I had a reason," Lew continued and then turned to Harris. "Charlie and I both appreciated the fight you were making on behalf of the Indians, and you had our sympathy from the start. While Charlie felt bound by a promise to guide Blake to the settlement, I had made no such promise, and I secretly schemed for a way to help you, if the chance came."

"Lew never could mind his own business," grinned Charlie.

"I thought if I played dumb I would have a better chance," Lew went on. "Dutch dropping his dope again was my first lucky break. I found it immediately—saw it slip out of his pocket. Dutch is a careless bird; he'd lose his temper if it wasn't ingrown. Anyway, I slipped the bottle in my pocket and waited for Dutch to start shaking."

"You took a big risk," said Charlie. "Dutch is as wicked as a snake. He would have shot you cheerfully if he had suspected."

"I knew that," Lew said. "But I had to take advantage when something finally broke my way. When he went to look for the stuff, I offered to help. After we had gone back four or five miles, I pretended to find the bottle. Up until then, he hadn't paid much attention to me. But then he actually fell to his knees and wept with gratitude. Then he grabbed the bottle and started to eat pills.

"Remember the night after we worked so hard? When Dutch was sore so he took an overdose? And then he slept right through Blake and you prowling about looking for men in the timber?"

"Sure," said Charlie. "He snored all the time."

"Well, I figured the same thing would happen, and it did. He got groggy and then slumped over in a stupor. He was simply dead to the world. In fact, I was scared for a while that he might really die and then it would look like I had killed him on purpose.

"At first, I intended to just destroy the notes Dutch carried. Then I got my other good idea. If I could just alter them enough that Blake would still think they were OK ..."

"I see the light now," Charlie said with a wide smile.

"I don't," cried Harris. "Go on!"

"The surveying course I took taught me to print figures like all engineers use. The notes one engineer makes look a lot like those of another. So, I took the sheets out of Dutch's pocket, built a small campfire for light, and then changed a few key numbers here and there, being careful to imitate Blake's lettering. I altered just enough that when the calculations come back, they will look OK but be completely off the money. And I did it so neatly no one will suspect a thing until the land commission examines them and sees they are hogwash. By then, it will be too late."

"I sure wish I could be there to see Blake's reaction to that," chuckled Charlie.

"Wonderful!" Harris cried out, clapping his hands with glee. Then his eyes misted over, seeing generations of Indians living their lives in the tamarack, happy images that crowded out the nightmare images of a forest of burned stumps, a dreary barrens.

"So, when I was captured by the Indians," Lew finished, "and I found you and Blake tied up, I knew the job was done, because I knew old Tatuma would take care of Blake's copy of the notes."

After another pause, he turned to the tearful agent and asked, "Tell me, Mr. Harris, what's the chance of a hungry trapper getting a two-inch-thick moose steak around here?"

"Best in the world," Harris cried joyfully. "Today, there's nothing in the tamarack country you can't have for the asking!"

The End